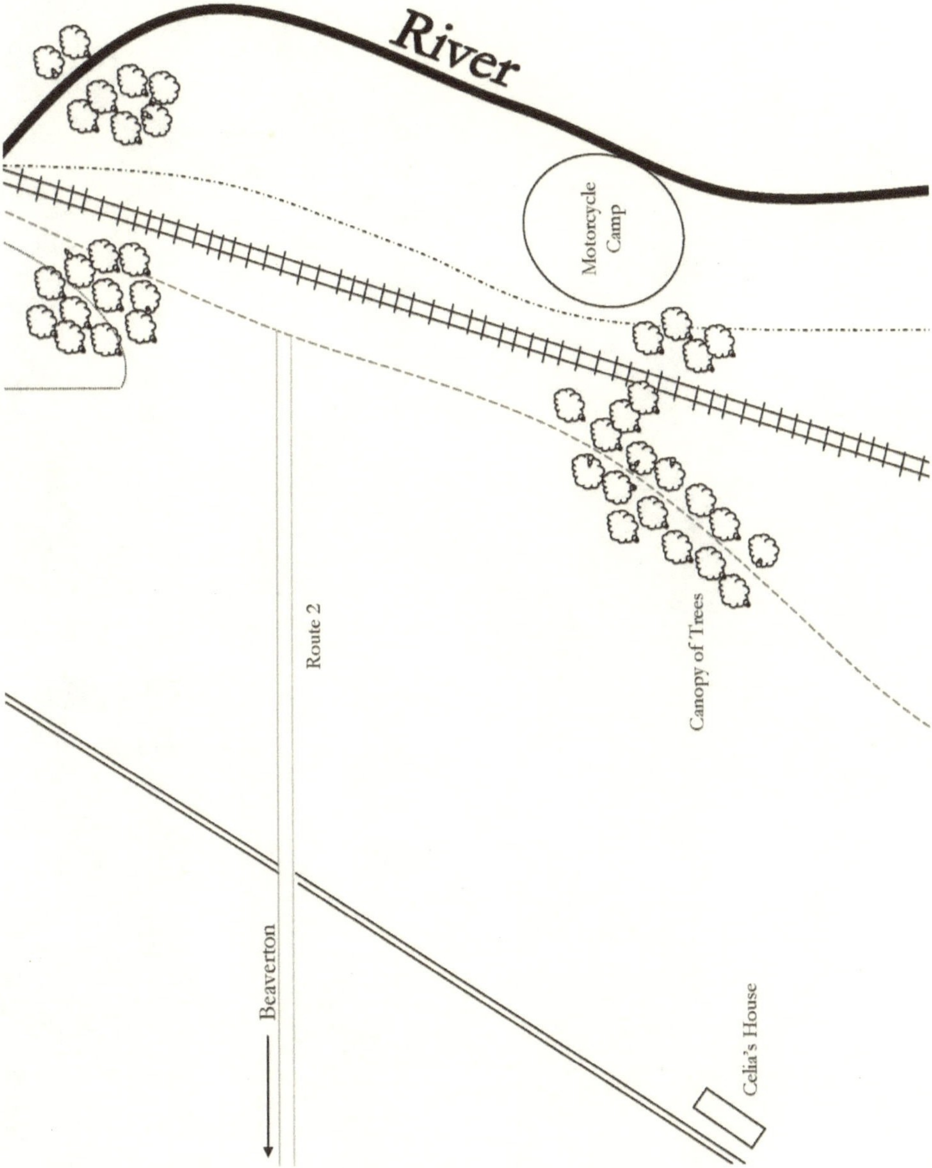

River

Motorcycle
Camp

Route 2

Canopy of Trees

Beaverton

Celia's House

DEDICATION

This book is dedicated to young women ready to start their journey through intimate relationships. I wish you wisdom and true love.

I wrote this book while my son was napping. We were both lucky to have most of his early years together. He still is the best thing that's happened to me, so I dedicate this book to him as well. I also wish to say thank you to my family and friends whose character(s) have given me a rich variety of personalities to pull from and show up ever so slightly in this book.

To those who helped along the way: Brooke Monfort, my editor; Bruce Bettinger, who helped replace my computer when I couldn't afford to; and the band, Little Village, and their song, "Don't Go Away Mad," which I played while writing this book, a very big *Thank You* for your support.

"A young girl receives most not from art but from nature"

—Uɴᴋɴᴏᴡɴ

"*The misery of a child is interesting to a mother, the misery of a young man is interesting to a young woman, the misery of an old man is interesting to nobody.*"

—Eric Hoffer

Celia, the Girl

Debra Peebles

CHAPTER ONE

Getting There

The first time I flew on one of Uncle Reesie's cruiser-flights-with-four-wheels was my mother's last. On this one particular day she had decided the right combination of warmth, sunlight and breeze was encouragement enough for her to venture into his car for a tour of Beaverton and its surroundings. It wasn't that she had forgotten about the last rambunctious ride from my Uncle Reese, or any of the rides before. It was this particular day and her eternal heightened cabin fever; the pollen numbing her better sense of panic and fear, allowing her to accept his invitation to view the scenic cottonwoods, dogwoods and birch trees rooted throughout the back roads of Rabbit County. She has always loved the wildflowers that decorate the dusty roadsides and presses those she picks into the books lining the living room shelves. The pale, weightless and flattened treasures will flutter down effortlessly whenever I inadvertently open a tomb, escaping, creating unintentional exposure.

Knowing Uncle Reese, he made the invitation as a way to pass the time between on and off duty for a few laughs while Mom (AKA: Curlers) hooted and howled, huddled and cringed underneath the dashboard, her right foot pressed firmly to the imaginary brake. He has always been a big tease. He will create a scenario and trap his victim as the punch line to his joke. Anyone can fall prey to

1

his teasing. The most pathetic wallflower can be as much a victim as the biggest bully, and he'll get as big a kick out of each reaction. He then retells the outcome over and over to everyone in town, reveling in the reaction he's gotten from his victim. I suppose Curlers was no different on this particular day either. Her memory lapsed in the glory of the day and an intense urge to see beyond her own backyard. If her faculties had been operating fully, she would have simply walked around the block to appease her wondering urges.

Perhaps she would have strolled over to *Barry's Quick Café* for a slice of chocolate cream pie and a cup-of-joe. Pops has everyone on a very tight budget, so she takes a few bucks out of the grocery allotment each week to cover her chocolate cream pie urges. Perhaps she thought on this particular day, Reese would spring for the treat after surviving the brunt of his auto thrills. This is how she thinks. I've seen this reasoning process time and time again—one catches on after awhile. I don't think chocolate cream pie and a cup-of-joe would have covered the cost of fear and terror that caused her body to shake and tremble, and then collapse fully on the living room couch after what she went through to see the sights of Route 2 that afternoon.

Uncle Reese opened the cruiser's front passenger door for her and she dropped daintily into the front seat using a contrived girlish manner that seems to appear whenever she crosses from our front yard out into the public. It is a false charm I suppose, or a gleefulness she learned to exude as a young girl to get the thinks she wanted—big or small. I enjoyed it then; I was only four or five years old and thought this meant we were about to have a good time. It is only now, in my growing maturity, I have discovered this charm is only meant for people outside the gates of our own home. I realize somewhere along the way this coy demeanor is never used on any of us within the immediate family. I suppose it is easier to be demanding and impatient with the regulars; which is not to say this charm is false, I'm sure it's a part of her nature brought out only when it is called for to those with less of a discerning ear than we who know the routine.

Uncle Reese opened the back door and with a wink of the eye said, "The County Sheriff's Department hasn't fit the cruiser for seat belts yet." I didn't know what a seat belt was, and Curlers didn't seem to hear him.

"I hope we can make a little time for a break at *Barry's*. I'm really in the mood for some chocolate cream pie," Mom said, letting him know with an added toothy smile what her priorities were even before the engine was running.

Reese didn't seem to hear her however. He turned the key in the ignition and gunned the motor all at the same time. I gripped my seat as if we were about to set new records, but to my comfort, we strolled up to the end of the block, moved smoothly around the corner and on down to Main Street. As we drove past *Barry's* to our right, everything changed.

Uncle Reesie honked his horn, shot a look over at *Barry's* then hit the accelerator, burning rubber and beaming a grin at Mom. Mom shot a knowing grin right back at him and patted his knee saying, "Now, keep it on the ground Reese, it takes more than a little burnt rubber to thrill me on a day like this."

Nothing would ever be the same after that.

Reese picked up speed hitting airborne as we approached the Main Street dip that signals farewell to everyone leaving Beaverton, while heading north on Route 2. I could hear Curlers gasp for air after losing most of it in the hollow as we plunged purposefully down and then skyward like a circus act out of a cannon. She went as ridged as a museum statue, solid in her seat. She didn't smell floral ambrosia, and cabin fever was out-of-sight, out-of-mind.

I wasn't enjoying myself much either. The deep broad back seat gave me plenty of space to toss around in, ricocheting off the walls like a handball. When we hit the dip, I went from pressed to the upholstered vinyl seat, to hitting the ceiling and back down again, sprawling out anywhere. As we landed on all fours, the chassis was an instant low-rider and the three of us lifted off and capable of flight—but no room for observation of aeronautics, the pace was full speed ahead.

I was pressed firmly to the Naugahyde upholstery while my eyelids fluttered up and down to prevent the heavy wind from drying them out. When I could squeeze a peek from battling visual windburn, I saw Curlers no longer held any interest in the scenery or employing her girlish charm. Rather, her whole being concentrated on the road ahead; no longer interested in carrying on idle conversations about Aunt Wanita or the Bergstroms (the richest family in town) and how spoiled they were, or, who got arrested last night and why. And, I'm nearly certain I could hear a whisper of her voice praying to St. Christopher to get us home in one piece. If he would only act on her behalf she would definitely consider giving up the chocolate cream pie money she had been pilfering from her grocery allowance. I hoped this was just a momentary lapse strictly based on fear because she always appeared late afternoon, calm and relieved having returned from a stroll to *Barry's*.

Uncle Reese, on the other hand, stretched out his legs, shot an elbow out the window, and casually gripped the bottom of the steering wheel with his right hand. I am sure he knew the anxiety he was causing both the stiff, ridged, wide-eyed torso next to him in the front seat, as well as me, glued to the back cushion where the freshly arrested usually sat.

"I don't know of anything better than a summer afternoon in Rabbit County. The majesty and pageantry of pine trees mixed with poplars, knowing some buck is watching from his afternoon napping place," waxed Reese.

"I don't know how you even have time to enjoy it at this pace. I can't believe you've taken a good look at the scenery around Beaverton since the last time you rode with *us* somewhere. Look at poor little Celia back there, she can't be enjoying this ride much either. As sheriff of this community, I would think you'd have a little more respect for our safety, Reese! I am your sister!" Curlers responded with a nervous yet bitter tone in her voice. She was still sitting fully erect with one foot surely on an imaginary brake and her right fist digging its nails into the door handle.

Uncle Reese turned around with a big grin, "Celia, you seem to be having a wonderful time back there. I don't want your mama to scare you. Relax and enjoy yourself while we're viewing this beautiful rustic setting."

"Reese, no one is able to enjoy the rustic surroundings while you're setting some kind of speed record for the State of Minnesota," Curlers said, looking over at him in exasperation.

"Uncle Reese, I'm not scared just tired of bouncing around back here," I said meekly.

Curlers turned around to gather in my hapless attempts to remain stationary on the slippery seats of the cruiser while fighting the heavy turbulence. Reese was still facing my direction, probably looking for something funny to say to cheer me up. Curlers turned back around first and focused in on the rear bumper of a car we had caught up to without warning of its impending presence. "Aauuhh! Reese! Look out! You're going to hit that car!" Curlers screamed.

Uncle Reese, both hands on the wheel now, snapped around and shot the cruiser into the next lane, apparently to avoid a rear-end collision. He swerved left even harder, barely missing another blaring oncoming car in the left lane. I guess at this point we could be called, "out-of-control," a term I'm familiar with from my driver's education course, and always reminds me of this moment— flying off the highway, over the gully, and landing solidly on Gus Everod's spring crop of corn. I hit the ceiling with a solid thud and whipped back to the seat cushion with enough force to leave an impression of the indented lines fashioned into the Naugahyde on my bare skin. It smarted like a slap from an open hand. I am sure Reese had his foot on the brakes by now and Curlers' shrill scream at the point of impact still echoed as we continued to throw soil and baby cornstalks out from under the rear tires. It seemed like eternity that I gripped the slick surface of the cushions with the rough impression of my fingerprints. Finally, I dug a hand between the seats and hung on until we swirled to a stop.

Everything went quiet. And, although I knew we were no longer moving, my head continued to roll and bump along the field. I jumped up and looked out the back window. Black dust had created a smoky scrim making it difficult at first to discern the uprooted cornstalks and the zigzagging trail we had routed out of the field. I waited for a clear view, concentrating on the cloud of dirt rolling out along our path.

Smack!

"God Dammit Reese, why the hell did you do that!" screamed Curlers.

I wheeled around to see Mother caressing the side of her face and eyeballing an explanation out of our escort.

"Well shit, you fainted, flat-out cold! I should have just let you lie there, because now I suppose I'll have to listen to your analysis of the situation," said Uncle Reese already on the defensive.

"No Reese, I don't think this needs any sort of explanation. I think the events speak for themselves. If I need to be scared half way to hell and back, I would have waited for the devil to call! You don't have to worry about towing me around. I'll never step foot in a car you're driving again!"

"Fine, call up your old man mid-afternoon and have him hustle your butt around. Some people don't know a favor when it chances up their front door. I don't need to be taken for granted. What do you think I'm supposed to say to Mr. Everod?"

5

CHAPTER TWO

Beaverton

Things have changed though. I wake up thinking about the car and how much I'd want to take off in one and cruise Rabbit County without escort of just about anyone, much less Curlers or Uncle Reese. It's a good twelve years since that day Reese last took Mom for a ride up Route 2. I got my driver's license last year and haven't been subjected to anyone else's hapless cruising. Still, most of the time I'm on foot because Pop's or my older brother; Keith always gets first access.

Instead, I move out the front door like a graceful cat, hoping I won't disturb the sanctuary my mother presides over in the cool darkness. Ahh, it's warm out here in the sunlight. I hesitate for a minute. Did she hear the creaks I made on the wooden porch floor or the quiet squeak of the screen door? I close it gently. No time to stop—hesitate and she'll be at the door hollering for me to get back in there because the chores are endless. Just the sight of my face must conjure up a work schedule on her endless path to cleanliness. Funny, no matter how much cleaning gets done it seems like perpetual upheaval. But truly—out of sight, out of mind. She'll never miss me if I've made my exit before she gets down to breakfast; she, in her morning glory, crowned with a laurel of curlers, a terry cloth train; hem dragging after years of wash and wearing, wash and wearing.

Geez, could this be the essence of the woman my father married 19 years ago? I'll have to remember not to get married—look what I'm in for.

How many summers left? Everything is freed up. Smells of morning grass, rain, air and photosynthesis, reproducing more of the same, until one day the North Wind shoves in responsibility. Summer changes everything—it owes it to you.

God, is this time good! The days labor out, each hour, each phrase we turn hangs warm and humid in mid-air. Thoughts grow slowly, without urgency or need for particular replies. Why think beyond the rise and fall of the sun for one complete rotation?

Every morning I wake up hopeful for a new adventure, a new prospect of some guy hanging on my every word and looking like meeting at the drive-in is the only special thing wound up in his summer—at least for today.

Maybe I'll meet him down on the railroad tracks...I don't know...too secluded. I only go there with my girlfriends so we can talk wildly, and laugh hysterically over yesterday's trails, and to pick up particularly tantalizing rocks the trains whip across three times a day without pausing to take in the significance of purple stria or the clear quality of the quartz. The rocks are washed clear after I get home and run them through the tumbler my uncle owns. I conjure up future earring and necklace sets after they're polished into a brilliant sheen. So far though, this is all a dream. Once the girls get laughing and carrying on, I usually forget the enterprise until I'm back home looking for something to do.

I usually end up begging by father for a little cash once or twice a week. I feel like a social misfit if I can't even pick up a pop at will. My father could easily be called tight; tight with a buck. He always acts like he's being hit over the head with a baseball bat. I mean a buck or two; running money for just a couple of days. Not big cash. I never pinch him for much out of humility or enormous pride. I don't know, maybe I just haven't got the techniques necessary to line my pockets with unearned money and feel justified. At least that's the way he guilt's me into accepting a small token of his esteem; but only a minor distraction in the spaciousness of summer. Most of my girlfriends' folks are weak in the money department too. No one dwells on it. We can always come up with what we need when we need it. We all sort of grew up outdoors. The neighborhood mothers shooing us out and on to our own devices once we were able to carry on a conversation and run across the small town streets. We always found plenty to do on a summer day with no expense to the folks.

There is a dance tonight at the Armory. Everyone is going to be there, the whole FFA (Future Farmers of America) contingent. The boys will get down from the hay-bailers, scrub themselves so clean that we town girls won't ever know that a few short hours before, heavy black dirt clogged their nails and stuck between their teeth. They will be so clean their cheeks are rubbed red. Some people say it's all those rich dairy products they eat that give their cheeks that rosiness. But I think they're scrubbing hard because they're trying to remove the farm from their faces.

Out the door, down the block, and without hesitation, I make my way to the edge of town. I head up over the railroad tracks and down the other side to the river. It's so peaceful in these tall grasses along the bank…I can really drift… There's a dragonfly, an iridescent blue one. I wonder if they think about anything, or do they just sputter about going wherever the food chain leads them? Who knows, maybe they're just looking for a good place to die.

Lying back I hear the river's current and watch birds play cat and mouse, bobbing and dipping, seeming to chase a mysterious leader playing foil to billowy clouds and moving gracefully in their mesmerizing directions. Every now and again a few independent souls break from the regiment, perhaps balking at such leader worship, or then, could they have spotted a midmorning snack?

I love to lie in these tall swaying reeds. They seem to dance to a melodic piece of music only the natural world around me can hear. I've always wanted to know what it would feel like if the blades fell over and blanketed me like a warm cocoon. My Grandfather says all the animals and birds—every living creature has a song. When it sings, it is a reminder to all of us that we are related, like cousins. The song this relation sings begins to pluck the strings that bind us all together as one soul. For one brief instant it fills the universe with joy. I believe I have a song to sing as well, and one of these days I'll set out to find it. Maybe it will come right here in the tall grasses.

Oh, but I have got to get a move-on! My mother's expectations are overpowering my reverie and pressing hard against fanciful dreams. A signal is filed somewhere in my consciousness to be on alert for my household duties. I press hard into the river bank. A chunk of earth loosens and plops effortlessly into the river, then dissolves in the motion of the slow moving current. Nature is so consistent. How estranged we humans have become from basic coexistence with nature. Gravity causes a chunk of earth to fall and quickly erode in water—the element we first developed from. Are we so estranged? Do we have instinctual memories of our struggle from water to land inhabiters?

I'll think about that later. I better head back down the tracks.

The rails connect endlessly on to everywhere and no where—no where imaginable, until they stop in a halting V-shape, I suppose at the edge of the eastern seaboard. I like the feel of the abrupt right turn the road to town makes, opposing the monotonous rhythm of eastern laid track defiantly opposing the Eastern Seaboard at its end, and saying there is something right here in between. I feel a twinge of excitement as I head off against the tracks, turning a cold shoulder, forsaking the new and mysterious distance for some strength in knowing the parameters of Beaverton.

It's still early, but up on the road leading into the center of town life has already gotten started, while everyone back at the house will only now be getting ready for the new day.

I walk on to Main Street, first past the Lutheran Church, the tallest building in town; quiet and ghostly, deserted except on Sundays when parishioners breathe expectant life into its sanctuary once again. I continue on past *Dell and Son's Barber Shop*, almost directly across the street from *"Dell's Beauty Biz*. This is no coincidence; the Dell family has Beaverton's hair styling business all to themselves. Grandpa Dell opened the shop sometime back in the 1920's and passed the interest on to Jim Dell, his eldest son. Jim married Colleen Schwartz, who went to beauty school in Bemidji, shortly after they were married. According to Curlers (AKA: my mother), Colleen caught the hairstyling bug from Jim and commuted from Beaverton to earn her degree. Prior to, she was gung-ho on housewifing and giving neighborhood teas, but once she had her beauty certificate in hand she was all business and telling all the locals what they should be doing with their hair. No one really appreciated her advice, but they liked having a salon in town for their stylin' needs. Jim Dell added, *"and Son's*" to the barbershop sign when the oldest Dell boy got hooked on clippers right after high school. Now-a-days, Jim can be found shooting-the -breeze with Norm Hildebrandt, owner of *Hilde's Auto Repair and Parts*, just up the street.

I like walking through town this early in the morning. Downtown the world is moving, unlike the neighborhood where nothing is doing.

At the gas station hangs the motorcycle gang everyone has been talking about: *Hell's Angels* or *Death on Wheels*, or some group like that. They rode in a couple of days ago and for some reason are staying around. I hadn't thought much about them until now. Practically every guy I know around here has a motorcycle and wears jeans, but now I see the difference, the cause for alarm. There's about six of them with a couple of girls too. They look rough, raw, wild—sort of untamed. A hot bath could be in order judging by long stringy hair and the dull, dirt-blown color of their jeans. They're laughing and carrying on as if being the center of attention is the whole point. They don't care who lives in this town or the lives we lead; whether the Gurney family lost their farm to the bank, or if Cappy Standing Horse froze to death last winter behind *Larson's Liquors*. They remind me of a big, old tumbleweed blowing through town; the wind pushing it here and there, dust and debris mixing in along the haphazard route. No one pays it much mind until it rolls onto a main road where total confusion radiates out from the center of the frail mass and on to the average driver. Do I slam on my brakes and wait for it to blow to the other side of the road? Should I bear around it or roll right over it, maybe snagging on my fender or under the car, then dragging it with me until I'm forced to pull it off? The apparition blows freely any direction the four winds' choose.

North, South, East and West, winds take their turn as seasons bow to one another. Every now and then, the Winds whirl uncontrollably, mostly during the change of season. Watch, when Winter changes to Spring, Spring changing to Summer, Summer to Fall, there will be one special day the Winds will be in council, encouraging the North, South, East or West to come forward and usher in change. Whirlwinds can be seen twirling as momentum grows. One day it appears on the street of town as tumbleweeds causing auto confusion, until it picks up speed and hurls on, zigging and zagging endlessly…elsewhere.

These bikers are like that too. They've blown in from out of nowhere and will blow back out, presumably not before confusion, anxiety and panic reign. It's the mood around town. Something is going to happen before they blow out Route 2 heading North, South, East or West. Uncle Reese, Sheriff of Rabbit County may have his work cut out for him.

I stroll past *Barry's Quick Café* and peer through the large front window to see what's shakin'. Barry's back is turned but his arms are moving frantically at the grill. I assume he's frying up eggs, flipping pancakes, toasting bread and sizzling up bacon; whatever it takes to produce breakfast for the early birds. The morning doves are pretty much the same crowd every morning so Barry has their order handy before anyone even sits down. Bernita is Barry's sister, and she's been the Cafe's waitress for as long as I know. She's always in right along with Barry. She's kind of the personality of the place, talking nonstop in her café uniform with her tall and skinny limbs hunched over the counter, a Pall Mall cigarette burning close by.

Bernita is sweet as pie. It doesn't matter what your name is. I don't know if she really remembers anyone's name because she will always call you "Doll." All the early bird farmers, businessmen, Curlers, me and even Barry are "Doll." Curlers has known Bernita their whole lives. They went to one of those Indian boarding schools together in the southern part of the state. They're more like acquaintances though, not like buddies at all. In the café, Bernita flirts and tells racy stories; cleansing herself of gossip on a daily basis. But outside of work she's reserved and keeps to herself. I guess she sings in the Lutheran Church choir and participates in some of their socials, otherwise, I never see her outside the Café. Curlers says Bernita had the hots for my Uncle Reese before he hooked up with Auntie Wanita, and that it broke her heart to see Uncle Reese and Auntie Wanita getting married. Personally, I've always wondered how these gals could hold Reese as their romantic hero. He's so unusual. Sure, a dynamic personality, but not exactly fitting the *knight in shining armor* stuff. And well, a little short in the looks department. Shows personality can go a long way.

I poke my head in the door and holler, "Good morning everybody!"

Barry turns around, smiles and asks, "Want a little breakfast, Celia?"

"I wish I could Barry, but I've got to get home to the chores."

Bernita inquires, "Are you out for another early morning walk, Doll?"

"Yes, Bernita, but I have a feeling her royal highness is about to take the throne, so I've got to get home," I reply.

"Hey Doll," she yells back, "your mother *is* a queen, so you treat her right, ya hear?"

"Okay, Bernita," I holler back as I let the screen door loose and step back into the sun.

Picking up stride, I pass *Perham's Outfitters and Dry Goods*. Then comes the *First National Savings and Loan*. The bank is made of large slabs of granite and it sits solidly on the corner. I make a quick sharp turn, and not break-ing stride, I head down Pine Street. Mr. Bjornson is out getting the morn-ing Minneapolis paper. His shirt has yet to make its appearance on his back despite the crisp morning breeze that seems to perk up in the north/south direction of Pine. Across the street, the Haviland's miniature collie is already out on its leash, and as usual, considers me a reason to sound off. I ignore him. If Mr. Bjornson wasn't in earshot, I'd probably yell back at the miniature mongrel. I cut across the middle of the street and head for the back alley toward home.

I grew up on the plains. So far I've spent my whole life on the Tundra. I like that word, *Tundra*. It's a word I learned in history class or heard it on public television; everything baron, flat and cold for miles on end. I remember looking over vast black fields with striped patterns—rows I now know had been indented by farmers' machines that had planted or picked the autumn crop of potatoes. I sat on that black dusty earth watching as Curlers and Pops picked up the leftovers the machines didn't pluck or the sorters had rejected. I remember seeing a painting in art class one time that resembled this scene called, *The Potato Pickers* by Manet, a French painter. He painted farmhands picking potatoes over gently rolling hills slightly dinned by dust—only, the tundra is flat.

My first memories of these outings I was two or three years old. My legs couldn't keep up with my folks. The indented rows were difficult hills and valleys to small feet, so I just sat and watched the scene. Those fields are still potato fields, but now I take them for granted, like I sometimes do the rest of this town.

And yet I can still feel how warm and consoling it was to sit in-between rows of the bare black earth in denial of the biting Fall winds that overpowered anything without purposeful intentions. If I stood to make progress in the direction of my parents, the foretelling wind grabbed a fistful of dirt, refined to sandiness and pressed it like pins to my exposed skin. It was meant to warn us, in a most fortuitous manner that Winter was following right on its heels and would soon roll down off the Tundra with little resignation, until exhaustion overtook it somewhere down south. I would then sit back down and cuddle into my rut as earth comforted my tormented skin, and warmed me to my heart.

CHAPTER THREE

Peanut

The kitchen window faces out to the backyard. I move through the lilac bushes, holly hocks, rhubarb plants and various tree types that make up our yard. I hope to make it to my room like a facile serpent looking for a cool rock to rest under before being spotted. But as I look through the screened back door, there sits Peanut devouring his morning bowl of "Sugar-Sugar-Sugar Flakes" at the kitchen table that sits abreast the large picture window.

The trick is to get past him without some sort of whining scene. He is chugging fast through the first meal of the day. Like all Saturdays, he is worried about what he could be missing on "Cartoon Morning." His concentration at times like this is total; he is fixated, in a stupor more or less, completely oblivious to the world at large. Any other day I might make attempts to get at the inner Peanut sanctum because this robot-like character unnerves me. To think, totally transfixed over some ridiculous cartoons is a waste of a glorious day. But Peanut hasn't even looked out the window to fancy the possible outdoor fun. For Peanut, that won't happen until after 12 noon—sometime after *Hedge Hog Hill World*. I will attempt to work around him. He will make an occasional scream when I step into the zone between him and the T.V. set. Curlers will grow frustrated with his automaton presents in the path of all cleaning expeditions struck out upon that day, and then she'll make the big move to turn off the set.

Normally Peanut is a rotund, red ball of energetic boyhood. He seems huge really, at least in contrast to Parrot, my kid sister. Huge, red and black, quite a stunning boy with black trim—black thick hair, black eyes and long black lashes. As a baby he never did a whole lot of crying, but he never seemed completely satisfied either. He was always moving, energized by some mysterious urge to flail, grab and pull. He never seemed bored, even if his crib or play-pen was empty. It wasn't necessary for us, his three older siblings to entertain him. He was always somehow pre-occupied. I could see from day one, he had a mind of his own—damn!

Yes, from the very start he contained dynamic presence. No, not all because his plumb baby-ness was overwhelming cherubic perfection; women's maternal hormones fluttering intensely at first sight of him. He had a natural charm he hasn't lost even now when his features have evolved to a large fleshiness. It's all some sort of mysterious sensuality I can't quite put my fingers on. Perhaps a nocturnal lustiness some people possess as a sort of scent/potion, an introductory handshake, even at an early age. Something like a wild animal using his greatest means of introduction and communication through sensory impressions.

Parrot, Keith and I accepted his powers from the start and carried on with our own childish maneuvers. Peanut is some kind of specialty child, and I, as his sometimes junior guardian, respond to his slight peculiarities in an off-hand, "he's a little peculiar but cute" fashion. And his monologues with the other world, I simply ignore.

Peanut, from as early as he could talk spoke of *Little People*, Moopits or Nunapees (Indians call them in their language), of inhabiting his sleeping suit, or as he grew older, inhabiting his room. Those "*Little People*" have haunted the landscape of Turtle Island for as long as anyone knows. They especially like children because all that Little People want, my Grandma once told me, is to play. She said they can be found in the dark shadows of trees and valleys on nights without full moons. They laugh and joke with each other and call out to the young at heart to "come play." She says they can be so annoying because it's hard to play with spirits.

Peanut is earth and fire in every sense, spoiled by his own inner world of delight, illusion and fantasy—intrusions resented. If he compromises his exuberance and spirit at all, it is only to the characters within, the unseen, or at breakfast before cartoons, in anticipation. He is a high-strung, emotion wielding, solid, compact kid. Passion to the women surrounding him; always after hugs and kisses I am too grossed-out to bestow. I never ask, just assume it is all a part of his particular puzzle; links from one end of the universe to our first moments on earth. Pieces or fragments of internal and external order, intricately connected together by millions of inexplicable tongues, linked to invisible grooves.

His make-up may be different. His bits and pieces often an annoyance to me, his older sister having to cater to his often unique instincts—an embarrassment really to my "oh so refined" nature. Peanut cannot be considered refined. All his emotions are processed, unwound and displayed as they evolve for all to participate in. My embarrassment alone I guess. People always gravitate to his charm like children to a sprightly puppy. Curlers knew from the start she had delivered a mystical genius into the world's midst.

I have eight years on Peanut so none of his particulars really faze me. Perhaps the age difference eliminates any real interest in connecting to his world and inviting him along to witness some of mine. I usually have the disturbing feeling that if Curlers views our making connections, she will line me up for steady baby-sitting and childcare, a situation I've worked endlessly to avoid. That teen occupation is not for me. I did my duty earlier in life. I worked six ways to Sunday, attempting to develop interpersonal skills with youth from ages three months to 12 years old. Everything from changing diapers to scrubbing some lazy old housewife's windows; from chasing six year old long distance runners across town, to watching every television station's closing address while moms and dads are out tangoing at "Gill's" up in Durham; all at the cool rate of .25 cents per hour. It's worth it to Parrot, she likes cavorting with the *wee ones. It* gives her a sense of control. Not me. The strain, my impatience at being tied down with anything but ideal children, makes it difficult rationalizing the "sitting service" as anything more than wasting my time. So I view Peanut in my peripherals, enjoying the picture from a distance, not gazing long enough to take on any responsibility.

I think I'll just cave-in to the struggle. I may as well pour myself a bowl of cereal and resign to the inevitable. At least I will be ready when Curlers dishes out a list of household duties to be done rapid fire the moment she sets eyes on us—Parrot and me. I hear her wondering about in the next room. She has descended the Master bedroom and I know the routine. She isn't fully awake, despite being on her feet. When she does come to, after a cup of coffee laced with thick cream and enough sugar to disguise the essence of Java, she'll scan the horizon for items to be included on the list: floors to be scrubbed, toilet bowl sanitation—all three bathrooms, ironing, vacuuming, laundry, walls washed, lawn mowing, furniture polished, mirrors shined, and on and on. Every bit is written down on note paper and divided in two. The lists are offered up to Parrot and myself like inmates at the Federal Pen: *Step on it and no complaints. In fact, I want to see a smile on your faces while you do it!*

Parrot and I begin each session bickering about which list we want to work. Somehow I almost always end up with the list that includes bathroom sanitation. Parrot puts up such a humiliating display of disgust mixed with anguish at the very thought of sticking her hand in a toilet bowl, that I cave in to the tantrum and fork over the more delicate chores.

From time to time, I flat-out refuse bathroom duty. Not even Parrot's whining or foot-stomping can change my mind in regard to going one-on-one with the latrines. I'm aware, as Curlers reminds us weekly, there are rubber gloves and foot-long brushes to use in those hard-to-get-to spots, but that doesn't alleviate our delicate sensibilities much. Parrot, on her occasional turn, will sweep through the entire list before I have even completed one item, then she drags out the lavs until Curlers can barely stand the aura she has created, or the maudlin atmosphere either bathroom evokes as we partake of their services throughout the day. By the time she gets kicked out of the house entirely, I have long since checked off each duty, mowed the lawn, and gone to work on hanging out.

If I have failed to mention what my siblings of the masculine sex are busying themselves with on such occasions it's because they are somehow exempt from such discipline. That's right, not a care in the world as far as household duties go. Why, you may ask? Well, I ask that same question regularly, and still no straight answer. Now what in the world do the folks think they're impressing upon these day-dreamers? It's women's work? Seems to me work is work. It's not more fun for me. I am in no particular way better equipped than they are. It's not like they're busy bringing home the bacon. It's completely unjust, and burns me to the core! They'll get theirs! They'll marry some vivacious playgirl who'll flat-out refuse to dirty her hands with lawn and garden, or household chores, then they will be introduced to the world of mop and broom. A whole new world will open up to them, and I will know true peace in my heart…

Today I meet up with Parrot in the backyard by the rhubarb patch. She throws herself sullenly on the ground and pulls out a thick stem of the red, tart, root. She is acting annoyed. I suppose over her banishment from the inner sanctum due to the sluggish work performance and lack of quality cleaning.

"I don't see why you should act so put down. If you would just get the work done and get it over with like I do, it would be over and done in no time. Geez, it's not like you're doing a bang up job! You're dragging around and acting like a poor suffering invalid. Actually, I really get the feeling you think you're too good for a few household chores. Well what about me then?" I ask, beginning to get worked up "If you're too good, then what does that make me—the family clean machine?!"

"Oh, just shut-up, okay? I hate doing toilets. I simply hate them. You might be able to stick your hands into the bowels of the monster, but I get the feeling some big slimy sewer creature is going to slurp up and grab my hand while I'm innocently scrub-a-dubbing," she replies, getting worked up too.

"Oh, please, how come this so-called Sewer Monster never seems to have an appetite when someone is sitting on the facility, huh? I'd expect that kind of excuse from Peanut, what with his overactive imagination and all, but you can't be serious!"

"So what you're saying is I haven't got any imagination?" Parrot jibes indignantly.

I'm about to reply when Curlers hollers out the backdoor, "Are you girls out there?"

Parrot and I look at each other wondering how to respond. A batch more of hang-around-the-house chores and Parrot's bad attitude could crossover in my direction.

Neither one of us respond.

"Tammi is at the front door looking for you!" Curlers shouts after spotting us stretched out along the holly hocks and rhubarb.

What a relief, I think to myself. That's a clear sign 'busy hands' duties are over...and the argument with Parrot. It was all making futility look like it was my only real companion.

"Come on," I say leaping up, "let's go see what Tammi has cookin' this afternoon."

Rounding the corner of the house, I am already refocusing my energy on some kind of afternoon free of worldly responsibilities. Parrot crawls along behind me, still locked in moody reluctance from her morning chores. She's always had a harder time throwing off distasteful mental cobwebs. I know once we come up with a plan though, it will gradually take hold and she will become a whole-hearted participant, or head up to her room and get lost in pulp.

"Hey, Tammi!" I yell rounding the side of the house and out into the open ground of our front yard. "Any news? Anything exciting happening around town today?"

"Hell, Celia, your enthusiasm could be infectious…if it weren't for the fact that this is Beaverton. As we all know it is slower than any snail around here, and always will be. I guess some people might find this charming, but boring is the real term for it," she spews, as though she were stating fact.

"Oh, here we go" I mutter. "I'm surrounded by malcontents and complainers."

"Let's face it Celia, we're going to have another long, dull, Beaverton summer. I'm stuck here with a family of mental deficients. My father can't afford, or just plain won't consider a family vacation anywhere, not even to one of the smaller ten thousand lakes. It's not that I want to be sandwiched into a car with the four of them. I definitely don't, but it's the principle. We can't do anything like a normal bunch of folks. No, we've got to be dull and routine, and without any hope of exploration, excitement, or inspiration at the very least!"

I slump over and collapse on the red cement stoop connected to our screened-in front porch. I lay back and feel the coolness of the slab and shade my eyes from the sun.

Parrot moves to take its twin on the other side of the porch steps, apparently as bored as I am with Tammi's continual whining over being miscast in her family tree. I roll my head in Parrot's direction. She looks over dimly, signaling the same dissatisfaction with Tammi's monologue.

"Hey Tammi, let's go out to Timmy Hern's place. He'll let us ride the horses and hang out in the woods around his family's farm," I suggest.

"No thanks,"Tammi responds, a little too fast. "I know you like that guy, but what nerd material. I just can't work up any interest in talking with him."

"Tammi, don't take offense, but I find the fact that just because Timmy has an extraordinary interest in books and science, you don't want anything to do with him. That's kinda shallow on your part. He's very easy to talk to, and very much a gentleman. Or, is it because he's growing up on a farm and smart to boot that bothers you?"

"He's just a NERD! No sophistication, not much in the common sense department, and couldn't get any, even if he was willing to pay for it. And it's not that he won't be in line to get out of here after graduation; I'm sure he'll be accepted to the college of his choice. It's just that he doesn't appreciate what it means to get out of this town. The importance of that is wasted on a guy like him!" Tammi states with confidence. "You can see what I mean, can't you

Parrot?" As she asks she turns her attention to a daydreaming Parrot, hoping to appeal to some common cynicism.

Parrot looks up slowly and simply says, "I'm not in the mood to go horseback riding."

Apparently she had tuned-out Tammi, or didn't want to bother getting involved in such a discussion. "Neither one of you has a car anyway, and unless we thumb out there and back…hey, which might be fun, I might consider that!"

"That seals it for me; I'm *not* thumbing to a nerd's place and back. I've got standards you know," says Tammi looking stern, her mind made up. "Getting all hot and sweaty standing out on that dusty old highway! Gimme a break!"

"Okay, okay," I interject. "Let's forget that idea. It's pretty obvious I'm the only one interested in really doing anything. Besides, what with the dance and all tonight, it could put a little strain on my evening plans, time-wise."

"That's right," pipes in Tammi, "I've got to make periodic appearances at home so they see I've been around. If it looks like I've taken off for the day, the old folks will nix my being out at night too. Don't ask me for the logic behind that thinking. It's just one of those unspoken rules I have to wind my way around *carefully*."

"Alright, here's my last idea. If you guys aren't up for this then you're on your own." I say in exasperation. "Let's head down to the river and do some sunbathing. It's nothing too strenuous for anyone, and if we use our usual spot no one will be around to bother us. I need to get away from the "Clean Machine" and the obnoxious smell of *pine-cleaner* for awhile. So, you are either with me, or you're not. I'm going one way or the other."

Tammi produces a faint smile and with a new found perkiness says, "Sounds fine to me. That'll eat up some time and I can still show up at the house for a couple of hours before dinner."

"Yeah, I'm in, but I'm going to have to have lunch first, if you don't mind Celia?" Parrot interjected, as if the whole expedition hinged on rejuvenating her taste buds rather than her depleted enthusiasm. I suppose after a morning spent altering her, "I'm above all this" countenance to a mere scrub women, really built up an appetite.

"Geez, we're all agreed then. We'll sunbathe down by the river, right?" I reiterate, making sure everything is clear. "At our usual spot down off the railroad tracks?"

"Of course," says Tammi. "How about we meet back here in twenty minutes? I'll stop off at home to eat and change into some roaming outfit and my swimsuit, then be right back."

"Sure thing," I reply. "If we're done first, we'll just head down to your house." Rolling down off the stoop, I head up the steps remembering my last purpose for being in my mother's domain. I holler back over my shoulder, "That is, unless the 'Big One' doesn't come up with some complaints about shoddy workmanship!"

"Yeah," agrees Parrot. "If things aren't ship-shape, we could be under house arrest and rehearsing swabbing the poop deck."

"What are you two talking about?" Tammi asks looking perplexed.

Tammi's long anguishing stories of drudgery and torture at the hands of her parental authorities never seem to include any indication that her routine torment has anything to do with household chores. Never once have I seen Tammi with the likes of a broom or the smell of bleach permeating from her hands at time like these, a Saturday afternoon. But then, whoever is picking up the slack at the Larson household, slack is all it can be called. Tammi's discourses on her inner and outer search for greater sophistication overlooks the interior affects of her family abode's lack of upkeep and orderliness. Noting this, I think its useless explaining what I am talking about.

"Never mind," I answer with a hint of contentiousness in my voice, "We'll see you in twenty minutes. Be ready!"

Parrot and I swing through the screen door on the porch simultaneously, mutually conscious of our interest in slinking across the house to the kitchen. As I open the heavy front door into the house, it produces a deep groan I hope is only audible to the two of us. We move from exterior heat of the outdoors to the exceptional coolness within.

During the summer, sunlight rarely touches the interior, shades are drawn and windows shut as Curlers sweeps through the rooms of the house every morning after she rises. Although I am a little unnerved by this practice, it truly works, and yet the din cast throughout the interior keeps me outdoors most of the day. My own room is filled with the day's sun. The shades are rarely drawn, even at night, and I shut the door as I come and go, to appease the dark she insists on.

We glide silently down the hall past the living room, dining room and den. In the kitchen, Peanut is at the table wolfing down what looks to have once been a bologna sandwich. An *Indian steak* (as we like to call them), has been cut into four squares, and the corner of each a bite is missing. Having sampled, Peanut must have decided the bologna was all he really wanted because the bread squares are laid open: mayonnaise face up and meat missing. I want to tell him the bread is the best part, but it's not a good time to create a fuss. So instead, I open the refrigerator door and peruse the shelves for something satisfying.

20

The neon orange-colored American cheese squares glow from their space in the door, and the thought of a grilled cheese sandwich strikes my fancy. I move to pull out a frying pan and notice Parrot is pouring herself a bowl of corn flakes. So this is the impressive lunch she so hotly desired.

I down the grilled sandwich at the kitchen table, keeping my eye on Curlers out the back picture window. She is on her knees rearranging the isle of flax in the back flower garden—her summertime obsession.

I look over at Parrot, still shuffling flakes around in her bowl, "I'm heading upstairs to put my suit on. I want to be out of here before Curlers comes back in. If you're coming I suggest you do the same thing."

Okay, Sis, I guess I've had enough cereal. I'll meet you out front."

CHAPTER FOUR

The Chase

We reach Tammi's house just as she is coming out the door. "Hey girls, prefect timing!" she yells out at us, and hops down the few steps to the front walk. I stop at the bottom of the walk way and wait for her to catch up, while Parrot strides on ahead, then hangs back at the street crossing.

"Let's hit the railroad tracks from here and follow them all the way down to our spot," I suggest as we catch up to Parrot.

"Fine with me," Tammi replies. Parrot moves on ahead in silence.

The street comes to a quick dead end as town turns to brush and tall grasses. The expanse preceding the railroad track and the river is made up of a variety of green and brown hues with flickers of purple, blue or red where early summer blossoms of wild flowers grow. We swish through the brush and quickly enter the thicket of trees that border east to west along either side of the tracks. This route to the tracks is faster than the other way which circuits through town. I often take that road–Route 2, which stops at the tracks just west on the out-skirts of town. The advantage to Route 2 is it's a clear path; no bushwhacking or thistles that can cut across bare legs, but it means walking through town, and that lacks the privacy I sometimes crave. I like this path we're on; it's quiet, deserted–eerily so, and always somber and still. The trees grow tall along this stretch and canopy the shaded bed of track below. River access is difficult from here as beyond this growth of trees the land drops immediately to the water. Here, there isn't a beach-like spot in which to drop our towels and bathe along the water's edge. At best, we'd have to dig our heels into the river bank to keep from falling in. Further on down, past the clearing, we'll have privacy and comfort.

Whenever I feel I need a place to retreat far from the worldly pressures of parents, school or guys, I think of coming along here…but I don't. Maybe I'm a first-class *chicken*, or it's something instinctual since I never take this route without someone else along. The path is too hidden, too shrouded and protected. Although, when I walk through the inner coolness, I feel as if I'm walking on a heraldic coronation path to my destiny. And perhaps it's not just me, because everyone grows silent on this walk through…to the light.

It's warming back in the sun as we trod on past Route 2's final destination, the tracks. Parrot is still several paces ahead of Tammi and me. She's mumbling something inaudible back in our general direction.

I bellow back up to her, "What's that you say, Princess?"

"I said: motor gang ahead, sweetheart," she yells loud and clear, fully turning in our direction.

In unison, Tammi and I crank our heads out and around Parrot's torso. Sure enough, Beaverton's recent arrival, a wing of a motorcycle brotherhood is hanging out a ways down the track. It's not the whole crew, at least not what I can see from here. Parrot stops and waits for us to catch up.

"What do you think girls? Should we keep going?" I ask, hopefully sounding casual and not overly concerned.

"Oh hell," Parrot pipes up, "they're just some guys on motorcycles, so what else is new?" She says this in her new droll talk, always somewhat bored, somewhat above it all.

"Yeah, I'd like to get a close up look at these guys anyway," puts in Tammi. "I've seen 'em at a distance in town, looking tough, but I have a feeling the closer we get the cuter they'll be. Besides, there are three of us, and you know: safety in numbers."

So on we plod like the Three Musketeers, three abreast and invincible. As we approach their scene, four of the bikers move to jump-start their Harleys, revving up the engines to decibels that drown out any hint of nature, or the possibility of hearing an approaching train. One last cyclist rounds his bike, but appears to catch sight of our previously unobserved advance. A tiny knot in my stomach declares its position as I realize *this* biker is going to sit and wait for closer observation. I don't know why, but this intense scrutiny makes me nervous and very self-conscious. I look away from his apparent interest to scan the other bikers maneuvering on the rocks and gravel of the tracks, and preparing to shoot a straight line down to Route 2. The three of us get the idea right away and step quickly to the outer side of the track railing. Parrot and Tammi move off right, and I make a quick hop to the left. The bikes rev up again, then move out single file, roaring past us like great chariots in the days of the Roman Empire. The *RoadWarriors* peel past us, throwing up dust and pebbles, looking sneaky and demonic. Nothing cute about any of them, especially the big gaps between their teeth, and tattoos placed helter-skelter without thought of designerly placement.

As they clear out, my attention again focuses on the fifth guy still casually seated and staring from his cycle.

Parrot, Tammi, and I reunite and retake our stride mid-track. And, although I may be embarrassed by his penetrating and licentious eyes, my contempt is growing from this overt and obnoxious intrusion into our privacy.

"Oh geez, what's with this guy anyway," I mumble as we are within a stone's throw of his bike.

"I don't know," says Tammi. "Let's just ignore him. Let's go on as if he isn't even here."

We stride silently closer…but the silence is awkward, so I pointlessly ask Parrot as we are abreast the biker, "Did you remember to wear your bathing suit?"

"Hey Honey, you're looking mighty fine today," the biker purrs. "You're just how I like 'em—tall, tight and cool. Go ahead and stick your nose in the air, I like 'em prissy too!" His throat like gravel stones, or more likely, chain-smoked to rough sandpaper!

Parrot, Tammi, and I exchange glances. Who was he talking to, "*tall, tight, and prissy?*"

"That's you, Chickie! You with the long black hair," he says, answering my silent question in a slithery, serpentine manner.

We have passed his perch by the time this declaration is aimed at my back. I mumble, "That's great," to the girls, then yell back, "You BOZO!"

Shocked, I gulp down hard, incredulous at my own brashness. His bold arrogance struck a distasteful cord, forcing me to lash out with no restraint or concern for possible retribution…for one split second. Tammi and Parrot stiffen with the realization that I truly uttered those words. And…from behind we hear. yell..

"*What'd you call me?!*"

I hear him jump-starting his Harley's engine. He revs her up quickly. Without even turning to look we know he isn't moving to join his crew.

"I'm outta here!" Parrot squeals!

We take off down the tracks half listening for the sounds of a revving cycle. We beat it out of there like three rabbits high on fear—our feet hoping for any traction the rocks surrounding the ties will allow before they flip into flight behind us. I stroke left down into the woods below the railroad track's embankment. Arms and legs flailing spastically, I move out and catch the blurred colors of Parrot's hot pink shorts and Tammi's orange sneakers racing off to the right and into the reeds and rushes of the river that lay immediately below the railroad dike.

I'm quickly aware of the reality of thrusting into the dense brush and canopy of pines and half-dead elms I hope will be safety. I vaguely feel the scratchy, abrasive weeds bristling at my bare legs.

The motorcycle roars. The rider twists the throttle and thrusts the machine down the track in our direction without hesitation.

Maybe if he catches us he will just tease and laugh at us for being such chickens. Or, maybe he will chat us up and flirt, then go back and laugh with his friends at our girlish behavior. But then, I'm not interested in spending any time finding out because I could be wrong and end up with slash marks from the knife of some overly sensitive misfit. After all, I'm sure he's been called worse names then BOZO!

My body is moving of its own accord and the sensation of muscles lifting limbs, pushing feet off the ground, has disappeared. All I know is I see a dark hiding place among the denser part of the woods ahead. The tree limbs hang low enough that it surely escapes anyone's view from the track above. Adrenaline has taken over and one goal drives me—**run**! I should have been clocked. Miss Berg, the track coach, would have me practicing the quarter mile for All State Championship the first day of school.

I hear the motorcycle coming and I press hard at the only strength and control I believe are left in my limbs. I just can't let him spot me before I'm halfway home…

WHACK!!

UGGHH!! Ooew, I've hit something! And gasp for breath…as everything… goes… black…

I stiffen up as I come to. My eyes focus at the maze of branches and blue sky above. It's still, quiet and cooler in the woods. I hear the motorcycle off in the distance, which is apparently motionless at the moment since I can't hear rocks grinding together with tread pressing over them. But I sense the *derelict* searching for a view of us from his trusty mount.

I lay still, splayed out on my back, recovering the wind that shot out against the wall of fear I pressed hard to burst through, and on home to freedom. I lift my head ever so slightly to glimpse the force that could thwart me so resolutely from my escape. Ahh, geez, some farmer is running wire fencing quietly through the woods. I suppose he means to keep his cows or any other livestock from wondering onto the tracks and down to the river. Well, bless his heart.

In the distance I hear the cycle turning around and moving back up the tracks. He's moving along slowly. I can feel his eyes moving back and forth from one side of the track to the other, which must means he hasn't spotted Parrot or Tammi either.

Ugh, I feel dizzy. A dull ache is growing from left to right, just below my chest where the wire fencing tried to sever my bod in two. I would consider moving further into the woods and perhaps complete safety were it not for the increasing pressure across my chest. I'll just lay here hoping I'll recede far enough into the womb of Mother Earth that I simply metamorphose to camouflage, and invisible to the leers of distant eyes. He is riding closer and within view from my hiding place. I become the leaves and earth, no longer filling my body with bones, blood and guts, but flattening out into forest compost. I'm holding my breath. I hear him continue on I think to the clearing where the chase began. He stops…waits… then revs the cycle's motor… Finally I hear the thing buck; hanging in mid-air for one split second…then roars off on the old dusty road to town.

I lay and listening a bit longer 'cause I want to be sure the man and beast have hit route 2 to Beaverton. Lifting up gingerly, ugh, everything seems to hurt. Breathing deep and on my feet, do the lungs have the capacity they knew before the chase? I guess I'm okay. At least I can get home. I'd better find the girls first. I'll hit the tracks and case the river. But there they are! Parrot's head pops up over the other side, and Tammi's pops up immediately after.

"Man, that guy's crazy!" Parrot blurts out.

"I told you *not* to run!" throws in Tammi.

"Hey Tammi, I don't remember you saying anything of the sort," I counter. "Just what do you think would have happened *if* we would have waited around to find out? He seemed downright bent out of shape about being called *Bozo!* As if a guy like that doesn't get called a lot worst names every single day."

"You know, Sis, you're not looking so good!" said Parrot, scrutinizing my brown-turned-to- ashen complexion and twisted clothing.

"I don't know what happened with you guys, but I ran full speed ahead into old man Warchek's wire fencing. All I remember is getting snapped backwards and flying freeform through the air. Then it all went black!"

Regrouped atop the track, our eyes fix sharply at the far end where we originally past the motorcycle gang and finally heard "Bozo" make his exit.

"Let's cut through the field," I suggest, pointing my thumb off to our right. "If he or his pals should still be looking for us or come back, we'll be sitting ducks walking on the road into town."

We head down the embankment and into the tall grasses and weeds of the open field. My legs have already been scratched up from the bushwhacking I've done today. I'm not even trying to avoid the sticklers or pricklers we now brush through to home.

"If we hear a motorcycle we can hide in the grass, and probably not be seen. Let's hurry though, I'd rather get out of here walking than have to crawl out of this field on my hands and knees," I say trying not to show the pain I feel.

"I think you're being paranoid," says Tammi. "We're letting him have some good laughs at our expense. He's probably with his pals right now, laughing about how scared we looked when he revved his engine. All he wanted was to see how high we'd jumpand it was probably pretty funny because we shot up fast and high."

"Look Tammi, I don't know why you're being so casual about this. How much experience have you had with this sort of stuff anyway? I know you must have seen the words, *Hell's Alive* written on their backs. I've heard plenty of gross stuff about them; things that make me pretty *paranoid*. I wonder if Uncle Reese knows they're around here. And besides Tammi, I didn't see you stopping to talk. It looked like you took off in a shot right alongside Parrot and me."

"Well, once you guys started running, I had to. But what I'm saying is: if we had ignored him, and casually kept on walking without paying any attention, he would have lost interest and moved along without much commotion. After we took off like helpless sheep, he could see he got our attention and wanted more."

"Look, he got my attention as soon as I heard him gun that motorcycle. From then on my instincts said, *'this man means trouble'*. The chance that he only meant to be cute was no longer on my mind," I say defending my earlier flight.

"…He was kind of cute, wasn't he?" chirps Parrot, changing the subject only because her short attention span is onto another angle.

CHAPTER FIVE

THE DANCE

Parrot is in tow, but I don't mind. Keith is walking up ahead looking like chaperoning the two of us is the last order of business on his dance card. And that's just fine with me because losing him is a natural.

I made my concessions to Curlers—bring my tag-along little sister under the "protective" eye of my stronger, older brother, Keith, and I wouldn't have to hand in a questionnaire of details concerning the dance and its participants. After all, Curlers has lived in this town long enough to know what a summer dance at the Armory means.

As far as I'm concerned, it means heavy flirting and admiring the new motorbike some boy's father endowed him with as a gesture to his coming of age. The guys think it means showing of their manhood, kind of like those birds during mating season hoping a female will take an interest. At the very least, it signals to other males that they have their stuff. They fluff up their feathers and prance around sticking their chests out. When I see the local guys out on their new bikes, it reminds me of those birds. They drive up and down Main Street looking confident on a brand new shiny cycle—showing off their manhood. I guess dads are saying, *welcome to the man pack, son*! All the girls just laugh and hope the right guy will ask us to hop on back for a ride. But if it's the wrong guy that can be kind of tough because you wouldn't want the right guy to spot you sitting on someone else's bike—he might think you're occupied. And to complicate things even more, you've got to put your arms around the guy's waist to hang on, creating ideas you're sure you don't want him to have. It's a balancing act alright.

None of that is Keith though. He'll meet up with some pals of his and they will be lured to the stage like zombies in a trance; listening intently, catching every nuance the band from Durham, a town up the road, can make. These guys don't even move to the beat. Maybe they don't have rhythm. Or maybe they're really interested in some girl, but disguise their feelings by somehow keeping one eye on the band and the other on this mysterious love they can't actually introduce themselves to.

As we near the end of the block, I holler up to Keith to hold on just one second. "I've got to stop for Tammi."

I don't always remember knowing Tammi. Her parents were farmers until a couple of years ago. They went belly up and the bank took everything they had. I guess it was pretty traumatic because it seems like every time I see her dad he's talking about, *'those assholes, the bank people.'* He moved the family into town after he was forcibly removed from the property and rented the house at the end of the block from the Bergstrom's—this town's land barons. Mr. Bergstrom just happened to need a foreman to run the potato sorters at his potato chip factory, so Tammi's dad had something to fall back on, but it wasn't farming… I guess he's still bitter.

Tammi went to elementary and part of junior high at a little school house that teaches some of the farm kids who live too far away for Beaverton's one-and-only school bus to pick them up. Part of the drive means going down dirt roads that are unusable during the spring thaws, although most of the farmers get out with snowmobiles or tractors, and keep a vehicle sitting close to the good road.

I met Tammi awhile after they had moved into town. Actually, Peanut met Tammi's little brother, Donald first. He brought him home to look at some kind of insect he had captured in a jar. Donald came to the house after school, sort of tagging along in his well worked-over tennis shoes and obvious hand-me-down wardrobe—at least two sizes too large. Apparently, Donald's mother felt he could grow into them before the true colors faded completely from childhood use. I was concerned for our health because Donald looks like a mutant creation from the local waste dump. Perhaps the mess contrasts too severely with his fair skin and blonde curly wig-like hair, having never benefited from a comb or brush. Donald is the youngest of five Larson children, and not all that is fair about him is appearance. Donald is more or less—and often more, a really average kid. In school he's usually quiet and speaks only when spoken to. Yet, on odd occasions (probably during a full moon) he can lack the self-control and discipline of any of the worst kids in school. His grades are below average, but his teachers know he's picking up some of the information because on tests he always answers the hardest questions correctly, and fumbles through all the easy ones. Despite the crusty coating that hangs on him like a bad winter cold, I sense an inner kid who can walk and chew gum at the same time. Actually, it scares me a little to know that Donald is not what he seems. I guess my attempt to put him in an easy category forces me to review his contrasts every time I see him, and feel he could possibly have my number better than I have his.

It seems Mrs. Larson no longer has the inclination to oversee her kid's appearance and upkeep. This humiliates Tammi to no end, especially since they're living in town now. Out on the farm, I figure she was more accepting since no one would have seen them but the immediate family. I hardly ever see Mrs. Larson myself, even though they only live at the end of the block, and Tammi and I have been hanging out for the last four years. At this point, I'm not sure I really care to get to know her. When the brood first moved in, I kind of wondered what she was so busy occupying herself with that the Larson compound could be so disheveled. Now I sense that Mrs. Larson has some sort of overwhelming discomfort with the in-town world, which may be even more debilitating than Tammi's own discomfort with her family. I feel as if their powerful self-consciousness could fill a room full of static so great they would be able to light all the bulbs and turn channels on the TV set. I'm not really comfortable joining in on this kind of intensity. Just viewing the upkeep of the family and Tammi's apparent disdain for either one of her parents, leads me to believe I too will acquire the same sort of feelings for them.

I don't want to view all this negatively because on the other hand, this may not be entirely true. Tammi has a concrete curfew and she abides by these rules strictly. And like clockwork, every Sunday, the family squeezes into their Ford and attends the Catholic mass, decked out in each one's finest—with or without the benefit of bath or shower. So I have to believe her parents have some concern for her welfare.

Tammi isn't like the rest of her family, and resents having come from a farming background. She has never actually come right out and said this, but when anyone mentions life on the farm, she always takes the opposite point of view. It's funny, secretly, I envy her rural education. I have always wanted to know more about animals and making plants grow. Something in my nature gravitates to the roots of life, and I feel as if I would be that much more prepared if I knew how to work with the earth. Tammi cringes at having anything to do with dirtying her hands. And although we are hanging out pals, I dislike the embarrassment she wears like a badge because her family farmed.

"God, get me out of here!" she mutters storming out the front door past Parrot and me, heading straight down to the end of their front walk. "They're all just crazy! How did I get so lucky to be a member of that bunch of animals? How can I survive one more year of idiots delight?"

Parrot and I shoot each other a frown. "I hope we don't have to listen to this all the way to the Armory," I say to Parrot. "I've got boys to think of."

Keith didn't wait for us as we stopped to pick up Tammi. He strolled on up to the corner of Pine and Main Streets, casting a quick glance back as he took a right turn towards the armory and disappeared from sight. He's probably relieved at ditching us and out of his hair for awhile.

"Don't worry Celia, I'm fine. Once I'm out of their view and vice-a-versa, everything becomes shiny and bright. The world feels fresh and open to all my own interests. I suck in a deep breath and forget all about them. So you see, I'm happy and charged up for a hot time on the dance floor. What happened to your brother? I thought he was our escort—isn't that what you said this afternoon?"

"Yeah Tammi, but you know that was mostly for my mother's benefit. What would he want with us around? And what would we want with him? He can be just like a nagging wife if he takes duties like this seriously. We'll catch up with him sooner or later."

"It's only that I told my parents he would be our chaperone… And…I suppose it would ease my mind knowing they weren't going to show up at some point and embarrass the hell out of me by insisting I go home with them," says Tammi, defending her inquiry of my nerdy older brother.

I have the feeling Tammi harbors some especially warm feelings for Keith, but for whatever reason, never brings it out in the open, or openly chases him. Sometimes I watch her flirting with him; getting real close and smiling up into his face with her pale green eyes. If this moves him at all, he never lets on.

Personally, I can't help but go on and on about whomever looks good at the moment. I probably bore Parrot and Tammi to tears, but I can't help myself. I become consumed with the notion of a guy, and someone has to listen or I will explode. Besides, talking it out kind of takes the edge off; releases the energy and dispels the myth—their myth, the male as superior beast myth, the whole I am cool and dangerous and can do it without shame of retribution myth. I can feel free like the way I think they feel free, by exposing my inclinations for them.

"I suppose I'll end up hanging out with Keith," blurts out Parrot. "You two will probably disappear on me and I'll end up tailing the zombie around."

"Oh, come on Parrot, you're going to have fun," I tell her, only half believing my own words. "Everyone will be there. You can't always sit home and read those trashy romance novels. At some point you're going to have to do some real living. When you do leave home, you're going to suffer from arrested development, and then you'll be completely lost in the greater world if you hide yourself away now. Besides, one of the only reasons I got to go out tonight was if you were in tow. It's not that big a favor for you to go along with me, is it?"

"No, but I do expect some kind of return," she answers back.

"Hey, I let you wear my new size 34 B cup bra, didn't I?" I'd already bartered with her. "Yeah, but it scratches, and is giving me a backache. So I think I want a favor that feels a little better than this. If a favor is as uncomfortable as this one, then it's not worth it."

We're hitting the corner of Main Street and Pine. Tammi starts twirling and skipping, flinging her arms and jumping to some imaginary music or rhythm only she could hear, happy to be away from authority's view. Every so often the breeze catches the hem of her skirt as she pirouettes up the street. The wind raises her skirt high enough to get a bird's eye view of her underwear, beefy thighs and butt. Tammi doesn't let loose like this often. Although, once in awhile, in the middle of one of her usual tirades she'll interrupt herself and break into lively banter about the state of pure ecstasy.

Tammi can go at top speed maligning everyone and everything that annoys her. These endless bursts seem to come immediately after lunch. I don't know if this has to do with some association with food or guilt at having eaten lunch altogether. I don't know, but her negative mood can leave me low and dragging for English class, which follows lunch break. I've never adjusted to her afternoon swing upward. By the time the departing bell rings for freedom, she is giddy and glowing with enthusiasm where anything is game, and she'll take her rightful place as entertainment chairmen. So watching her prancing and swirling down Main Street, she is back in the swing of hopes and great expectations. I smile and loosen up, knowing we have the best time in mind, even though we'll each find it in our own way.

Parrot is on her own. If she doesn't have fun, at least she's out of the house with a chest enhanced by my more mature bra size. And, knowing Parrot as I do, she will test the new image out for a couple of hours then boredom will overwhelm her as she realizes the novelty is mostly her own. She will head home early, tired of begging for attention by unnatural means. She probably has some case study in mind. What type of individual notices her chest size, and what kind of attention does it get? It will all be theoretical and conclude whether or not she can continue to *enhance* her appearance this way.

Strolling up Main Street the Armory comes into sight. It looks solid and resolute against the ambient setting sun.

This is my favorite time of day. I suppose it is for most people. Suddenly everything is silent, holding its breath as if uncertain the day will become night once again. A chill permeates the air for just an instant, announcing the next phase of the cycle is upon us. The crickets, frogs, bats—the night creatures herald the coming with proud vociferating; and the grasses, rustled by the change, release their finest scent, bidding a fond farewell to radiance—for one more rotation. I feel as if I can float above and beyond the vast fields of crops and suck in the delicious scent. But sounds of a crowd gathering outside the Armory halts my flight and reminds me of my purpose.

"Oh, Shit!" Parrot implores sharply, yet under her breath. "There's the guy from the railroad tracks today!"

"Yeah, it is him, isn't it?" I say spotting him. "Tammi, look who's on that Harley by the Armory on the sidewalk," I holler meekly up to Tammi who is still prancing up ahead of us.

"Oh, god, it's that *jerk*! Well, let's just ignore him. He's only a big teaser and thinks it's funny scaring the pants off girls like us. I think if we show him we don't scare that easily he'll move on to some other weakling he can work over," Tammi concludes.

"Maybe you're right and we're overreacting to his tough boy image. I wonder where the rest of his zealous followers are? Where's the bike brigade tonight? He doesn't look nearly as cold and ugly as he did earlier. He seems a little lonely off on his own."

You know, I think he seems like a sad outsider watching the local kids gather for the dance. At this moment I feel as if I can read his expression, and acceptance is all he really wants. Instantly, I loss all fear of him. I know I have what he doesn't have, and feel strong knowing his weakness.

"He's kind of cool, coming off like he's some kind of mama's boy when underneath that sweet routine he's probably a genuine killer," says Parrot.

"Yeah, let's just avoid him and act like this afternoon was about three other girls," I say playing up her opinion. "I don't even want to make eye contact. Parrot, now don't go running home alone. When you start getting bored let me know and we'll make sure we all go home together," I say in my best authoritative big sister voice.

"Oh you bet! I know you and Connor Johnson will find each other, and from then on I'll be cast off and adrift in a sea of ferocious barracudas."

It's Parrot back to whining, so I have to say, "Look Parrot, there's no need for such drama. But incase we're underestimating that guy on the cycle, and he really is a pervert, it's better to be safe in numbers. Connor may not show—I'll just die if he doesn't—but of course that is where you can find me if he does."

"And where is THAT? On the dance floor? Hanging on his cycle? Necking behind the Armory? Just where is THAT?" Parrot asks in a *'let's-get-real'* tone.

"Parrot, Parrot, Parrot! Geez, I'll be right here. If worse comes to worse, Keith is suppose to be chaperoning, you know. He'll be easy to find I'm sure."

Tammi slows down and we silently join to cross upper Main Street and on over to the Armory. I press a most sophisticated look on my face, a look of cool aloofness, a look of *'Oh yes, another summer dance—I'm almost above it all'*. Really, I'd die if I missed this. I glance about for Connor, hoping to disguise my exploring eyes with happy waves to various friends already queued up at the door, quietly searching the crowd for the farmer boy of my immediate pursuit. My eyes inadvertently come to a rest on the one soul here I would as soon never see again—the Motorcycle Maniac. Fate isn't doing me any favors. His stare is purposeful with a sarcastic smile. Moving too quickly to turn my glance away, he winks, in utter disregard of my disdain. A chill shoots through my body, shaking the very solid earth on which I stand. If I could run from here without creating a scene or concern, I would. The idea I conjured up of a motherless child is now vanished. What I thought I knew, and what he truly knows are worlds apart. What I have in Beaverton might be just what he wants, but could he get it even if he tried? Parrot maybe right, he comes off like a *mama's boy*, but then again, he could be a cold hard killer.

I suck in the summer evening air hoping a little more wind will unthaw my legs now frozen to the gravel drive. I must find Connor, or Tammi and Parrot, at the very least, Keith, for safety in numbers. As I move through the crowd of Beaverton and the surrounding area's finest youth, it occurs to me this is my town, and all these people are my friends. I have known them all my life and feel protected as I bid each a good evening.

This guy might be scary only because he is different. He lacks approval because he isn't one of the familiar. Should I give him the shadow of a doubt? I can hear myself casting judgments that I know only grow out of fear and not foundation—although, this afternoon seems like a touch of foul play to me. Maybe Tammi is right. He *is* just a big tease and we were good victims. I can't/ won't look back to see if his stare is still burning.

No, I'm going over to see the local guys all hanging out in the parking lot comparing bikes. I turn and see Parrot is a short step behind me. For a change, I was glad she was close by, not only for my own protection, but hers too. I spot Bruce, just a buddy and a moose of a guy, "Hey Bruce, glad your Mom let you out tonight."

"Celia, I haven't needed my Mom's approval to do much of anything for quite awhile now," he responds, "unlike yourself, with a small-fry sister tagging along."

"Have you seen Connor Johnson around tonight?" I quietly inquire.

"Maybe."

"Yeah?" Where'd you see him? How long ago?" I ask, trying not to seem too excited.

"Come on Celia, he isn't your type. He's just a shy guy trying to sneak by. Give him a break," Bruce says mockingly.

"Hey Big Bruce, you wanna give me a ride on your bike?" chirps Parrot, pushing out her falsies.

"Funny kid. But, I don't need any robbing the cradle stories going around. Your Uncle would come after my butt just for thinking about giving you a ride. What are those things hanging off your chest, there?" he says trying hard not to laugh.

Parrot turns slowly and deliberately toward me then asks, "Tell me again how he got through the eighth grade?"

I'm about to ask for a truce and further my inquiries to the Connor situation when we bystanders hear drums begin to pound from out of the Armory's windows and door. Everyone perks up with renewed excitement, naturally activating teen hormones and distracting the routine flirtations and constant flow of juices nourished by the possibility of a hot band and dance moves.

Over my now cautious shoulder, I holler back to Bruce as I move toward the music, "Are you going to be here awhile?"

"Are you saying you care?" he shouts back.

"Of course I care, Bruce. I think of you as one of my better bike buddies. Life wouldn't be the same without you!" Oh god, I hate this schmoozing stuff, but if I'm wrong about this biker maniac, I want some tough guys on my side.

Parrot and I stroll in closer to the door. People are all crowding in, adrenaline flowing from head to toe as the music pulls us magnetically near. I spot Tammi, all bubbly and animated, lost in flirtation with transfixed Gary Perham, son of Frank Perham, "*Outfitters and Dry Goods*".

Tammi is only interested in town boys, and the Perham's are one of the oldest families in Beaverton. If for some miserable act of fate she ends up staying here after high school, at least she is going to marry a townie. No hay-baling, black finger-nailed, sod buster for her. She has already set her sights on military service to remove herself entirely from the scene.

"Tammi, are you coming in with us?" I holler out from the line already formed to press in.

"Nah, don't wait for me. I'll be in shortly," she hollers back.

"That's the last we'll see of her tonight," Parrot relays sarcastically.

"Oh she's just checking out the territory, pretending to have a deep intimate conversation with Gary while seeing if anyone else is noticing her," I respond.

Looking disgusted Parrot says, "Geez, you guys are too weird for me. What a waste of time."

Finally nearing the entrance, I feel a body press in against my back, and hot breath close to my ear. As I turn to see who could be so rushed to get to the dance floor that they are willing to crush me, I hear, "Hey honey, I hope you're going to save the first dance for me. You're kind of tall up close like this, aren't you?"

I snap around quickly for a look at such a nervy guy. There he stands, cocky and bold... and brazen—Motorcycle Maniac looking down at me with complete confidence, as if my interests were naturally all his. I take one long look at him in his weathered biker's jean jacket, a pristine white T-shirt, and probably his only pair of blue jeans, cleaned for the occasion. He wears heavy cycle boots that give me a creepy feeling he could kick someone to death with them if he wanted.

I reel back around without muttering a sound.

Viewing Parrot out of the corner of my eye, I see she has witnessed his intrusion. We walk like zombies into the Armory looking straight ahead. I tremble at the direct contact he has made with *me!* He has isolated *me* out. He has picked *me* out to work over with whatever his gist is. Is there anything about me that says we have anything in common? I am horrified, angry, and insulted, all at the same time. I can feel my head start to throb and...someone places their hand on my shoulder...

"How about this dance? What do yah say? How about this dance?"

I swing around, ready to make a stand and take my chances. It's Connor with a big boyish grin stretched across his ever so relieving face.

"I didn't mean to scare yah, Celia. You look kind of angry. I was only asking if you care to have this dance. I wanted to get to you before anyone else did," he says apologetically.

"I have to admit you scared me a little, but I'm glad you came. Sure, I'll dance with you. I was hoping you'd be here to ask me."

The band moves quietly into a slow number. In a way it's just what I need: a moody song I use to press lightly next to someone stronger I can hang on to for a while until I pull myself together and relax. Connor feels a little shaky himself. I suppose dancing with me is overwhelming. I've never known Connor to have a girlfriend, so this is probably a whole new feeling for him. In a way it's flattering for me, since he's not a mush-face, dunce head. I expect his shyness has led other girls to overlook him, but I find the quality to be quite sweet. He is tall and lean, built like someone who has spent a lot of time working with his muscles. His blonde hair already sun-streaked from planting season, is fine and short, contrasting my thick black braid. I like the difference. As we meld across the floor and gaze out over the auditorium, I spot Parrot slunk against a wall staring nowhere. We rock in another direction. There he is …staring at me. He knows he has my attention; winks and blows me a kiss. *What a gross character! What nerve!*

I turn my head immediately and re-focus to see Tammi's face, all big and round, and turned out like a moonbeam, giggling, as she and Bruce waltz emphatically about the hall. Connor and I swoon around again and I see Keith off in the distance, silhouetted by the glare of stage lights. He stands still and erect like a tree against a full moonlit sky with the bright stage lights outlining his form. I am sure back at home he will give me a complete synopsis of the music, the scene and who was cool and who wasn't. We turn again and there is Parrot, still slunk against the wall, yet this time with one hand on her hip looking exasperated. As we swing toward the spot the Maniac was standing, I peek up from Connor's shoulder to survey his presence. He's gone! Gone at least from the audience he had made of my movements. What a relief. Maybe he's just outside. I don't know. At least he's gone beyond my personal boundaries, my own space. I can relax and be here for Connor…until Parrot makes it impossible to stay any longer.

Parrot, Tammi and I leave skipping high and as wide as we can all the way down Pine. It's probably the only fun Parrot has had all night long. But Tammi and I are delirious with the excitement of the dance. I decide to put the cyclist out of my mind and concentrate on my wonderful evening with Connor.

Tammi throws herself onto the grass of the Anderson's front lawn and I follow right after her. Parrot halfheartedly flops down too, making it obvious she is tired of our antics.

We lay in the shadow of a tall Elm tree looking up into the summer night sky. The quarter moon appears luminous and bright despite its demure size, while the bountiful stars fill the Prussian blue sky with the noiseless sparks of millions of exploding fireworks. The vastness and majesty overwhelm our skittish behavior, awed by something greater than earthly pursuits of boy chasing—at least for now.

Parrot speaks first, "Wow, look, did you see that falling star? "I wish I may, I wish I might, get my wish on the first falling star I see tonight!"

"The Northern lights will be aglow soon. I always love laying out and dreaming about other worlds during that time of year. It's strange to think there could be other worlds alive and well, maybe even more advanced, and we don't even have a clue to who or where they are," I wax. "They could be incredibly homely, or beautiful beyond our wildest dreams, and they could be thinking the same about us."

Tammi adds, "Yeah, someone in New York or Los Angeles, even Minneapolis could be looking up with complete sophistication from alongside their backyard pool, while her husband fixes them a Martini, and wonders the same thing."

We return to silence.

Up the street comes the sound of footsteps traveling quickly along the sidewalk near our hiding place. Transfixed, we lay motionless as they draw closer. I raise my head just high enough to observe Keith clipping on past. He stalks by our retreat without even turning his head in our direction. Tammi and Parrot are watching him too. We burst out laughing for no particular reason other than his appearance on the scene is enough to jolt the three of us back to reality. His stern demeanor is laughable next to our dreamlike state.

We shoot up from the ground and run towards him. I shout out, "I'll beat you guys back to Tammi's house!"

The race is on.

As I whoosh by Keith he mumbles, "You guys are not cool."

Back home again, I curl up in my bed with just a light sheet over me to repel the chill that comes on once the moon is full and high in the evening sky. I lay awake drifting through the events of the evening dance: *does Connor think I'm too aloof, or does the Motorcycle Nut think I am at all interested? How will the dance change my presence in the world tomorrow? Will Connor's interest, or mine, last past the summer?* Early speculation can jinx it all, so best not to think past the immediate. Besides, Tiny, our sweet little mutt of a dog, is up on my bed and digging a sleeping space in the hollow of the fetal circle I'm creating, laying on my side.

CHAPTER SIX

The Cyclist

He is rough cut alright. His blondish hair thick with the consistency of sweat and dust, blown back as the wind might form it at 80-miles an hour. He wears a sleeveless, well-worked over vest that exposes some highly developed biceps and triceps leading to, I imagine, a well defined chest. I sort of think it's a nicely put together physique wasted on a baboon. But not everything about him is coarse and raw, run over by the cheap thrills of motorcycles from one age of development to another.

I picture him in a black suit and tie with shiny black dress shoes, ready for Sunday service. Amid the dirty denim Levis and greasy chains, I sense something of refinement. I don't know if it's his long square nose, not yet broken, sitting atop a rather squared up jaw lending just for an instant a courtly and noble air. It all makes for a second look, a better look, a deeper insight. And, maybe it's nothing more than that; looks atop a powerful machine. For a moment or two he seems important, intelligent, as if belonging with this group of dangerous guys is only a short study on how the other half lives. He has caught my attention, whether I want it that way or not. I don't want to read anything into his character that isn't there; that might create wishful thinking, ultimately leading to real trouble. My folks would never see him as anything other than a bum chasing his irresponsibility from one end of the country to the other—he, having his fun with me, and then packing it all up for another chase down the road. And even this explanation could give him too much credit...

CHAPTER SEVEN

Uncle Reese

Reese Joseph Sitting, my uncle, my mother's older, "full tilt" brother. Uncle Reese is sheriff of Rabbit County, all 3,210 residents, or so it says on the sign when you come across the county line.

Uncle Reese, or Reesie as we call him when we want to bring out his playful side, is a full-blood with a strong and striking resemblance to James Brown—soul singer—and I guess you could say Uncle Reese has a whole lot of soul too. Uncle Reese is a towering figure a 5 ft. 6 inches tall. His hair is a jet black mane set atop a solid square block of a face, and at quick glance most everyone would call him pudgy. But Reese's ability to fill out his uniform is deceptive. Granted, the threads of his navy-blue official's shirt are not just taut; winding their way around his torso, belly and chest, from button back around to buttonhole. It looks as if with one quick move, Reesie could explode through this upper girdle garment with pieces of blue cloth, thread and buttons flying everywhere. Knowing Reese, he thinks he cuts a fine figure. Having seen him once or twice in a swimsuit, I know pudgy is not the word to describe his build. Below his flat and stocky hips jut out two long sticks doubling for Reese's legs; really a sight if caught on those rare occasions when he ventures to expose them.

Uncle Reese is also the funniest man I know (everyone thinks so), and that's probably why his sheriffing job is colorful. I imagine he has the routine law enforcement tasks to attend to, although I've personally never seen him in a fluster. Everyone has complete faith in him and knows he will be on-the-spot and get to the bottom of any crime in his own way. Yet he's funny! No kidding! He's so funny that sometimes I try to avoid him and duck out of sight when I see him coming. He can make me laugh so hard at practically everything that rolls off his tongue that it actually hurts. I break out in tears and double over trying to ease the workout my belly gets at non-stop laughter.

It's this sense of humor that makes Reesie acceptable to some of those people with highly refined and discriminating tastes. I know this is only Beaverton–population 3,210 (including local farmers), but some little biddy or church denizen feel it's their calling to maintain appropriate deportment for those of us who never curtsied through finishing school, or spent more than a day or two in a metropolis the size of Minneapolis (the nearest bearer of current trends). I believe Uncle Reese knows he is disarming in appearance, perhaps even scary, but then, everyone in the county is comfortable with which side of the law he's on.

Not to paint a completely solid picture; it is humor alone that got him through his "platinum blonde" era. Not to say he had a particular interest in blondes of the opposite sex. No, one day he just decided he would become a bottled blonde and see how the other half lives. A peroxide version of James Brown; a striking and disarming contrast to his natural dark coloring and official sheriff's uniform that lives on Reese between exiting his house, until he closes the door behind on his return. If he owns any casual duds, he rarely ever puts them on. And if on those rare occasions he dons stretched out sweatshirt and slacks, he always wears his badge. The sheriff was a real eye-catcher as a blonde, but the kind of 'eye-catching' the State Sheriff's Department found a little too bizarre for their outfit.

Curlers said Reese was only going through some changes during the peroxide days. His wife, Aunt Wanita lost her sense of humor, I guess. Talk around *Barry's* said Uncle Reese spent more time in the squad car then around the house. At some point Auntie Wanita began spending spare hours getting to know the truck drivers over at *Gill's Diesel Palace* as they caravanned their commodities off to far vistas. I guess one guy must have caught her eye because she radioed Gill from somewhere in Saskatchewan, Canada. She said she was trucking her way west with a hot ticket and would he mind transmitting the word on over to Reese—she'd be in touch with the divorce papers. Shortly thereafter, Reese went Platinum.

I overheard Pops telling Curlers he was at the jailhouse when Sergeant Burns drove over from the Rabbit County Courthouse, just west of Durham. Pops said Burns started out laughing and pointing at Reese's hair, then began losing his jovial spirit and asked, "What, are you in a local pageant or something? I didn't think you needed to change your hair color for the Corn Dances. Aren't you supposed to be working that event?"

"No, I'm not in a local pageant, Burns," he replied sarcastically. "I felt a need to make a few changes around the place, maybe formulate a new perspective, and shake it up a bit at the old grind."

"Well, crap, Reese…I heard about Wanita running out on you and all, …and if you need to take a couple weeks off for R and R, and maybe dye that Marilyn Monroe job back to black, I can have Verne Jorgenson come over from Heron Cove and cover for the time," put in Burns.

"Hey Burnsie, don't get sober on me now. This hair switch is only to keep the local riff-raff guessing. I've been pulling in the same Joes lately, so I thought I'd go incognito for some fun. Really, this has nothing to do with Wanita sticking her thumb out for a free ride to anywhere. No more balls to chain is the way I've put this in prospective. My head is 100-percent company man."

But everyone knew Reese was venting his loss through his hair.

"In that case Reese, it ain't regulation. I could catch it from my superiors if they caught a glimpse of the style changes you're going through. I get enough complaints about your driving methods—which I overlook 'cause you run a pretty tight ship. But this may not wash."

I had to agree, Reese's driving methods were fiery. A few complaints had been logged by those denizens of decorum and the lawbreakers Reese had provoked. But the hair switch was really embarrassing, even if we all knew he was "wearing his heart on his sleeve/head." It was hard to respect a law enforcement official with big styling problems.

Uncle Reese was best behind the wheel of the official county automobile. His long legs reaching easily to the floor peddle and yet, as viewed by the outside pedestrian, his short body held his erect head just above the dashboard.

Despite the great pride he took in his police work, Uncle Reese couldn't help but joyride almost everywhere he went. Curlers, as much as she always needs a ride somewhere for just about any reason, won't even consider Reese and the cruiser. He owns a rather spacious American sedan of some sort, large enough to sail on the open seas—he rarely drives it. The cop cruiser is a signal around town that Reese Sitting is on duty and ready for trouble; trouble almost always meaning someone on a drunk and inspiring disorderly conduct. Now and then he patches up some kind of husband-wife ruckus or girlfriend trouble, anything else is speeding past the school grounds where he usually pulls a few offenders aside and warns them of how awful it would be to hit one of their fellow townie's kid. It works for a while, and then sooner or later, they need reminding.

Some people just aren't meant to follow the rules–and Reese is no exception. Reesie's right foot just seems to naturally fall to the floor once the engine is running. He whips along with siren sounding and cherry-top blazing every time he pulls away from the curb. It's just natural; he sees the road and peripherals faster and more clearly than the average driver and tries to keep pace with his vision.

CHAPTER EIGHT

The Car

I want the car almost all the time. I wonder now and then if this feeling will ever wear off. My father is so aloof about getting out and around in the old family "Buick" that I know at some point it will be just another thrill that I too will take for granted. Curlers rarely drives because Pops always has the vehicle. I know she would like to break out of the compound now and again just to feel free for a couple of hours, and not because she likes the feeling of control over a powerful machine. The "Family Car"—I don't know why we can't afford one more for the rest of us. Keith, my slightly older brother is my biggest competition for wrangling a few hours of cruising pleasure from the big beast. I don't really see why I should be competing with him for its use. Keith is mostly a homebody, almost bookworm-ish, and his handful of friends are the same. They quietly get together writing and creating cartoons for some kind of underground newspaper they put together. So, why does he need the use of wheels? I mean, I've got to get places, take the girls for rides about town, and to the lake. I have my social standing in the community to consider.

Keith is star-struck, and I mean literally, mentally caste amongst the constellations. His concerns are celestial; one spaceship out-witting the former. While I have more earthly bodies to follow—the car is a necessary aspect of my identity.

Keith doesn't seem to understand that. So we grovel over rights to the keys on the off-change that Pops will pull it to a rest a few hours each day. And even if he does park it in the drive, that doesn't necessarily mean he will extend the privilege. Every so often, the old man feigns a pleasant airy quality which usually means he is overwhelmed by the notion his insurance might not cover the grim aspect of collision, although he never lets on that any such thing has crossed his mind. Nor does he let on that our driving skills might be challenging for the average cool natured passenger or fellow driver. He might even say something about the peer pressure to drive recklessly through the town of Beaverton. But instead, he harbors the keys deep in one of his back pockets, jingling pointedly every time he moves. I can only do so much begging however, until I get tired of humiliation, relent, and walk to my destination, muttering obscenities all the way. Keith never seems to spend any kind of time in the beggar's mode. He either gets the car or he doesn't. He silently leaves the house heading in a purposeful direction, like a long dark shadow.

The Buick is a big old monster and nothing like a shiny new convertible hot off the assembly line. Not Pop's style in the least. It's kind of annoying; never having a cool automobile to show off around town. This model is a good five years old and I don't suppose we will ever do better than that. We, a middle class family. Pops is the local elementary school principal. I have poorer friends whose fathers keep in stylish wheels one way or another. Not Pops. He's on a savings bender and squeezing out a new car is heresy. He sees spending as the depths of absurdity. I see a new car as the sparkle on my reputation. And, a little something smarter looking than a big old family car would put me right in the golden category. A Volkswagen bug, a Mustang, a 1951 Chevy pick-up would really set me apart, according to the farm boy contingent. But it's all just dream material because we'll never be that cool.

Last Fall I took Tammi, Parrot and Cyrus Eagle out for a little spin. We had nothing better to do, and I thought we could take a look around for what might be cooking at the "Dairy Quick." I felt in absolute control behind the wheel, when I decided to give everyone a thrill at the corner of Main and Ojibwe. I shoved the gas pedal to the floor, ready for the unnerving sounds of rubber scratching concrete. She wasn't having anything to do with it however, and dropped her entire U-joint in stubborn humiliation of my cavalier handling of the equipment. Pops appeared quickly on the scene, as if Miss Buick and he had some hidden alarm system built mysteriously in her chassis. It was disturbing, unceremoniously caught without a chance to come up with a workable story.

I couldn't sneak her into "Norms" for repairs, or claim it felt like it was going to fall sooner or later, or that it could have happened to anyone, and too bad it happen while I was driving her. I could hear Parrot, in the back seat snickering quietly into her hand.

That left me on foot and without a moving view of the area for several weeks. It's not that Pops grounded me, because he knew the humiliation factor taught me the biggest lesson. I had been caught at the scene. Visibly, the family car was not a hot rod, and I proved that to myself and in front of my friends. The humiliation was a powerful feeling. I wouldn't need to be told not to pull stunts like that. I wouldn't want to be embarrassed that way again. So instead of tying me down to the homestead for days on end, he simply denied me the keys. I would insist with, "why not?", and he would simply say *no* and walk away.

I had a similar problem last summer. Curlers and Pops felt the family vacation ought to be used to catch up on life at Mom's family home. The six of us crammed into the Buick, topped it off with suitcases and various give-away items (necessary to keep our name in the good graces of family tradition). We sped out along the interstate road system heading west; Pops manning the helm, Curlers eyeing the wildflowers, Keith cringing by a door with motion sickness while Peanut and Parrot poked each other silly. I sat listlessly in the middle concentrating on my next male victim when we returned home. That's why I like these family jaunts. They give me the opportunity to ruminate on the local scene from a distance, forcing the guys to sort of miss my presence, and after my return, put a little mystery and spark into my renewed existence.

We headed west to Fort Yates, and as we did, the air grew dry and hot. We moved quickly from the cool summer breezes of the lakes to the rolling grasses of the prairie. I looked out passed Keith to golden reeds and swore I could see a herd of wild mustangs raising their tails high and racing the Buick in the direction of a setting sun. The vast horizon expanded out beyond the here and now to the intangible forevers of the grand heavens, built billowy by clouds atop clouds. I breathed in the smells of thistle and sage growing freely among the prairie grasses, and dreamt of riding out on my painted pony; free, strong and defiant, master of my earthly fate. I dreamed out beyond the visible and the prairie carried me along to bluffs and ridges, high above mystical canyons burning with purple, red and yellow hues. I could run and twirl and dance upon the buttes as larks and ravens alike urged me on with their own displays of exaltation.

We made Fort Yates sometime late in the afternoon.

Everyone hugged and kissed and talked of old times; how Curlers was spoiled as a child, running about the dirt floor of the old log cabin, the apple of her father's eye, the cherished feather on his war bonnet.

Then she, her sister and brothers were shipped off to Catholic/Bureau of Indian Affairs boarding schools a good distance from home. Grandpa couldn't keep the kids, even if he wanted to. He roamed the territory for wild horses that he broke for the military until sometime around World War Two. He was often gone for weeks at a time, even months. Grandma died earlier of tuberculosis, leaving her young family virtually parentless, with the family elders left to take care of my aunt and uncles. When government officials showed up to collect the kids, it seemed almost for the best.

This sort of reminiscing went on for several days. It was interesting at first, and I was naturally curious to get some clues as to why Curlers turned out the way she did. But after several days of hashing over the past, the maudlin atmosphere forced me out of the cool interior and onto the open plains.

I ran into Parrot hanging on the bumper of the car parked on the dusty shoulder of the dirt road to the house. She was displaying her best glum, cantankerous and without access to another- lousy-pulp novel demeanor. Personally, I began to question her bizarre fixation with junk reading and this thing for romance at the quest of a heroic male pin-up on the back of a dashing stallion. I would sometimes suggest Jane Austin, the Brontes, Thomas Hardy, Henry James, D.H. Lawrence…serious, human-being sort of writing about romance; a more intense, deeper, investigative piece of work, something conjuring up a language that matches the intensity of a union between the eternally star struck heroine and her hero. But she only rebuffs my offers, like I'm not getting the point in real trash reading. I can only leave it at that. If I am going to read these romance novels, I want to be transported wholly and fully, with the flow of language to carrying me back to Victoria or Edwardia; rather than left sitting in my chair awaiting liftoff to rose gardens and row boats on gentle ponds with wicker baskets full of wine and strawberries and roasted pheasant, packed with embroidered linens and fine bone china.

"Hey Parrot, let's walk over to the trading post and grab a pop. What'd yah think?"

"Nah, I don't feel like walking anywhere."

"Ah, come on Parrot, it'll take up half the day. I can't sit around any longer or I'll go stir crazy. Besides, you haven't anything else to do either."

"Yeah, but I'd rather sit here doing nothing than walk a couple miles to the trading post for just a pop."

Typical Parrot reasoning.

Then a bright idea struck my restless, '*I've-got-to-do-something*' fervor... The car had been sitting silent for 24 hours. Its peacefulness was more than ready for an interruption. The fluids were coagulating and in need of engine heat to make them viscose, functional and performing reliably. I strode over to its resting spot (the quasi-dirt-cum-gravel plot fashioned for the various autos and trucks, working and rusting), I noticed as I moved by the passenger-side that the keys were still in the ignition.

"Well then Parrot, I guess I'll take the car into the agency. Are you up for that?" I said rather cockily.

"Yeah, okay. I suppose if you're driving I could tag along. You got any money?"

"Sure, I'll buy you a pop" I said in a '*just get in and I'll handle it*', tone.

I started the clunker up and backed her into a corner of the gravel and dirt lot. I stuck it in first gear, not bothering to glance up at the house for fear that one or more of the residence would shoot out into the sunlit expanse, gesturing frantically to park and leave it at rest—such alarming energy and gesticulation, a contrast to the awesome simplicity and silence of our surroundings. The contrast would infuriate me, so I couldn't look up and chance altering my carefree escape with the "family" car.

We drove into the Agency, blowing dust behind us all the while. Parrot wasn't worried about getting caught without asking for the car and disappearing unannounced. She knew it would be my head that would get chopped off.

We pulled up to the "Post" feeling independent and able to create our own agenda. The trading post had a few regulars seated out in front and eyeing our "visitor" quality for a clue to our identity. We slid out from the Buick's front seat, shut the door and headed self-consciously towards the weathered porch they were sitting on. The porch roof sloped far enough out beyond the building to give the loungers shade all afternoon. We silently reached the screen door, aiming for the darkness within.

"Hey, you girls from around here?" asked one of the corralled cowpokes with a bored yesterday look on his face.

"Nope," replied Parrot in the direction of the inquiry.

We stepped through the door pursuing our target. It was dim, dry and dusty inside, with the same kind of stillness we sensed from the fellas outside. We walked around eyeing the merchandise, which didn't take long. I spotted the red pop case and felt a rush of coolness as I approached; just knowing it held my satisfaction. I lifted up one of the rubber rimmed lids. In the depths of the cooler, and submerged in ice water, stood a variety of thirst quenching drinks. Parrot moved quickly over to my side and began rummaging around for the perfect selection. I pulled out a *Nesbit Orange,* my hand wet and refreshingly cold from the encounter. Parrot eventually spotted the root beer. I moved to the counter up front near the door, the floorboards echoing my intent to the old women manning the place from behind her stitching.

Parrot holler up to me, "Can you afford a bag of potato chips?" Her voice shook the store and seemingly all the dudes outside. I wanted to say, "*keep it down,*" but I knew she hadn't raised her voice. Rather, the silence projected her words to decibels greater than those actually broadcast. The group in their chairs turned to spy through the windows and the elder proprietor looked up from her sewing.

"Sure, I'll buy em," I mumbled, trying not to standout more than any two strangers do.

Parrot put her goods on the counter. I looked at the old lady who had already put a price together: "a buck and a quarter," in her thick native accent. She seemed less interested in our stranger appeal and quickly went back to her stitching. I felt uncomfortable with the depths of the silence exaggerated by the acute interest of the waiting gentlemen outside, so I stretched my blue-jeaned gams and made the door.

Attempting to get behind the wheel before I actually took those steps, I opened the screen door quickly. Parrot trailed somewhere behind me, nonchalant and oblivious to the hyper-stillness. I felt if I stayed around the Post too long, my tracks would surely solidify like a wooden statue, not released until someone new came along and moved them.

I glanced at the boys as I made for the car. My hustling by only seemed to motivate one of them to inquire, "What's the hurry ladies?" And another, "Can I come along for the ride?"

Parrot shot back, "It's no fun where we're going."

I swung open the driver's side door which gave its usual vocal acknowledgment at being handled, and moved swiftly to the ignition and gas pedal. Parrot however, put a little swivel in her hips as she approached the car and glided on over to the door. I peered at the audience now chuckling and winking, tickled at her girlish, immature, gyrations at seduction. I couldn't help think Parrot was sliding a little too easily in and out of the romance novel reality. I guess it was obvious to the boys that it was all show.

Once I had the car started, I eased back in my seat and calmly stuck the old auto into reverse, slowly moving her passed the boys and onto the main road. A cloud sailed quietly over the afternoon sun and cooled our ride to a pace that paralleled the looming cloud's shadow. I spotted a sign: **Lake,** and turned in the direction the arrow indicated on the sign.

It was no bigger than a large farm pond really. I could circle the perimeter and rejoin the road in just a few minutes. I found a quiet place to pull under one of the few trees providing a moderate amount of shade. Parrot and I could devour our chips and pop in tranquility. We could see for miles in any direction including the sky's monumental reflection from the lake's surface. The place looked to be other's preferred stomping ground as well. From my perch atop the hood of the car, I could see empty beer cans, previously burnt wood, candy wrappers and miscellaneous refuse. I kinda felt like I was trespassing on someone else's property—and truthfully, I was.

It was cool under the big tree and warm beneath my seat from the heat of the engine. Despite the signs of others having been here, it was remarkably still and empty for a community with so much time on their hands. Parrot broke the silence, "Sis, what are you going to do after graduation? I never hear you talk about it. Not like Tammi, who can't talk without mentioning how fast she'll be long gone the day after school lets out. She may not even wait for the ceremony."

"I don't know. I have the feeling Curlers will shrivel up and die if I don't go to college. Maybe I just don't think I need to rush it. Pops always says, *The best education is experience*, and I think he's right, but I have a feeling he'd rather I became more experienced after college. That's not to say he'll pay for it. He's been typically quiet about where the dough for this education will come from. I don't know though, I haven't really set a goal for what I'd like to specialize in."

Truthfully, I hadn't really done any sort of concrete thinking about my future after high school. Until that moment, after high school seemed like a distant dream, like watching an old black and white movie. It was a lovely movie about white picket fences and ladies talking so sweetly you wish you could bite into them to see if they taste like candy. I felt my future would just happen. I would roll into the opportunities at the right place, at the right time. The intense kind of planning like Tammi was doing wasted good energy and blocked out natural vibrations that could lead down my path to adulthood. But I didn't know quite what to say to Parrot because I wanted to maintain a strong ambitious picture of myself in her eyes. At least that's the picture I thought she had of me in her world. This explanation of my future was right on line, but I knew if put into words some folks might find it a little flaky—maybe even deflating to my inquisitive younger sister.

"I'll start working on my options mid-school year. I've got time. And, Beaverton isn't such a bad place to be from. I'd like to hear other people's escape plans. I wouldn't mind having one more good year there, free to enjoy the guys and life without having to have a full scheduled routine to abide by, like school or work."

"Not that I'm antsy to see you go, or anything like that Sis," explained Parrot, "but I'm kind of planning ahead on how I'd like to decorate your room after you move out."

"Your acting like you'll be happy to be rid of me! Well I'd stop dreaming about my room and anything else I leave behind because I don't plan on vacating for at least a year. You know, sometimes you seem really ungrateful for having me as your older sister. You could be sitting back on that log I found you at earlier today, without pop or chips and still mumbling to yourself. I took a big risk just so we could get a little relief from the family sanctum," I said, getting more and more exasperated.

As I was about to mount another testament in defense of my hurt feelings at Parrot's opportunistic outlook at my future, a caravan of cars entered the road around the other side of the lake.

The vehicles consisted of two pickups and some sort of major sedan, much like our Buick. The passengers looked about my age, only they were hooting and howling and raising hell to beat the band. I had to admit they made me a little nervous. They honked their horns and one driver would floor his gas pedal and set the tires burning rubber around the tranquil water—beer cans flying like automatic ejection machines were equipped on all open windows. They spotted us the first time around. Someone hollered out, "Hey, you girls want something to drink."

"No thanks," was my quick response.

"What, are you, too good for liquor?" one shouted.

"No, I'm just not thirsty right now." I yelled with strained patience. They didn't seem to care if I rejected their offer or not. It was just a friendly formality in the introduction of themselves and their intent. Along with the team of drinking dudes and reckless drivers were a number of girls as carefree as the rest and apparently flattered by their inclusion on the spree.

I sort of felt this frenzy would only have been half as wild if it were only guys along for the thrill. Listening to the girls scream every time one of the caravan careened around the corner of the lake made it that much more amusing for the guys. As an outsider, I thought, these babes were being just a little too dramatic and flattered by the antics. But inside, I knew if a couple of dudes around Beaverton took me joy riding I would have been just as silly.

I turned to Parrot, "Well are you about ready to blow this pop stand?"

"No way! This is as much fun as I've had around here all week. If they ask if we want a ride, let's say yes!" she urged, looking like this is the kind of excitement she'd long been missing.

I have to admit she started to trouble me. This wasn't the Parrot, my kid sister, I thought I knew. I had long felt Parrot was a mini version of myself—not that I always liked that. At times I gleaned at my own uniqueness and flaunted it like an authentication to my creative sensibilities. Yet, I took comfort in feeling a shared sense of the world with Parrot; a kind of sacred camaraderie I could depend on when everyone else seemed disloyal of my efforts. Lately this dependence seemed to misfire. Parrot too, was grappling in my grip. All I felt I taught her about the world—for her own survival she was shedding for some kind of brat appeal. I was appalled, and no one else seemed to see this but me.

"They don't scare yah, do they Sis? They're just out for some fun." She poked.

"No, they don't scare me," I said, trying to appear at ease while ten or eleven partiers swerved recklessly around us.

"Good," she said. "Then let's ask em if they'll give us a ride around the track. Looks like a cheap thrill to me."

"Cheap thrill is right," I retorted, now annoyed. "I have a better idea. I'll show them what this Buick can do, alright?" I put this to her with an air of total confidence in my driving abilities. I could handle a car as well as anybody, and I wouldn't have to squeeze in with some flirtatious, half-lit guy; one hand on the stirring wheel and one hand on me. I assumed Parrot hadn't taken this into consideration—or had she? In any event, she emitted a girlish giggle and popped into the back seat. I didn't pop into anything. I sauntered over to my door, all the while building energy and confidence in my new proposal. I don't know if she saw the concentration now drawn from my forehead to chin, but I knew it was there.

I stuck the keys in the ignition and turned her on. I gave her some gas and revved the engine up with a roar, if only to alert the gang that I had some intentions of my own. Parrot pressed forward and rested her hands and chin on the front seat, alert to possibilities I think I wanted to avoid. With one flashy gesture, I pushed the car into reverse and peeled backwards aiming blindly for the road that had now become a speedway! Yes blindly? In that one thrusting moment: the timing, the planets, the stars, synchronicity, metal meeting metal, one speed freak meeting another, stranger entwined with stranger; change, risk, bravado and remorse all came crashing together. In my bold willingness to prove my metal with the rez crowd and my mouthy sister, I overlooked one important factor—look where you're going!

Showing off got the best of me! I was shoved full force into the steering wheel, my head bouncing effortlessly forward. Parrot shot momentarily against the back of the front seat, then pressed resoundingly against the back seat. I guess she was okay since I could hear her chortling in the back. Although, I was too overwhelmed in my efforts to judge my own condition and do a serious diagnosis. My first reaction was to overcome all personal remorse of injury if only to present a responsible picture to the guys outside now surveying the damage.

A picture quickly developed beyond the moment of the hell I must be prepared for when Pops becomes part of the incident. I felt the bottom drop out of the rest of my summer; chores without end, caretaking duties with Peanut, and looks of distrust and disloyalty. That would be the hardest for me to handle. "Oh, SHIT!" I muttered out loud. What else could I say?

Parrot gasped at my profanity in characteristically sarcastic fashion to let me know that I'd fallen off my high horse. I stepped slowly out of the car. Sheepishly I minced to the rear of the Buick.

I said hello to the rider's in the car I'd hit now gathered around the hood and fenders of our respective damage. My voice was as weak as a young singer leading her first tribal song sitting in with the elders. But they must have heard my squeak because they all looked up. With that same effort I asked, "Whose car is it?"

"Hey, it's mine," spoke up one of the guys leaning against the hood of the car I had struck. He looked me over quickly with a sarcastic grin etched broadly across the portion of his face allotted for lips.

I stepped over to his side of the accident and released the apology that had welled up inside. I really couldn't tell how he was feeling at the moment, and I took a pretty good guess that he didn't know either. The crew were all laughing and poking at each other so I tried to smile and pretend I too was part of the party. Somehow the whole event just seemed to be part of the game to them—and I'd lost. I turned around to take a remorseful look at the Buick fender. I stood dumb-struck. A twist of fate, a little luck; this collision had merely scratched a meaningless dent in the Buick's bright chrome. Otherwise, she was just as she'd always been. I stood starring, mesmerized by the sun's rays reflecting off the silver chrome and striking back at me, mid-iris. Could this really be? All that noise, all that ego-crushing, that flailing around at impact, hardly testimony to a near imperceptible dent?

"I don't know Kenny, looks pretty serious to me!" Someone said, giving the whole group an opportunity to double over in laughter. I turned slowly to eyeball his car, thinking they were still playing games with me since the Buick had virtually no damage. I must have taken the impact harder than the car. This was disconcerting in itself since I always take great pride in my level head and calm demeanor in crisis situations. Not that I've had much real experience in that department. Turning, I kept my eyes at bumper level as I brought his car into my peripheral view. It was a deep blue car with a little rust around the edges. But wow, as I directly fixed on his front end, I couldn't help a gasp from deep in my stomach. I had wreaked total havoc to his left front fender. My heart sunk again. Pops would have to find out. The old man's insurance would have to cover the damage.

"Ahh, geez", I squeezed out. "I guess I didn't see you coming around the curve. I can't say I took a good look to see who was coming, for that matter. I'm really, really sorry. I guess that's what I get for trying to act cool. What should I do now?" I asked, ready to take a big spoonful of the bitter medicine that would follow.

I'm sure it would be a matter of doses. Running away was out of the question. I had a full life invested in Beaverton. I would have to succumb to prolonged finger shaking, head hanging, and an uncomfortable ride back to Beaverton— until this thing blows over.

"Hey, don't worry about it", said this guy Kenny. "You tried to roll but you didn't have what it takes. It just makes my car look better for the demolition derbies. This makes it kinda look like a mean machine, like it's been to war. Serious, don't worry about it!"

"You can't be serious! I mean wow! I can't believe this! If you're okay with this, God, I couldn't be more grateful. I was preparing to catch Hell from my father and all my relatives. Man, thanks again!" I said stunned and amazed at Kenny's devil-may-care attitude.

Or, was it the booze talking? Why wouldn't he want to collect on the insurance money? He wouldn't have to put the check back into his car. He could probably run on it a couple of weeks around here.

I didn't want to spend much effort considering his whys and wherefores. Whatever his reasons were for dropping the problem, personally, I felt like picking daisies in a vast field of green.

By now the group had wondered off lakeside. Kenny moved toward his vehicle and shoved the driver's door shut with his perfectly worn cowboy boots. I hadn't notice the other guys stripping down to their BVD's until I turned back for the driver's side of the Buick. No one seemed all that amazed at Kenny's cavalier attitude or the damage to his car. I was still bewildered and under other circumstances would want a deeper reason for this gift, but everyone had moved on. I was the only one who didn't seem to understand the gesture. Perhaps it was too much trouble, too much red tape, too white, too much a violation of the natural rhythms of day-to-day living. It certainly would have been trouble, questions, answers, estimates, raising rates, haranguing, haranguing. But from what I had gathered from the Old Man and Curlers, the responsibilities of owning a car.

Parrot was still sitting in the car snickering now and again, prepared with ammo for the future. I yelled down to the swimmers, "Thanks again. You don't know what this means to me!"

They looked up half interested, then moved on to more basic topics of interested.

Someone yelled back up, "Why don't you girls stay for a swim? It'll cool you down."

"Nah", I yelled back, "I've had enough excitement for one day." No one seemed to hear, they were absorbed now with splashing the girls who were dipping their toes in or wading ankle deep, unable to make the first big crash into the cooling water.

I turned to Parrot after I got the car running again and started maneuvering around Kenny's still sitting in the position of the wreck. "Boy what a hot break that was! Do you suppose we could keep it a break? I mean, do you think you could manage to keep this from getting to be a hot topic with the folks? I'm going to have enough trouble explaining where we've been with the car all this time."

"Ah, come on, who do you think I am, a rat, a snitch, a tattle-tail? I think we're both going to have to take on a long drawn out lecture about taking off without letting anyone know, or lack of concern for other people's auto needs. Don't worry, I'll keep it to myself, although Keith might get a kick out of this."

"Please, definitely not Keith, he can't keep anything to himself. The instant he's let in on a little gossip he turns around and blabs it all over the place, especially to those you don't want ever hearing about it."

I got back on the road, tense from the mishap and apprehensive about our pending lecture. I still wondered why that guy Kenny was so relaxed about his damage, and yet, I felt one day I would understand. I needed a little more experience I guess. Pops never did let on about the accident or appear to notice the slightly dented bumper. Although every time I passed behind the rear of the car I focused in on the blemish. I admit, I had gained a bit of respect for the old "Buick" after all that. I was impressed by its ability to take on that kind of force and come up with nary a scratch. If Parrot had ever let my two authority figures in on that afternoon, they never mentioned it to me.

My driving skills have improved remarkably since then. No more fancy tricks or speeding off to the lake. I follow the rules just like I was taught in Driver's Ed. No illegal turns, cutting down the alley ways, passing on a yellow line, and no swerving for cheap thrills. I am the model driver, and actually, I feel pretty good about that.

CHAPTER NINE

Parrot

Well, I call her Parrot. Her given name is really Louise Ryan, the Ryan being her middle name. I use to try calling her Ryan, and I still think it sounds so sophisticated, but I could never get it to stick. Pops started calling her Parrot when she was two or three years old because she squawked and screamed about everything, and I suppose because she talked nonstop, repeating everything anyone said. I imagine the folks had to be careful about what they said around her for fear family secrets might be spread around. Use of profanity of any sort would later weave through her vocabulary without restraint.

We grew into what we are now—pretty much together. She was brought home from the hospital a small, petite and quite lovely girl baby. I felt awestruck as I peered up on tip-toes looking over and into her fresh bassinet. She was much better than any of my doll babies.

I don't remember when she first gave me a sense of purpose. Perhaps I needed more activities, or a better sense of who I was in the world, but when Parrot came along, I felt I had to take her under my wing. Perhaps I was treating her to a variation of the education my older brother counseled me in, until he realized I was a girl and ended his protective bent for good. Up until recently, I considered her tutelage on my shoulders. She riled at my insistence on conformity to my idea of right and wrong, perfection and sloppiness. I suppose she wanted to define her world her way.

Like the bird, Parrot has developed a luminous color sense. She loves anything bright and brilliant; shocking pinks are her favorite, but full yellows, chartreuse and radiant orange are the stables of her wardrobe, which she absolutely insists on during shopping days. She knows when she's got the right stuff on because her chin points higher to the ceiling, and struts around showing off her new duds; one available hand locked on her hip, cruising her imaginary runway. This all contrasts a thick head of hair, parted in the middle and pulled back into what she describes as a *chignon*. I can't help but bring her back down to earth by saying, "you mean a ponytail." At which, she glares through her black rimmed microscopic glasses, often slooping down her nose, disappointed that I'm incapable of playing along.

Parrot likes angles, the angles to everything. Nothing appears new or inspired to her. Everything is pointed and has a motive whether obvious or in need of uncovering. It isn't that she intends to get to the bottom of it all, but mostly angles are a necessary means for observation of the world at large. From the moment she descends the stairs to the breakfast table—and descending is her angle, she views us, her family, as the greater public working out our day-to-day lives with schemes and manipulations to get from one point to another. I guess you could say her approach is cynical; nothing developed out of purity or honesty and integrity, but I suppose she doesn't want to succumb to a sweetness and vulnerability I have to believe is her bottom layer.

I don't spend much time with Parrot's friends nor have I observed her social skills outside the family circle. However, her friends appear devout, giving me the impression they are offered a view of the bottom layer. To me, these friends tend to be cowering, coy and shifty-eyed. They periodically gather in her room to whisper and laugh hysterically about their schemes and angles—at least that's how it appears as I stroll past her room. They immediately stop all talk and don't even lift their heads to see who may be eaves-dropping. Sitting frozen in their seats, I sense their eyes roaming the territory for outside spies. Parrot doesn't entertain regularly, nor does she participate in group activities much—only between dull chapters of her latest pulp acquisitions—romance novel, does she venture out.

My first real memory of her picking up the romance novel was the day the mailman delivered a box of the complete set of "Victoria Holt" romances. I was stunned to find at what lengths Parrot would go to keep abreast of prince meets princess. But it was only the beginning. Apparently the school library, inspired by Parrot's obvious interest in reading, loaned her an order catalog and placed that first order of the definitive "Holt" romances. From that time forth, Parrot has received a box every month. My question has always been, *"where does she get the money to pay for them?"* Funny, the folks don't seem to have that question. I am sure that sneaky whispering the girls do in her room has something to do with cash flow. Parrot opened her first bank account at Beaverton's First National around about the time those first books arrived. It seems to me Curlers started getting occasional phone calls from Parrot's baby-sitting employers saying their kid's piggy banks were missing, *"Could Parrot possibly have seen it?"* Or, they noticed a pack of cigarettes missing from the top of the bureau, *"Could Parrot possibly account for them?"* I could, I could account for their disappearance.

The pint-size hoodettes would gather, in between dull chapters, while Curlers was off selecting banana crème, chocolate crème or lemon meringue at *Barry's*. They would pass a fag around, smoke the place up, then spray some cheap perfume purchased for the occasion about her room to overwhelm a discerning nose. No one seemed to catch on (except myself), leaving me baffled by my folks gullibility.

Despite some basic differences, Parrot and I can hang together pretty tight. Most of my deeper secrets I confide in Parrot—even before Tammi. She will keep them all pretty close to the hip—unless she needs to work me over for some "angle" infraction. If that is the case, then the folks will get the word on everything. This doesn't occur very often however, 'cause Parrot really does like trailing me around, and I will ban her from trails in an instant if I think she's going too far. It's a delicate balancing act all right.

CHAPTER TEN

The Drive-In

"Jeez Pops, I've made it clear I thought—at least to Mom anyway, we're going to the *Shining Star*. Connor is a very safe driver. He doesn't speed like a lot of these other guys do around here," I insist, trying hard to remain cool.

Connor is outside revving his cycle's motor and laying on the horn. Pops mysteriously appears from behind his newspaper just long enough to give me the word, "Don't move an inch from the couch. That guy is coming to the door or you're not going anywhere. I want to know if this guy can speak English. I'm not wild about you going off on a motorcycle."

Connor hits the horn again and I sink back into the couch, frustrated that Pops has suddenly decided to do the responsible thing. I didn't even know he was present on earth let alone aware of my evening plans. Apparently, he has tuned in; perhaps the noise factor has annoyed him enough to inquire of this evening's agenda. Connor will eventually come to the door, of that I am sure. But how long will he stand out there and impress my father as a manner-less teen?

Pops peeks from behind his editorials again and offers up, "I hear there are some Hell's Angels types hanging around town, so keep an eye open."

I know, believe me, I know, I say to myself.

Slumping back further into the couch, I'm feeling like this game could go on forever. My integrity is lost somewhere amongst the multiple columns of the daily news, or maybe hidden in the squares of the crossword puzzle Pops is so transfixed by. I mean, doesn't Pops trust my choice in male companionship. If I can't pick a trustworthy guy by now, it might be too late. And Connor, if he would just overcome a little of that shyness; or is it awe, in dating a town girl like me, that makes him a touch shaky in the courting scene. It doesn't matter all that much one way or the other 'cause I'm now getting bored. I'll give it five more minutes, then head out to Connor and his bike and tell him I am no longer in the mood to do anything. I can go to the drive-in with Tammi and a couple other girls, and probably have more fun without the hassles of Pops or Curlers approval in the company I'm keeping. I have an hour or two before dusk in which to round up the girls. Plan B could go into effect and is beginning to sound mighty appealing.

The idea routes its way through my system as the screened porch door swings to a close and jolts me to my feet. Pops throws his newspaper down and firmly states, "Sit down, I'll get the door!"

At this point I don't care. Do what you have to do, I say to myself; let's just move this show along a little faster. I know my father's approval isn't a factor, he'll do some sort of ceremonial handshake and we'll be on our way. But that handshake, and Pop's eyes meeting Connor's will set dating standards without a word purposefully spoken, yet letting Connor know that he'll find him if any funny stuff occurs while his little Celia is in his hands. Can you imagine the fiery flames that would shoot from Pop's eyes, and the angry wooden handshake he would offer up if Connor were instead that Motorcycle Maniac?

From my burrow nestled in the couch, I hear the groan of the heavy hardwood door open simultaneously with the anticipated ring of the doorbell. I imagine Connor's face as he realizes Pop's deliberate readiness at the door with his arrival. I can hear Connor coughing up some immature and embarrassed explanation for his sorry manners and laying on the cycle horn. Pops isn't interested in waiting for Connor to describe his hesitation, he readily injects, "That's not a good way to get my attention young man! If you're trying to get the rest of the neighborhood to notice you, it probably worked. Celia has been waiting patiently for you to come on up to the house and meet me. I hope you don't feel put out by that, but I think it's the polite way to start off a date, don't you?"

"Well, ah, ah I'm sorry Sir. I guess I was in too much of a hurry. I'm please to meet you Mr. Elkhorn. My name is Connor Johnson—you remember me from elementary school, don't you Sir?"

"I remember your Dad, Bud Johnson, and it seems to me he'd expect his son to do the right thing."

"I'm sure he would Sir, and I'll come to the door from now on."

"Okay, good. Celia is there in the living room. Oh, one other thing: I'm not wild about Celia riding on the back of a motorcycle, to tell you the truth. Could you do me a favor and take it easy. Keep it on the ground, okay?"

"Oh sure, Sir, she'll be safe with me. I wouldn't try anything wild with a passenger like her behind me," Connor says, puffing up his chest to reclaim his dignity.

That's about all I can take of Pop's third degree and Connor's whinny tone. I shoot up from the chair, whipping past Pops with a, "I'll be home after the movie." Grabbing Connor by the hand, I yank him out onto the porch, swinging the screen door open and take the steps in one large leap. "See ya later," I yell on the move.

Coming to an abrupt stop at the cycle, I let go of Connor's hand. I look up into his flushed florescent pink face and feel in full control of the situation. "Connor, let's get moving, alright? Sorry, I hope you weren't too humiliated by my Dad?" I ask, knowing full well he felt awkward and embarrassed, yet, leaving me confident that if I chose I could relieve his discomfort with a few reassuring words, or let him grope for balance and returned identity. He hands me a spare helmet he has attached to the back of his bike. His hands are noticeably shaking as I reach for the head gear and decide I better say something soothing and gentle before we take off or it could be a scary rather than exhilarating ride. "I can hardly wait to get out on Route 2 with your bike. It's really a neat bike, how long have you had it? My folks would die if I ever bought one of my own."

"I've had it about a year now," Connor says slowly, methodically, perhaps in an effort to gain composure. "Yeah, I can outrun most of the guys around here. Your dad would be really happy to hear that," he says soundly, relieved to be talking on a subject he felt confident and comfortable with. "My dad put the initial outlay for this bike, but I'm paying him back slowly. After I pay it off I'd like to trade it up on a Harley and maybe do some biking around the country before heading to college, or real farming."

I'm fumbling around with my helmet buckle, feebly trying to secure the strap under my chin and hold the head piece in place while listening to his future plans. Connor has his own helmet fastened, and I sense him focusing on my difficulty with uniting buckle and strap simply by touch. I know he's questioning whether or not to lend a hand. How controlled are his hands? Will his knees hold up? I guess we haven't reached a level of comfort with each other yet—but he'd better help buckle my helmet or we'll be standing here a lot longer. "Connor can you buckle my helmet, please. I can't see where this strap should go?"

"Oh yeah, sure. Sorry, I should have offered. I'm so use to doing mine that I never think how awkward it is the first couple of times you put these on."

Bending over my helmet, and as he reaches for the strap, I see his hands are still shaking. I peer up into his face and reflect upon the flushed crimson color made all so obvious by his pale skin and the whiteness of the helmet that frames it. This sort of closeness must be a new feeling for him. I guess he could use a little re-assurance. I reach up and squeeze his damp hot hand and smile into his face, hoping to slow his racing heart. He looks down, smiles back, then breathes in deep, releasing the anxiety of new moments.

Okay, the helmet fits and Connor slips effortlessly onto the cycle and raises it upright off its stand. I throw my right leg over the rear as nonchalantly as a cycling novice can and sit down in the spot left between Conner and the back bars. I gently place my hands at his waist and look up towards the house, feeling someone's eyes burning from behind the front window curtains. Sure enough, there stands Curlers, looking stern and alienated by the close proximity we are now taking, mounted on the powerful and quick reflexes of a male teen hood's alter ego. I smile and wave, letting her know I see her and will not let her over-bearing presence prevent me from enjoying myself.

We shoot off toward the paling sky, feeling obscure and yet an implicit spark in the universe and given the opportunity of this moment to observe its enor-mity. The evening sun is now low to the horizon, as the moon and stars press to appeal to our vision. We speed into the dusk free of bindings and confines; liber-ated, formless and independent. And, as if a switch has been flipped, the heat of the day becomes in an instant, the cool of the evening. Twilight air presses force-fully against my limbs creating wings that suspend me in this atmosphere—then I soar out and back down onto the bike. I look out beyond Connor's torso and feel the pointed shadows that loom off the trees, fences, stop signs, diner, barns, silos and posts, soon to expand beyond their sharp, crisp boarders, absorbing all bright shapes and forms until once again the morning sun reaches up behind us, coaxing the dark with dawn.

The bike moves nearly of its own volition. Connor leans into it, hardened like a steel statue welded into—drive. For one brief moment we hang atop Route 2's crest, stunned by the opulent neon lights of the *Shining Star Drive-in Ciné*, aglow against the din of a northern summer night.

Without notice everything changes. The ethereal freedom of the ride abruptly closes to the energy of life at the scene. Who will I know? Who is here with whom? Will we see the movie on the back of Connor's bike, or will someone invite us to watch from their spare back seat? Do I look like a basketball head with this helmet on? I better remove it fast before I'm noticed by too many people I know. Will Connor make any moves on me? Will I respond? There are so many possibilities, making an appearance is just the beginning. I want to appear sophisticated, effortless…and myself. My heart is fluttering at the excitement. I have four or five hours of complete freedom and independence over how I will spend them. It is my time and I can fold and mold it to suit my interests without a determined outcome thanks to Pop, Curlers, Parrot or the boys.

We pull up alongside the ticket gate and once again Connor becomes life-like as he stands to dig into his fresh denim jeans for the wad of bills clustered tight to the interior of his right back pocket.

"That will be one dollar," says gravelly voiced Norma, the owner's wife, always stationed behind the entrance booth; a cigarette burning, cough syrup to the right and money box in the middle. I better get this helmet off, at least before I'm spotted and permanently labeled—"helmet head". Of course, it's not that I don't want to be noticed at all, but I'd like to come off a little more style conscious.

The once baron gravel rows of the *Shining Star* are nearly full to capacity with cars and their movie-going passengers. At two o'clock this afternoon all would have been stark and void, except for the zombie-like silhouettes of sound boxes hung silently atop their erect poles. The drive-in always does the business on a summer night—especially weekends. Something fun will always happen—guaranteed. Beaverton has one movie house across the street from the First National Bank, on Main. The theater is okay. It gets every B-rated movie to come out of Hollywood—never first run stuff. I don't mean to put it down because I go almost every weekend in the winter, but the drive-in is a very important social activity.

Connor maneuvers us into a spot almost directly in the middle of the lot. He parks at an angle so the bike is sideways to the screen, that way we can lean against it or sit side-saddle on the bike while we watch the movie. It doesn't seem all that comfortable, at least not to watch the movie. But then, I don't care. I don't usually see the whole show anyway. I either find friends to hang out with, or laugh at what really goes on in the back seats of various cars. If I go with the girls, we mostly gossip or yell obnoxious stuff a people we know.

Oh wow! There's Tammi out with Gary Perham. Things must have worked out at the dance. Who are those guys in the back seat? Oh, its Bud Brooks and Kyle Bird, both star basketball players for the team. I like the car!

"Hey Connor, I'm going to say hi to Tammi over there with Gary Perham. You don't mind do you? I'll be back in a minute." I hand him my helmet, not expecting an answer to my off-hand inquiry. The gravel beneath my tread rustles and quakes with every step, making progress slow and self-conscious. I see Twyla LaPointe sitting pretty tight in George DeBerg's pale blue pickup. She and George have been close for a couple years now. I think everyone assumes they will get married soon after senior year, and do whatever young newlyweds do. Trés boring. She sees me and waves.

Darkness has all but descended, except for a sliver of orange fighting to stay just a little longer. I can feel the crowds anticipation mount. Everyone holds their breath, suspended in time waiting for the first few frames of the show to flash up on the screen. Yet, the first minutes are always a let-down 'cause it's only advertising for the concession stand.

I step over to Tammi's side of the car and lean down into the window, half hoping to give her a scare. She is snuggling up close to Gary who is giggling down into her coy face. I poke through the window and in a loud authoritative voice ask, "Well, I guess your mama knows where you are tonight, right?" Tammi, first jumping away from Gary, looks over to see who is checking up on her.

"Celia, very funny! I didn't know you were coming tonight. If I'd known, we wouldn't have picked up these two eggheads in the back." Bud and Kyle are shooting popcorn kernels at each other and generally oblivious to my appearance and anything else going on around them. "Are you here with Connor?" she asks, turning her attention less to Gary and more toward me.

"Yeah, we're here on his motorcycle; which was a great ride, but watching the movie might be rough. I'm secretly hoping we'll find someone we know with an empty back seat."

"Gee, sorry Celia. Like I said, if I'd thought about it, I would have asked if you and Connor wanted to come with Gary and me. Those guys in the back are too obnoxious to be true," Tammi says to me, convincingly disgusted.

Looking up over the roof of the car and back toward Connor and his bike, he seems to be staring down at his cowboy boots for lack of a better place to reflect his dejection.

"I better get back over to Connor. He's looking a little lost without me. If you run into anyone with some extra space in their car, send one of those goof balls in the back seat to give me the word, alright?"

"Okay Celia. Say, I may stop by in a little while to take a break in the Ladies Room," Tammi emphasizes.

"Sure, sounds good," I holler back to her as I skip off towards the bike. Seeing Connor looking bored and glum makes me feel responsible for injecting some spirit and plain old fun into the evening. I skip up smiling and turn my attention to enchanting his lonesome persona. I kick his boots with my red sneakers and ask, "I hope your thoughts haven't strayed too far from here?"

The red sun of the summer sky has disappeared beyond the night with only a trace of its glow visible to colored twilight. I look up to Connor's face silhouetted by the rising moon and the glowing star that trails it at this time of the year. A broad smile reclaims the somber downturn of his contemplative face. "No, I'm standing here waiting for you. I hope it will be comfortable hanging out on this bike for the movie. I can throw my jacket down on the gravel and we can lean against the bike when it cools down a little more."

Great, why didn't one of us remember to bring a blanket along? Maybe we'll run into someone with a spare backseat yet. But despite the awkwardness, no privacy, lack of space on the back of his bike and a gravel floor to cushion my buns, I am happy to be out under the stars testing my ability to handle the world without the ongoing assistance of the folks at home. I don't know whether they will approve of all I do or say, but I know the independence feels good, and I am going to want more and more of it. I am happy to have a guy giving me attention while he seems flattered that my flirtations are meant only for him. Impulsively, I grab his hand. He looks down at me, and I smile reassuringly up at him. We lean back on his bike seat, holding hands, gazing up at the big screen, all the while realizing our attachment and what it now means.

The feature movie is coming on. I have yet to catch the name, but what I can pick up without a place to really hookup the speaker, it's some kind of monster thriller. It's in black and white, which to me, always makes everything seem a whole lot more ominous. The shadows loom out from the depths of some monstrous dark inner world.

I'm not that interested. More interesting is Connor's palm growing hot and moist in the grasp of my cool hand. Even so, I know he's attempting to relax. It seems that I have hit a point of male weakness. I know my ability to compete in the world is set by male standards; and it doesn't bother me to have to work within those standards. Somewhere deep inside, I know my most valued achievements are those that stand out from the nearest male competitor. The successes I have had amongst my female gender are hard to see as anything out of the ordinary—the expected, lackluster and diminished in comparative stature. But, quietly, right here at this moment, I catch a glimpse of something females hold the standard for; have the superior knowledge of, strength and natural aptitude towards. I don't know if I would call it romance or the comfort in closeness, it just seems as if we girls can reach over and share a warm and comforting familiarity without having our character threatened, without rewriting the pamphlet on our female-hood, as it appears most males most do in order to just hold hands—especially in public. They always seem to quake in their boots while a rosy glow overtakes their face; reassuring themselves that other guys they know do it too. Men may have set the standards on 'bringing home the bacon', or workplace etiquette, but how does that compare to expressing love or kindness for one another? I don't feel particularly put off by such lack of emotional awareness. No, on the contrary, I think I like knowing my fearlessness on girl-boy issues gives me an advantage in the lessons of life many guys may never have. It gives me a little more confidence in seeing beyond the normal achievement standards men have set. So for a flash, Connor feels like a wee babe in my hands, and I can see playing him like a puppet on a string—if I were that kind of a girl.

Connor looks down sweetly and offers, "I'm going to throw my jacket down here so we can sit and lean against the bike. It's got to be more comfortable than this."

"But don't you think you might get a little cold?" I ask, trying to convey my interest in his welfare.

"No, this isn't anything. Really, it's my favorite time of the day. It can get so hot out in the fields during the afternoon sun, I look forward to this," he assures me.

"Okay then, I'm all for it."

We unload our hands carefully and Connor removes his jacket. In an instant we are released from our bonds, aware of our separateness and crouch down to our courtship on the gravel of the drive-in. I have never felt freer in all my life. I look up to the stars and know this moment is perfect and complete.

The movie on the screen seems as far away as some of those stars above. I peer up at its height and width, regarding little more than shadowed movements dancing across the moonlit panorama. I nestle my body closer to Connor's, hoping to provide some warmth from the crisp summer night. He seems more relax now. Perhaps being off his feet comforts him from the possibilities of stumbling during my romantic overtures. He reaches over and grabs my hand, letting me know he likes it. I focus up at the screen just in time to see the gigantic furry monster crush half a dozen buildings in one heavy step.

"Hey Celia, are you ready? Celia? Hey Celia, you want to go to the Ladies Room?" Tammi's loud booming voice startles me from the peace and tranquility of Connor, the night air and our privacy. I guess she's ready for the lady's room. She's undoubtedly bored with the movie already—not that I can blame her, and coming up for air from those two maroons in the backseat.

"Come on Celia, I need some girl company away from those guys. Look Connor, I'm sorry to drag lovely Celia away, but we won't be gone long. Celia, he understands, you can pick up something for Connor at the concession stand, okay?"

"Alright Tammi, I'm coming, but you owe me. Connor, really, can I get you something while I'm up?" trying to direct my attention back to him.

"Yeah, sure. Here's five dollars. Have whatever you want. I'll have a tall coke and popcorn–no butter. Hurry back though, alright?"

"Hey Tammi, how's it going in that big comfortable, cushiony car?" I ask sarcastically. "Have the boys settled down now, or is the monster movie pushing them to rambunctious extremes?"

"Oh, they're doing okay," she says, talking above the noise of sneakers pressing against gravel. "I just wish we'd gone to the show alone. Cuddlin' up to Gary would be much more comfortable with a little more privacy. Hey, but you and Connor seem to be getting to know each other better. To tell the truth, it looks like he's really stuck on you. He's got that doe-eyed, puppy dog love look in his eyes. So what 'cha going to do about it?"

"I'm going with it," I say. "I like the way it feels, and I'm having a great time tonight. Don't go off and blab it around though 'cause you know, I could change my mind tomorrow. Besides, I have to keep my eye down the road. My future is so up in the air."

As we stepped into the brilliant glow of the bug light's intense beam, my eyes re-adjust from the outer darkness. I scan the possibilities that lay within the concession stand. Tammi taps me on the shoulder, "I'll be around the corner in the Ladies Room."

"Oh, wait, I'll go with you. I'll get the eats on the way back," I say, moving back out into the darkness. As I blink, I make out a familiar figure sitting atop a cycle and leaning against the tall rear fence that confines the *Shining Star*. I follow closely behind Tammi as she walks confidently around the back, seeing clearly despite the quick lighting changes. The ladies room is dimly lit, which is just as well because it always appears to need a fresh coat of paint and the sink faucets drip rust non-stop all summer. I step quickly into an empty dank stall. There are a couple other girls milling about the mirror area smoking cigarettes and re-checking their hair-dos. Tammi and I know them from around town. I don't say anything to them and never really have. I've always considered them troublemakers, but I don't know why...maybe the pumped up hairstyles and heavy make-up. They make me feel as if I need more time to mature and grow up. They look as if that took place for them a long time ago. So I feel sorry for their need to be so old before their young. And of course, everyone knows they do it all with the guys.

I self-consciously sit down to pee and make it quick, never even letting my fanny touch the seat. I zip up my jeans and pull down my Beaverton High sweatshirt and shout over to Tammi, "I'm going to the concession stand, meet me there, okay?" I don't even consider washing my hands in the dripping brown water of the bathroom faucet, and fling open the moth-covered screen door, whose squeal drowns out Tammi's response.

My eyes blink purposefully crossing over into night vision outside the restroom. And as I blink, my stride is cut to a quick halt by a figure I stumble hard into. My vision adjusts instantly as I careen into this large warm body. I know this collision is no accident by their solid stance. The figure quickly grabs my shoulders and presses me up against the concession stand wall. It is pitch black as the side of the stand is in the shadows. His heavy body presses hard against mine. His weight and my paralyzing fear, make struggling away useless for the moment.

"Hey, I've wanted to see you for a couple of days now! You're sure lookin' pretty tonight. Whatcha doin' with a scrawny guy like him? You were with him the other night at the Armory. Well, at least ya like choppers. We have somethin' in common, now don't we? I can take you places on my bike I'm sure you'll never see with that sweet little farm boy. You're more women than he'll ever know what to do with, and I'm more man than he'll ever be, and it's all yours!"

I stand frozen to the wall. His words are jabs, repulsive from a lack of sensitivity and monstrous egotism. What is he trying to do? Is he thinking he can force me to like him? Why did he choose me? Does he think fear will inspire my interest? He's repulsive with his cigarette breath and wind-burned appearance. Where's Tammi? What can be hanging her up in that hole of a bathroom? Primping, I suppose, while I'm out being threatened?

"You are sweet aren't cho? How about lettin' me try a little sugar? It won't hurt. Come on, I think you'll like it!" He pushes his face into mine, but I turn my head away before his lips hit mine.

"Look, get away from me! The girls you're looking for are still in the bathroom putting out their cigarettes!" I say, shoving him as hard as I can—and he falls back off me. "My uncle is sheriff here in Beaverton, and he usually makes nightly rounds of the drive-in. If you don't leave me alone, I'm going to report you!"

"I'm a lotta guy, honey," he responds in his cocky fashion. "I think you're my kinda girl. I like your long silky black hair and those dark brown eyes. I'll be waitin' for you whenever you're ready," he says with a smile and a wink of the eye, turning away and striding to his machine.

I lean back against the wall and breathe in deep. Tammi pops out of the lady's room smelling like heavy cologne and lipstick perfectly replaced.

"Geez Tammi, what took you so long?" I blurt out, exasperated and wondering if anything violent had happened, would she have been there to save me, or even witnessed the scene?

"Look over there. Over at that biker leering at me like I'm a prime steak—done medium well, just the way he likes it cooked," I say with contempt.

"Oh no, it's him, isn't it?" She presses in a hushed tone.

"Yeah, Motorcycle Maniac! While you were in the bathroom, he accosted me as I came out. And I mean accosted! He cornered me against the wall and pressed his big ole body up against me so I couldn't move, then told me I was the girl for him! Can you imagine? That ape without any speakable qualities is out for me! I thought he was half joking before; someone to trifle with and scare a little, but he got physical!" I said, trying not to overreact.

"I don't know Celia, this sounds dangerous! I think it's time to report this guy to your Uncle," Tammi implores.

Just as she knit her brow to reflect on my dilemma, those two other girls stroll out of the bathroom. They have already lit up cigarettes and start a strut I know is as phony as the bleach they use to re-color their hair.

Oh, yeah, one is named Lanette and the other, Shannon. Both girls were hardly making it through school and dropped out last year. Deep down I know they probably miss being in school–at least for the football and basketball season. I wonder if they're here with some local divorcees. But they aren't heading up to the cars and trucks packed single file in front of the big screen. No, instead, they work their way back to the fence and lean up against it, eyeing my worst nightmare. There you go sucker, I think to myself…just your style.

"Come on, let's get out of here," says Tammi, tugging at my arm.

"Yeah, I'm coming," I reply. I take one last glance back. Lanette and Shannon have now moved over to his bike. He is lighting their cigarettes–again; obviously their way of introducing themselves and asking for trouble. But that's okay, it was what they'd been grooming themselves for.

"It's probably close to intermission by now. Connor is going to think I deserted him. Let's hurry this up, get our snacks, and head back to the peace and security of the guys," I rush.

"Alright, but think about it Celia, your uncle needs to know this guy is out for you. HE may be a bigger problem then we really know. It's better to play it safe. Uncle Reese can keep an eye on him in case he turns out to be LOCO," presses Tammi, sounding uncharacteristically concerned.

"I guess, but maybe he'll go for Lanette and Shannon. They look like his kind of girls, and maybe they'll take care of his interests. I think I'll let it go, but if he bothers me again, I'll go to Reese," I respond, trying for optimism.

We walk up to the concession stand counter. I order a large buttered popcorn and two large cokes, and add some chocolate covered peanuts for Tammi out of the kindness of Connor's treat. Together we mince silently up to Connor, still sitting patiently on the ground and up against his bike. I throw my head back one last time toward the shadow of the back fence. The spot is empty—void of the Motorcycle Maniac and the girls. I release the wrinkles in my brow and my shoulders drop to—*at-ease*. The thrill of an evening out with friends returns instantly in his vanishing. I turn back to greet Connor, and wish Tammi a better second half of the evening as the sound of a cycle engine guns down our back isle. I don't need to look. I know who it is and his intent. I stand motionless, not wanting to make eye contact and provoke anymore discourse.

But, he stops behind me and shouts, "You'll be mine yet! I can wait!"

Someone in a car behind him yells out their window, "Turn That Damn Machine Off! We Can't Hear!"

The Maniac guns his engine more and yells back, "Fuck You!", then takes off. I never turn around.

The movie is over and the lights are exposing the shadows. I don't remember much about the rest of the film after the Maniac pulled that humiliating stunt. Connor asks how I know that big dope, and all I can say is, "I don't."

It is a double feature tonight, but I don't feel much like grounding it anymore. My fanny is cold and sore and besides, that cycle nut took the romance out of our evening. I don't want Connor to think I spend my spare time flirting with scary elements like the biker, but somehow I feel his guard click in after the biker drove off yelling his intentions. He is at least questioning our familiarity, and for whatever reason, I can't explain my troubles with this guy. I know if I don't word the situation just right, I will involve Connor in what might turn into really risky business. Although it might be egotistical to consider, a fight over me could prove dangerous for Connor, and somehow, I think he knows this.

"No, I don't know him. I think he is some biker thug, hopefully just passing through town. He keeps turning up at places I go and sort of taunting me. Tammi thinks he's a big tease and keeps pestering me 'cause I take him too seriously."

"Forget Tammi. He's bothering you because he wants you!" replies Connor, obviously miffed. "You are the best looking girl in town and you seem distant—sort of hard to get. I'd be kind of alert, if I were you. If he tries to lay a hand on you, or make you scared, tell your Uncle Reese, who, by the way, is hanging out over by the ticket box talking with Norma. If that guy had given you any real trouble, Reese would have been able to help."

"Okay, I know I had better start to watch out. I guess I shouldn't take Beaverton's tranquility for granted. Nothing that scary ever seems to happen here, but there's always a first time. I only wish he were interested in someone else!"

"Do you feel like staying for the second feature?" I ask, changing the subject.

"Not if you don't."

Oh good, I think to myself. He isn't too turned off or intimidated by the incident. "Actually, Celia, I should be going. Tomorrow evening I've got a baseball game against Deer River and I'd like to be sharp. If it wasn't for a lot of field work I've got to do, I wouldn't worry."

"That's okay," I interrupt, "I kind of feel like getting to bed early myself."

"I'd really like it if you'd come and watch though. I'd pick you up and we could ride out to the ball park together. What d'ya think?" he asks with enthusiasm.

"Sure, sounds like fun. I haven't been to a baseball game all summer. Who are you playing for?"

"*Perham's Dry Goods.* They've recruited a bunch of us high school guys and we've been looking pretty slick. I don't know…it's just fun!" he concludes.

We reach for the helmets and thoughtfully ease them into position. Connor silently pushes his bike out of our spot, heading toward the ticket box and the exit. Once past most of the rows of viewers, he turns on the motor and revs it up. His consideration and politeness makes me feel warm and respectful, and pleased I'm going out with him. I hop on back, wrap my arms around his waist and clinch my hands together in front. I feel warm, loving and secure, at least in this moment.

We pull up in front of my house. Every breath moves to disturb the absolute stillness of midnight. I get off the bike touching every moment in slow motion; the lifting of the hip, the angle of my foot, each phrase pulling from the comfort of freedom, independence and speed. I am aware of the next step before it happens; immediately longing to repeat the last and assuming the comfort, ease and predictability of life inside my parent's house will soon replace this moment.

I step out from the bike hoping our goodbyes will be meaningful. I glance up at the house, scoping out the porch light and the faces that may be watching from behind the curtains. But all is still.

"I had a great time Connor," I express enthusiastically. "I'm looking forward to the baseball game."

"How about I pick you up at 5:30 tomorrow evening, okay?" he asks, reaching out and taking my hand.

"That will be good for me," I reply, smiling up at his boldness.

With that he moves in and asks, "Do you mind if I kiss you goodnight?"

"No," I reply quietly, "I was hoping you would."

He bends down, gently placing his hands on my shoulders. I move in like our dog Tiny; cuddling up for some extra closeness, wrapping my arms around his body and gently meet his lips. We look into each other's eyes, smiling at our new familiarity and its freshness, and a perfect time to go, just when you want desperately to stay. I whisper a final "goodnight", release my embrace and shoot for the house. I hear Connor's good-bye catch a bit of the breeze rushing past my ears, and his engine roars as my hand grips the knob of the inner door. I never look back until I catch my breath on the steps to my room…where I relive the evening…till sleep overtakes the night.

CHAPTER ELEVEN

Morning Walk

This is a beautiful morning. The sun radiates from behind the barrier of the shades, overpowering the sheer fabric curtains with brilliant, illuminating streams cutting across my sleeping room and up the wall I now nestle against from my bed. A cool westerly breeze breaks the sharp, hot, eastern rays with soothing cool air that overwhelms the dreaminess and tranquility of early morning slumber. I throw off the warm covers and expose my bare legs to the cool breezes. The freshness breaks the spell cast upon me by last night's dew— only perceivable in early morning light.

I grab last night's jeans and sweatshirt that had been thrown carelessly on the floor, and quickly dress. I want to get out into the world, to feel my existence in the earthly scheme of things. Perhaps to shake off the subconscious dust left from last night's dreams. I slip out of my room and quickly, silently move out the side door that opens above the basement stairs. I have Tiny along with me as she too is eager to herald in the majesty of this fine day.

Tiny leaps and twists in mid-air, so completely caught up in the spirit of morning sun, dewy grass and general buzz of critters sounding off with the sights, sounds and smells of a new day. Suddenly, Tiny picks up a scent and busies her nose at getting to the bottom of it. She squats down and leaves a little signature of her presence at this spot…and that spot…and on to other spots.

I chase her zigging and zagging down our block. We reach the end and without looking back for my approval, she tears off across the open field that abuts the road Tammi, Parrot and I had taken to the railroad tracks the other day.

Tiny sees me sprinting through the tall grass and reeds as an opportunity to bolt full speed on ahead; short stubby legs a blur in hyper-motion. I reach the road far behind her. She cruises the border disguising her impatience by searching frantically for scents, looking anxiously back for my approval to move on to our usual resting spot by the river. I catch up and say "Okay" and she resumes her zigs and zags from one smell to another, searching for that particular doggy delicacy sure to be uncovered somewhere along the way.

Strolling along marveling at my chance to be alone and at peace with thoughts for just a little while, I wonder if Connor is out on his tractor already; as a good farm boy, he probably is. I wonder if he is as cute sitting up on that mighty piece of equipment as he was last night sitting down against his motorcycle. I wonder if he becomes strong and willful as he works the cattle in and out of the barn— far more willful than the shy guy who could barely steady his hands to help with my helmet. I think about Tammi asleep in the room she shares with her sister. I'll be over to see her later this afternoon, sometime before the ball game.

Tiny reaches the tracks before I do and stops. I jog across the road and up the left shoulder to catch up. The road curves off to the right following the tracks and the river behind town. I bend down and feel the track for mystery trains possibly rushing in our direction. The steel bar is cold and still, without any indication of high-powered locomotion or impending surge. Tiny shoots down the tracks passed the path that leads to our spot on the river bank. As I look up the tracks to catch a glimpse of her speed, I catch hold of the glint and sheen of motorbike chrome and endless reflections of the surroundings on black chassis. Oh no! I sure don't want to run into those guys—especially when I'm all alone. I stop and stiffen, motionless, paralyzed by this inopportune meeting. Should I go quietly leaving Tiny to roam on her own? This is my town. Why should I be afraid of walking along a path I have taken fearlessly all my life? Should I boldly walk up and summon Tiny to my side? I recognize the bike. It's his. The Maniac's. I don't know. The idea of having to put up with his aggressive come-ons this early in the day could ruin my bright outlook.

What could Tiny be doing? She hasn't popped up from the river bank so apparently something has caught her attention. Everything is just too quiet and still. Not even Tiny can be heard darting up and down through the brush and reeds, barking or yelping at the river's wildlife or the strangers. I feel an urge to catch a glimpse of what these guys might be doing down along the bank. I'm going for a closer look.

Slipping off the tracks like a ghost, I ease over the rocks that vocalize every shift in the bed, and moving down the track's incline on the right. In the tall grass and weeds at the side of the gravel path, I feel surer of my silent footing. I have learned in my days outdoors to tread effortlessly and lightly in order to get closer to the animals that inhabit the woods around Beaverton. The deer, the beaver, the otters, the pheasant and prairie chicken can be sneaked up on if your movement is stealthy and silent. Putting these lessons into some real use gives me a sense of power, cunning and self-confidence. Of course, I would hate to be caught prying into the ridiculous life of *misfits on wheels.*

I tread even lighter and crouch down as I ponder the idea of getting caught. Off in the distance I hear the low pitched wail of a train signaling its impending presence on to the scene. It must be the daily eight o'clock heading for Minneapolis, right on schedule. I should find Tiny. I always worry she will jump on the tracks just as the train thunders through town.

The bikers can hear the train coming too. I wonder if I'll be exposed as they look up for the train. Between the track and the river is dense brush and trees of Birch, Cottonwood and Willow. The trees look like saplings, but I think they've been there for years, never achieving full growth or development because the soil is always wet along the bank and can't provide the roots an opportunity to mature. But the tall reeds and cattails are dense, growing strong in the dampness, giving me plenty of cover as I create a path down to a place where I can hear activity; the rustling of grasses and low voices talking in short, sporadic clips. I feel like a spy, and if caught—held for ransom. If not, I could uncover the secret schemes of mass destruction by deranged thugs.

I turn quickly down and into the woods. The train bellows its oncoming intentions, allowing my movements to go yet unheard.

From just above my hiding place I hear, "Hey, Moose, you got everything tied up tight this time, don't ya?"

"Sure, I ain't no slouch, Big Dude," one of the bikers hollers back.

"Okay, I'm just tired of fuckin' careless work. Ya got it? Like Smokie's over there," another replies impatiently.

Ducking low amongst the reeds, I can see the hurried activities of three bikers. They're busy tying something up in a sheet. Good grief! Whatever it is looks to be just about life size! A chill runs through my heart down to my toes with a burning sensation around my ears. I kneel down to catch my breath as the train whistle blasts a louder version of the last.

"Come on!" I hear from the river bank. "Let's toss this in before the train gets here!"

I look up from my vantage point. I can see two bikers, each holding the end of the long bundle as they swing it with apparently needed strength, into the air. The wrapped load sags lugubriously in the middle. The bikers swing the bundle up and away from the river and hold on as it comes swaying back hard over the rippling current. They swing it up and away once again, lifting the bundle even higher than before. As it swings out over the river, they let 'er go flying with a crest that gravity forces a direct descent to the morning stream.

I'm sick. I can't help but believe they have just thrown a body, wrapped and tied in sheets, into the river—either dead or about to be. I turn and run up the side of the hill at full speed, flying passed their bikes on the tracks. I'm running headlong for home, regardless of whether I'm spotted or not, totally arrested by the possibility of *murder*.

But who, why and how? In an instant the blare of the train whistle brings reality roaring back. My reflexes catapult me in one leap to the other side of the track. I tumble head-over-heels down the side of the hill as the train churns passed me. I come to a rest amongst some bramble bushes whose thorns pierce my clothes and skin. I am shaken, even scared and take off again across the field.

When I get to the road where just a short time ago Tiny and I were blissfully strolling, I stop to look back. I left Tiny! I don't recall seeing Tiny the whole time I was sneaking about the woods. Where is she? Normally she sticks pretty close. She'll run ahead of me sniffing deliberately from scent to scent, then rip back for acknowledgment, then set off again. After she first bound down the river bank, she never returned. Oh Tiny, where are you? Those awful men couldn't have you? I turn back slowly towards town and head home, all the while the train surges past.

CHAPTER TWELVE

The Search

Parrot and I searched the grounds by the river for hours to no avail. It's as if time has stopped and all my powers are soaked up by the dilemma I face. Must I let anyone know? My parents of course, will take the news of Tiny's disappearance like most everything: "*It was your responsibility to keep her on a leash. You know the rules.*" And I feel silly telling my friends because they will know I was just being lazy and didn't want to admit it.

I was at in the wrong place at the wrong time. I wish to death that I could live the whole day over again. I would start fresh and hang around waiting for commands to come from the goddess getting her beauty rest before descending to the depths of the breakfast dishes. She would have quickly hailed me before the sink to take stock of the situation and ordered to make quick work of it. Well, maybe I can manage this dilemma a little easier than I first thought. Perhaps Tiny will show up on our doorstep having spent the day running wildly through the woods. Maybe she has broken loose from whatever has held her and is now hiding in some safe location waiting for the right moment to sneak back home.

My heart is beating hard. I can feel my whole body vibrating and shaking, thinking about what really could have happened to Tiny if she hasn't escaped.

Poor Tiny…my sweet little dog. I always think of her as mine alone. She will tiptoe up into my bed late at night, then sneak down just as dawn brakes, revealing her forbidden whereabouts. After all, NO PETS ON THE FURNITURE! I loved curling up next to her after dinner in front of the TV set; she, resting from the day's chase and wanting to spend time like the rest of her family, in peaceful repose. I'm not ready to lose her. I brushed back the tears and wished I could disappear into the corner of my darkened closet.

My place: the closet. I go there and huddle in the dark when I need absolute peace and solitude from the world raging outside—my dark closet. In there I float. I can hardly feel the floor or the walls that encase my physical body. It's dark and black in my mind just like the closet. I don't have to be aware of how I look, and if anyone else is sizing me up; my parents, my siblings, my pals or some guy. I curl up resting my head on my knees and grip my legs tightly together. I wish I could dart through the door and slink down the hall to my room right about now. I would slide into the closet and collapse like a wilted rose in resignation of my misery.

I turn to Parrot, trying not to show my anguish and desperation, "Maybe we should go home and check the yard to see if he has made it back to the house? Right?"

"Yeah, okay, but once we get there, I'm staying in. I'm tired of this stuff. Besides, I don't know why I'm helping you anyway. It's not as if you'd ever do this for me. I'm missing the finishing chapters in, *"Love on at String,"* the greatest romance novel ever! I'm going to take a hot shower and pull out those cinnamon rolls I bought at *Barry's* yesterday, and forget all about YOUR problem. What kind of punishment do you think you're in for anyway?"

"Oh thanks. After all I've done for you—which I don't need to go into right now 'cause you know I have and you're just trying to avoid getting into trouble."

"You can get as mad as you want, but I'm not going to have anything to do with this," Parrot, chickening out as usual. I want a comrade in this mess, but I'm on my own.

As we mince silently back to the house, I raise my sullen head as soon as our yard is in sight.

"Oh Tiny, please be there," I plead.

"Maybe you'll get lucky Sis, but I sure don't see her from here. Could be she's in the backyard. I hope she is. That is the best dog in this whole dang town. But I'm not going to start crying until I'm sure she's gone for good. For your sake, I'm not going to let on that I know anything about this."

"No, I don't see her from here, either. She's gone for good," I say, letting my worst, yet hopefully uncertain fears out in an effort to at least prepare Parrot, knowing how emotional she becomes over ambiguities much less intense than this one.

"I just know it. I'm not really worried about Pops and Curlers. I'm more worried about the guys who did this. What if they come after me? I did see them all together and a pretty good birds-eye view too. I'm going to spend the afternoon looking for Tiny. Maybe I'll head over to Uncle Reese's office for some help, and after that I'm going to be at home until next fall, when school starts. If anyone wants to see me they will have to come find me. I don't care how much torture Curlers can heave at me—cleaning deluxe, dishes galore, babysitting Peanut noon, night and day. I'm not going anywhere until I go to college. It'll be hard on the boyfriend front, but it's better than being the playmate of redneck/serial killer/demon cult types. Yeah, I better talk to Uncle Reese.

Parrot strolls up the walk, her shoulders drooping and her usual expression of, *I didn't do it*, now sags. I view her from the corner of my eye as I head for the backyard, and hopefully Tiny. She kicks the screen door open with her foot, not bothering to catch its handle as it swings back, hitting the frame with a sharp whack. I continue on, zombie-like, my ears taking in the screen doors offense until it is again at rest, silently erect and forgotten.

"Tiny! Here Tiny! Time to eat!" I call.

Nothing. Dead silence. The harsh, rotting feeling in my stomach interrupts the usual steady stream of sorting and dividing I take for granted. Nothing left to do but see Uncle Reesie. I turn and check the backyard again, just in case Tiny has made it back in this brief instant without my knowing.

As I walk up the single step into the Rabbit County Jail, I take in the bars that secure the windows and doors inhibiting violence from outside or in. I feel safe, if only for the time being. What reason can I find to extend my visit beyond the few moments I need to tell my story? Uncle Reese will ask me a few questions made short and officious to accompany the nature of his investigative work as sheriff. I can then dawdle, idling away some time at the county jail. I can offer to clean the place up a bit, polish and wash the floors, about the only thing the jailhouse ever needs done.

I don't know. I'm beginning to have doubts maybe this will all sound so silly repeated out loud to Reesie. He takes his work so seriously—honestly, sometimes too seriously. What if he needs actual evidence of a crime to take police action? What if my story ends up sounding like a lot of muddled, high-strung panic without any real cause for worry—other than I lost the dog?

The sun has brightened the white-washed county jailhouse to an uncomfortable eye-squinting glare. I feel salty driplets of perspiration rolling down my side as the day's heat intensifies. I try piecing together the story I'm going to offer up to Reese. Looking through the large window of the old wooden double doors; ancient and dog-eared, having born the duty as sentry for far longer than the lives of those who live here remembers. Sun's rays bounce off the glass and I must cut through the diffraction to get a view of the darker room inside. I cut a piece of darkness by casting a shadow across the window with my hand. I peer in blindly, scanning across the room until I reach the desk. As I look up at a dark figure stationed behind it, I can see they've already spotted me. Too late to turn back now, Reesie sits opposite the door, feet up on the desk, leaning back in his regulation government chair and grinning at my efforts and consternation. I swing the door open, trying to look confident.

"Well Celia girl, welcome to the county jail—home of the shiftless and wayward," Reese says. "I, as resident analyst, can turn any frog into a prince and any scullery maid into a princess. And how about yourself? What can I do for you?"

"Oh, Well….ahh," I'm fumbling and trying to remember the story I hope to convince Reesie is worth investigating. I proceed ever so self-consciously toward the coolness at the center of the room where the Sheriff is seated and apparently looking over some kind of charts.

"Did you want to make a few bucks straightening this place up? It's about that time again. Or actually, you know what I really need done? My car could use a good wash and waxing. I'll pay you for it?" Course, I'd think you'd have that boy…Connor Johnson… right? …busy fussing all over you on a lazy afternoon like this. Didn't I see you two out together last night? At the drive-in?" he inquires.

Gee, Uncle Reese, I guess this town might be too small, like Tammi says. I mean, a girl can't have a little private moment with a guy before the whole town is talking," I say, maybe a little too defensively.

"Whoa, don't get your hairs all in a knot on my account little missy. After all, it is my duty to be observant. You know I check out that drive-in regularly. Say, I've been thinkin' about doin' some interior decorating around this place.

Come over here. Take a look at these color samples. What do you think of this color *Tangueray Green* on the walls with this *Champagne Peach* for the trim?"

I step up to the desk and lean over the opposite side. "Well, I don't know, they kind of sound like they'll inspire more drinking in the already drunk and disorderly, don't ya think?" I respond. This color coordination was just what I needed to take my mind off the Maniac. "Look at this neutral beige color over here. All your office furniture would work well with a more understated wall color, ya know what I mean?"

"Yeah, yeah. First of all," Uncle Reese says, ready with his own theories, "I don't care whether the local drunks approve of or are inspired by my color scheme. Actually, *Tangueray Green* might be really nauseating to a stoned bum trying to sleep it off. I don't want to have to clean up any more stomach altercations than I have too. But still, I'm here day-in and day-out. If I'm not making my rounds, you can find me here. You know that, right? I often just throw some clean sheets down on one of those cots in the cells and bunk over. In which case, I wake up looking around and thinking how grubby this place looks and I might appreciate it more if it were given a fresher appearance. I guess beige, or as the tonier people would say, *e c r u*, is subtler. I'm tired of understated though. This office furniture is way too subtle, that's why I want to give the walls a bit more of an accent. The boys over at State Headquarters might prefer *e c r u*, but they're so seldom here. I don't think they'd mind much. As long as I get the job done—and I do, so *Tangueray Green* and *Champagne Peach* it is! Now, what was it you came in here for?"

This little discourse had really taken the edge off. I might find Tiny running along the road on my way home. "Well Uncle Reese, Tiny seems to have disappeared. I mean, she could have run away, but I was walking with her along the river and never saw her again. Do you think you could keep your eye open for her on your rounds?" I skipped right over those nasty little details in between on how I saw that suspicious stuff down by the river while I was walking Tiny. Why would they want to bother with a sweet dog like Tiny? It didn't even occur to me to tell him about that hoodlum trailing me about.

"Geez, Tiny's disappeared, huh?" Uncle says, cocking his head to one side and turning on a look of official concern. "I wasn't aware of that. I thought your problem might be something different... Oh well, sure, I'll keep my eyes open, and you young lady, keep your eyes open too. Ya know what I mean?" Reesie says kind of stern.

"Oh sure, I'll be looking everywhere, and hope the folks won't freak out. I don't want to sound too worried, but I took Tiny on that walk, and you know everyone will hold me responsible for her disappearance. I went home and got Parrot to search the area with me, but Tiny never turned up."

"Now Celia," Reese pipes in, "I wouldn't get too worked up. She could have tracked a deer down by the river and chased it further out of town."

"Yeah, I know," I respond. "The part that worries me is those motorcycle guys were hanging out at just about the very spot she took off towards. Not that I'm trying to point a finger at them, Reese. It's just coincidental that they were there and Tiny disappears at that very spot."

"Well shit, girl! Why didn't you mention that right off the bat?" Reese says, suddenly looking alert. "Don't get me wrong, that little crowd of "has-beens" don't bother me a bit. Somehow I know these guys might be the first guests to get a good look at my interior color scheme, but, as of yet, they seem to be minding their own business and mostly taking a tour of our little part of the State of Minnesota. Can't arrest anyone for that!"

I suppose he had a point there. I fidget around with the color charts he has lined up on the large oak desk in front of me. "That's all I really came about Uncle Reese. Just let me know if you need any help painting these walls, okay? I think you should go with the colors you like. I think they'll really brighten up this place. It always seems so dark in here!"

"So you see what I mean, don't you? I need a little relief from the dull and the drab".

And as if to complete that thought, Uncle Reese jumps to his feet, places his fists on his hips—legs spread to an officious stance, and in a tone of decisive forth-rightness says, "I'm heading over to *Perham's Dry Goods* to place a paint order. After I finish there, I'll put in a concentrated effort around the community for Tiny. But, don't expect me to be shagging through the woods or along the river bank for her. That's your job—covering those hard to get to areas. I imagine if she's in one piece she'll come crawling home on her own. If not, and I want you to be prepared for her possible demise, leave her where you find her so I can examine the scene. Got me?"

"Yes, Uncle Reesie. I'm crossing my fingers she'll be home when I get there," I say agreeably. His dominant tone puts me at ease. It makes me comfortable knowing someone with more expertise in these matters could be taking over.

Reese minces quickly over to the door. Uncle Reese, for having such long legs always walks in short quick clips; never striding out smoothly, but needing twice as many steps to get to his destination as most people with longer torsos and shorter legs. On the other hand, the stride makes the sheriff's demeanor more effective.

"Now, if you have the rest of the afternoon free," Reese begins in a new controlled tone of voice, "how about pulling the sedan out of my garage and giving her a wash and waxing. I'll pay you $5 bucks for your services."

"Sure, Uncle Reese, that might be what I need to take my mind off of Tiny."

"Great," he shoots back. "Here is the key to the garage door and this longer silver one is the car key. Now, take her out slowly watching through the side mirrors to be sure you're far enough away from the sides of the garage as not scrap any paint off. Alright?"

"Shoot, Uncle Reese, I know how to pull a car out of the garage!" I can't believe he's giving me instructions on driving. I've had my license for a year now!

Uncle Reese turns and shoves open one of the heavy wooden doors out of the jailhouse exposing the world outside of this room washed over with a sheet of brilliant white light. He takes the first move out into the open and his body becomes a black silhouette against the white scrim. I head out too, feeling reassured by Reece's assistance, yet at the same time, I can't believe he has so little faith in my driving abilities.

"Celia, don't take it personally, I'm just lookin' out for my car! I'd advise anyone pulling my car out of the garage to take care. It's kind of a tight squeeze out the sides. Just calm down girl!" he insists, which sounds kinda like he's half mocking.

"Well, okay Uncle Reese," I reply running down the steps and passed him out into the heat of the sun. "I'm going home for lunch and see if Tiny has shown up. After that I'll be out washing your car if you have any news. See you later." I continue on, jogging up the street toward home. I'm not going to look back, assured the case was in the best possible hands around.

As I hit the front porch I'm aware of the silence; the lack of energy cast by the absence of my small beloved dog. She hasn't returned, and I don't have to look around to know it.

Parrot is coming down the front stairs from the second floor and flits right on by, giving me the impression she doesn't want to speak; annoyed I suppose by my carelessness with Tiny. Well if she had only been the one to walk her, instead of me, she'd know just how anguishing the whole experience has been. "No sign of Tiny since I've been out, has there?" I ask.

"Nope," she murmurs through a crusted frown.

"I spoke with Uncle Reese," I shout down to her from several steps up. "He said he would cruise the local area looking for her, and that I should check the back woods, like along the river bank."

So, what are you doing here then?" Parrot tosses out in a scowl.

"Thanks for your optimism, Parrot. I hope you'll be forever blessed with good fortune," I jibe back, trying to remain unaffected by her doom and gloom attitude. I want to believe Tiny is going to return either with the help of Uncle Reese or she'll show up at the house after a little cruise from the homestead.

I turn and finish the stairs. I'm so disappointed in Parrot's lack of understanding. I'm going to throw off the doomsday caste she's permeating. To wash Reesie's car, I better change into a sweatshirt and beat jeans. Uncle Reese lives two blocks behind ours. Not far out of the way is Tammi, I'll stop by her house and try arousing a little energy and enthusiasm for washing down someone else's car.

Okay, everything can work out, I think as I bound down the back stairs to the kitchen. I whip open the refrigerator door hoping some delicacies will catch my eye then meet and greet these hunger pangs. Even just a morsel not yet sucked in by the eating vacuums—my brothers. It's not looking good. Curlers hasn't done the weeks grocery shopping up in Durham yet, the nearest town with a major store. I crouch down for closer surveillance of the lower shelves. Bull's-eye, two chicken wings and a leg left over from last night's dinner! Quick, I got to get a lunch bag to put them in before a sibling arrives and grabs the loot from my hands.

I drop the three pieces from their platter into the bag, stick the dish into the sink and scoot out the back door. I veer around the side of the house marching up to the sidewalk heading toward the Larson house. Maybe I can get Tammi to pack her own lunch, 'cause it might be hard to share the three pieces of chicken.

Approaching Tammi's front walk, the sound of a familiar yet intimidating roar of a motorcycle engine breaks my purposeful assent on the Larson house. A Harley. *His* Harley. I turn and see him coming down Pine. I hope he's oblivious to my presence so he'll move on past. I stop in my tracks thinking, if I'm still and quiet he won't turn his head. He'll focus straight on down the road and further even to his destination.

It seems to be working. No…, shoot, damn, he's spotted me! Damn…! He's driving on past a few feet. I scoot quickly up the walk toward Tammi's steps and her doorbell. Too late, he's making a u-turn in the middle of the street obviously with the intent to come back around as if we have anything to talk about! I'm going to carry on and ignore this grand gesture.

"Hey Cutie-pie, I've been looking all over town for you. How about hopping on back and going for a ride? What d'ya say? I won't hurt cha. Really, we can go wherever you want and just talk. You're not afraid of me are you? Seriously, I just want to know what you're all about. Can't blame a guy for bein' curious about a girl like you, now can ya?"

All this time I am ringing Tammi's doorbell. No one's answering! Damn! I don't remember Tammi saying they were all going somewhere today. Maybe she was trying to get hold of me while I was out looking for Tiny or talkin' to Uncle Reese. Go to Uncle Reese's; that's the ticket. I can make it that far, then duck into his place for cover, or tell this guy my Uncle is home and he's the sheriff of Beaverton.

"Now I know you can talk, Honey!" he starts up again, "'cause I've seen you gabbing with your girlfriends and that farm boy."

"Hey, look! I've asked you to leave me alone, right?" I say, getting my nerve up. "At least that farm boy's got manners. I don't see that we'd have anything in common to talk about anyway. You've got a bunch of gang girls with you who seem to be just your type. So what would you want with me? Do I look like that type of girl to you?"

"No, Honey, you sure don't, and that's one of the things I like about you. Not that I'm putting those chicks down, mind you. They're doing just what they want to do. No one is forcing 'em to tag along. But you're kind of refined and haughty, like you need to be broke; like a colt that's done a lot of swishing its tail and prancing about and one day it's time to put the saddle on. Well I'd like to be the first one to put the saddle on you. I think you'll give me a hell of a ride!"

Shoot, where's he coming from?! I don't need taming, and I'm sure not going to let him near me. Put a saddle on me! Not him, not in a million years!

"Hey look," I say, now getting angry, "I don't know what you're talking about! What has *ever* given you the impression I'd let you near me? What is there about you that you'd think I'd be charmed with? You look like you just blew in out of a dust bowl. Like I said, that *farm boy's* got manners. What makes you think you can ride into town and pick me up, just like that? Forget it. What's to talk about?"

That must have left him speechless because he wasn't saying a think, just staring at his handle bars. Good, now let me head for Reese's.

He revs his cycle motor and moves off from the curb as I walk on. I am halfway down the block as he pulls up alongside me again. *Now what?!* I think to myself.

"Hey, why don't you let me bike you to your destination, okay? Unless you're scared of me? I promise I'll be a gentleman the whole time. Then I'll leave you alone."

"Look, I am not scared of you. Okay, you can give me a ride, but you also said you'll leave me alone, right?"

"Yeah, you can trust me."

This could be one big stupid move, but I'll ride to Reesie's and that will at least get him off my back. I move over to his bike and slide on to the back. It's roomier and seems more powerful than Connor's bike and truly makes me nervous. This guy smells manly and I feel way over my head in the macho department. He's not like a growing boy, he's not tall but solid and compact, sure of where his weight and center of gravity is at all times.

"You're going to have to hold on a little tighter than that, Sugar, for your own good. Like I said, I'm not going to try anything, trust me."

I spread my arms around his front waist, not putting up a fight, hoping he'll just get moving and get this thing over with. I hope nobody I know sees me...

He revs her up, working the engine to a blaring roar, for sure louder than I had expected. I look around to see if anyone I know is watching this uncomfortable scene–especially Pops and Curlers.

We shoot off like a bucking horse, faster than I anticipate. Before I've adjusted to this unexpected ride and the bit of a thrill I'm getting, the biker shouts back at me, "Where you goin' anyway?"

"Take a right turn at the corner of the next block," I shout forward. I must admit I am impressed with his sense of control and lack of concern for what anyone else seems to think of him. It's probably impressive to me because I always feel so self-conscious. His kind of cockiness is pretty unusual around here, it's so bold and almost out of control. It's scary and exhilarating all at the same time. I almost feel flattered that he's interested in me. I could almost like it. "See that pale blue house with the white picket fence over there? That's where I'm getting off." I say in a demanding tone.

As he pulls up to the curb, I jump quickly off before he can say anything about riding somewhere else.

"You don't have to run, I'm dropping you right where you asked me to, see," he says with a note of cattiness in his voice. "Your looks knock me off my feet,

Sugar, but I ain't going to grovel or get down on my hands and knees to get you to take a little sight-seeing tour of the countryside or nothin'. Shoot, there's plenty of babes begging me for a ride around the block, and they can be a lot sweeter than you. So don't go actin' all prissy or nothin'." With all that out in the open, he twists the throttle and shoots off down the street.

Geez, give me a break! As if I care how many BABES are interested in him. I'm not, and didn't I tell him that? Why get all bent out of shape? I didn't want a ride from him in the first place. I was actually hoping to ask him directly about Tiny—if he'd seen her. I wonder if he would have told me the truth. Nah, if he knew she was my dog, and he had taken part in doing something to her, he'd lie. He'd say he'd never seen her. Trust him…not hardly!

I walk up Reesie's driveway fumbling through my pockets for the garage door key. I wonder how much longer those degenerates will be spending in this town. If Tammi had been around I wouldn't have had to give him even the satisfaction of a ride. Oh well, I wouldn't mind having her here to help with Reese's car either.

Pushing the key into the lock, I'm happy to see it opens with one quick twist. Before me sits Reese's major bomber of a car. This is a huge sedan looking as nearly perfect as the day he drove it off the showroom floor. Now, why would he want this thing washed? The "thing" is long and extends bumper to bumper from as near to the front of the garage as possible without touching the wall. What does he do with all this space? Maybe some nights he creeps from the house and stretches out in the luxurious plush vastness of the backseat. Of course he couldn't hear his emergency phone ring from the luxurious interior reporting some emergency. It's certainly bigger than even the cruiser, where he spends most of his waking hours.

As I open up the front driver's side, I say a few words to creation asking for help in keeping from scratching an iota of paint from the body while I maneuver the prize from the darkness out into solar exposure.

I still can't see why he wants this washed. Perhaps a bit of dust has accrued since the last cleaning, but hardly worth working up soap suds for. I suppose Reesie just wants to give me something to do and take my mind off of Tiny for awhile. I can't complain, because he's probably right. I need to stay busy and out of sight from my parents until they realize the family pet hasn't been seen or heard from for most of the day.

I fire up the ignition, being extremely careful not to sit fully down in the driver's seat in my drenched cut-offs. I'll get a long sob story sooner or later from Reese on how I damaged his upholstery and that the car will never be the same. He has always been extremely careful about all his possessions. They become so precious that he can hardly stand to use them. I figure, why have 'em around if you can't feel casual and comfortable with your stuff, or they start to own you, and not the other way around. But, it's a lost argument with Reese so I'd rather "handle with care".

After locking the beast into the garage, I turn and head back down the driveway. It occurs to me that I'd rather avoid a lift back home by the motorcycle guy, so I look around just in case he's lurking from around some corner. It looks all clear. I think I'll take a shortcut and slip through the yards straight across the street, back through the alley and do the same with that next block...until I end up in my own backyard. I should've done this on my way over to Uncle Reese's house. I usually do, but I felt like running my problem over in Tammi's mind just in case she could give me some advice, or at the very least, cheer me up. I'll give her a call; hopefully I can get it in before Parrot drops the bomb on the folks about Tiny. Or, maybe things will sound better if I give them the full scoop just the way it happened. Yeah, that's what I'll do. I'll muster up the integrity to give an accounting of her disappearance.

I swing open the screen door to the mud room, the entrance to the kitchen, and march aggressively into the house, determined to get the Tiny thing off my chest and let the chips fall where they may. Curlers is the most likely candidate to hear my story first since she's usually lurking about somewhere, cleaning this or repairing that. Unless she's at *Barry's* because it's that time of the day.

Darn. No sign of her down here on the first floor. I run up the front staircase pressing hard not to lose my enthusiasm for my task. Looking in her room... nothing. Wait, the front porch door squeaks and someone steps through to open the heavy inner door. I run back down the stairs to intercept one of the folks before anyone else can lay my difficult story on them. I guess hearing it from the horse's mouth is the best way, otherwise the interpretation could vary. I reach the entrance just as the door swings open and in steps Pops.

"Gee, hi Pops! You're home kind of early aren't you?" I blurt out, a little overly excited.

"Well, Celia dear," Pops begins, pleasantly calm, "this is the summer break so I only need to go into school for a few short hours a day. Besides, this is Saturday afternoon. "Why, are you disappointed I'm home?"

"Oh no Pops, nothing like that! I'm just not use to seeing you around at this time of the day." I suck in a deep breath because the time is now, or I'll end up explaining the Tiny ordeal to Curlers, who will take a dive off the deep end of hysteria, and after I'll feel morose and morbid—like Parrot. "Pops, you know the morning walks I take?"

"Yes" he responds, looking around the living room for the Bemidji daily paper.

"Well, I took one today around 7 a.m. with Tiny. I don't know if you've noticed or not, but Tiny hasn't been seen or heard from since."

"Oh really. No, I can't say that I noticed." Pop replies off handily.

"I was walking on the railroad tracks by the river, west of town—you know the spot, when she took off in the direction of the river, right where the motor-cycle gang happened to be carrying on. I didn't want to walk right into the middle of their party so I kind of hung out in some bushes to see if I could get a glimpse of Tiny. But, I never saw her again. That gang was up to some pretty weird stuff so I got a little nervous. When they heard the 7:30 train coming they started to head back up the river bank to where they had parked their cycles, and naturally I took off toward home, without Tiny. Pops, I've gone back and searched every step of that area for her, including most of town."

"How many times have I told you to keep Tiny on a leash?" Pops retorts dryly. "Not just because she could get loose and take off like this, but because I don't like her terrorizing town or getting into garbage in the back alleys. Now who knows what's become of her. I hope she wasn't an easy target for those biker delinquents. Has anyone notified Reese to the situation? Not that I think it should be a priority issue for our local law enforcement official, but if he happens to see her on his rounds he can pick her up."

"Yes, Pops, I talked to Uncle Reese earlier. He said he'd keep his eye open for her. Although, I didn't tell him how Tiny had run down to check out the motorcycle gang. I didn't want him to get too upset over something I'm not sure really happened." I say sullenly. Pops' response was what I had expected but I was hoping he would be more sympathetic to the anguish Tiny's disappearance had caused me. "I really can't say I saw those cycle dudes messing with her Pops. I mean she could have taken off after and animal or something, or just taken off on her own for awhile, although she's never done that before. Or, a farmer could have picked her up thinking she'd make a good farm dog..."

"Yes, these are all possibilities," Pop interrupts my explanations, "all the more reasons for walking her on a leash. It's going to be sad and disappointing to the whole family if Tiny doesn't come back. If its foul play by these motorcycle types then we'll let Reese figure out what can be done about it. If she simply has run off, and I hope that isn't the case, well, perhaps she'll return at her free will. In the meantime, I want you to announce at dinner to the rest of the family why she's not around, okay?"

"Yes, Pops," I say as somberly as I'm currently feeling, "I'll explain it to everyone." I slink out of the entryway and back on up the stairs and gently close the door behind me.

Throwing myself on my bed, face down on the pillow, I fight back tears built up over the day's stressful events and Pops' finger pointing at my irresponsibility. I want to run down to him already sitting in the heavy plump chair next to Grandma's old yellowing lamp, reading the paper and yell, *"YOU'RE WRONG! YOU'RE WRONG! Why must this be my fault? Just because I take morning walks? What about those motorcycle dudes? I made a judgment call. I'm seventeen; can't I make a few decisions and a few mistakes? How's about a little support? Huh?"*

Instead, I feel my temples throbbing and a greater desire to sleep…

CHAPTER THIRTEEN

The Baseball Game

"Oh geez," I blurt out loud, lifting my torso half up from the bed. "What am I doing napping?" I crank my head over to get a clear shot of the time on my clock radio sitting on the dressing table next to my bed. It was a gift from my folks last Christmas and has an alarm built in supposedly to drive me from my bed on school days. Actually, I wake up before the radio automatically goes on, then wait for Durham Rock to come on, then listen to as much of the Top 40 as possible before the folks pop a blood vessel over my incapacitation.

Anyway, I can hardly believe I have slept 'til 5 p.m. One hour and Connor will be here to get me for the game. I hope Pops doesn't expect me to make an announcement about Tiny to the family this evening. I should phone over to the jailhouse and see if Reese has any clues yet. Oh yeah, but first, I better give Curlers the info on the baseball game so she won't set my place at the table. I bet she'll want a complete run down on how we'll get there, what time it starts, and where are we going after? Then she'll tell me to be home at 11—sharp. It's not like she doesn't know the answer to all this stuff already, or what time I'm expected home. Parents get started on this repetitive syndrome sometime early on in a kid's life and forget that by the time we're this age it's drilled in material, hardly likely to be lost amongst the cavalcade of peripheral data housed in the brain. If a kid wants to break curfew it's not because they don't remember what time they were due back home, but because they'd rather stay out late and face the consequences later. The folks want to believe by repeating the rules over and over I will robotically appear at the front porch door on or before 11 p.m. The excuse I use most often is, "The time got away from me," not, "I forgot what time I was supposed to be in." I didn't get this far being a complete dunderhead!

I better make a move down to the kitchen to let Curlers in on my ballgame schedule. She'll tell me how she needs advanced notice and I'll apologize but tell her, I fell asleep before I had a chance, and that I'd be home early, and Connor is a nice, safe guy, so not to worry.

The real problem will be in not telling her about Tiny. This just isn't the right time to drop the bad news on her. She'll gasp and twist her face into high anguish—brow all knotting up. I'll stand there counting those furls in her brow, mumbling my story over and over as she pieces a distorted picture together in her mind. No, now is not right. It'll be 6 o'clock before I'll even be able to come up for air. Later, isn't good either. Pops will be mad 'cause I waited so long, and so will Curlers—double trouble. Two parents demanding my responsibility with two scoops of reliability on top. I really have no alternative but to save the story until later since I can't keep Connor waiting.

Decision made, I slip down the stairs and glide into the kitchen. Curlers is frying up some flattish brown meat as smoke billows from the hot, dry pan to be sucked up through the overhead air vents. As I approach I recognize the long thin slabs as Curlers' favorite meal—liver. Ahhh, what a relief I mutter under my breath, knowing I'll miss this meal as I launch into the night's venue with the chef.

"Mom, I know this is late notice and all, but I made plans to go watch Connor play baseball with his team. He's supposed to pick me up here at 6 o'clock," I start in a half-pleading sort of tone.

"Celia, I think you know how I feel about short notices. I've already started cookin' a piece of liver for you," she says, very matter of fact.

"I'm sorry Mom, I would have told you earlier but I fell asleep and didn't wake up 'til just now. Connor is probably on his way already and we won't be any later than 9 or 10 o'clock," this time really pleading.

"Okay, Celia. You've got my permission, but remember, no later than eleven."

"Oh, definitely not," I bounce back enthusiastically. "And, I'm sure someone will eat my share of liver!" Tiny would have if she were here, no matter how tough the consistency after Curlers cooks the life out of it.

"Say, Celia, have you seen Tiny today?" Curlers asks as I'm about to turn the corner and head back up to my room.

Oh no! I guess I can't make a sneaky exit out of here without being cornered on the question of the day. I wonder if Pops leaked our conversation to her early before I could let it out, my way. After all, he did say that I should be the one to let everyone in on the news.

"Well Mom, the last I saw of her was this morning. Has Dad said anything to you about her?" I say deciding to take an offensive approach to my explanation.

"Only that I should talk to you about her whereabouts."

"I took her for a walk this morning, as I often do, and she didn't return. But Uncle Reese is out looking for her, and I've scoured all the usual possibilities. Parrot and I have looked high and low. On my walk, that motorcycle gang was hanging out down by the tracks, near the clearing we go to down by the river. Well, she ran into that area and never came back," I said quickly but very concerned. It occurs to me that if I direct my story more toward the suspiciousness of the motorcycle gang, I might have more sympathy from the family. "I don't know Mom, that gang was acting pretty strange. I tried to get in close for a peek at what they were up to down there and Tiny's whereabouts. They were throwing something into the river all wrapped in sheets. I don't want to alarm you or anyone else, but it was a human shaped bundle." I blurt it all out fast, kind of steaming on out before I had a chance to censor or evaluate the meaning of what I was saying. I am feeling better about the whole thing though. I really need to get it off my chest to someone with more authority than I had. Also, Curlers was a good person to drop this on because my welfare would become more important than Tiny's. For her, the motorcycle gang will take on a persona of all evil next to the sweetness of her little Celia. Unlike Pops, who sees the irresponsibility of my action, Curlers will direct her attention to my potential harm. Both sides can be irritating. But for now, I need to get on with this explanation because I want to get ready for Connor.

"Mom, I know Uncle Reese has got a handle on the situation, and if anyone can figure this out, he can. Maybe Tiny is taking a tour of some area farms and these guys haven't really done anything with her at all. I can't just sit here and mope Mom. That won't help anything. I better get changed or Connor will be late for the game.

"Really, young lady, do you think I care whether or not Connor is late for a game. We're talking about your possible harm at the hands of some degenerate hoodlums. Having Tiny injured or dead at their hands is bad enough. Well, there will be no more walks to the railroad tracks alone. Do you hear me? I think you're being just a little cavalier about the circumstances when these guys could play havoc with this whole community." She pauses in her tirade, overreacting just as I thought she would. I glance over her shoulder and watch the kitchen clock's second hand click away as my time to dress and perk up my look begins to wear away.

I reach his bike just as he starts pulling the strap up from the buckle of his helmet.

"Hi handsome," I blurt out, half in relief of the anxiety I feel at leaving my dilemma behind—at least for a time. I feel a sense of calm embrace my body as I enter a world away from the guilt I linger in from Tiny's disappearance. At the ballgame there won't be looks of let down and disapproval; somewhere I can relax for awhile.

"Hey, Chic, are you all set?" Connor asks, and then goes on before I answer. "I can't believe your father let you out of the house before I got to the door. You think he's beginning to trust me, or something?"

"No, so don't get too excited over this little break in decorum." I say glibly. "I'm motoring out of the house because I'm anxious to get away for awhile. My father doesn't really know I'm out for the evening. But it's cool, my mother knows."

"Is there a problem? Are your parents coming down on you for something?" He asks gently, his smile dissolving compassionately to frown at the thought of my discomfort.

What a warm heart, I think to myself, and place my helmet over my untied hair. "I'll tell you later. It's been kind of a difficult day for me. I just need a change of scene for a little while."

He reaches over and pulls the helmet strap through the buckle. I feel kind of cozy in his attentiveness, but at the same time, uncomfortably helpless, like a little girl whose father is helping her tie a bow. I like Connor's care and consideration, and I know he means to show me he cares, but it almost makes me seem helpless—and on that score, I know I'm not.

I move away quickly so not to have to commit myself to one emotion or the other for long. Connor turns and throws his leg over the bike and starts it up, hopefully without sensing my discomfort with his sweet gesture. My face turns hot and probably blushes thinking about this momentary lapse of awkwardness. It doesn't last long as I jump on behind and situate myself in the center of the narrow seat, and up close to the driver—arms around his waist, ready to slice the wind in two and thunder up the middle.

Pulling away from the curb seems disjointed, as if the machine hesitates, ready to change its mind at a whim. But the cycle gets a head of steam up as Connor twists the throttle, pumping acceleration to the stop sign at the corner. Connor has his baseball uniform on. It looks a little geeky with its tight fitting knit. Connor seems notably confident in his sports attire, or, is he simply trying to give that impression as he rides through town.

Connor's number 10 is boldly announced on the front and back of his jersey in large navy blue letters placed just below the team name: GOODS. Maybe he's truly proud of being on a winning team and doesn't mind the whole town knowing it.

As we coast to the stop sign, I cast a quick glance to my right. There he is, recognizable in an instant! Dressed in denim and an aging cotton plaid shirt, our eyes meet as his Harley swoops past like a hawk eyeing the field mice below. I turn my head quickly to the front after flashing him a look of distain. *It can't work, it could never work*, I tell myself.

Connor sees him too, and follows his path up the street with his eyes. He waits a moment to move on, until he feels the cyclist has put a little distance between *our* intentions. We launch off from the stop and center ourselves upright after turning left, heading for the main drag, then down Route 2-North, and the baseball diamond.

We brake at the Main Street stop sign. I quickly look about for the other cycle, trying not to show much interest. Yet, I want to know if he's lurking somewhere, watching all my moves. Somehow, I feel vulnerable out in the open with Connor; anticipating a confrontation, I suppose. Maybe this guy will try and prove himself because I'm with someone else, someone he could threaten and maybe even do physical harm to, just to show me his strength and dominance. He'll be disappointed to find I'm not that simple, not like the girls who usually hang out with guys like him. He's nowhere in sight, and listening for him is futile over the roar of our own motorcycle engine.

Connor doesn't hesitate. I sense a feeling of power and control coming over Connor as I try pressing in closer to him, letting him know I believe in his manhood—or is it the uniform spurring him on?

The air is a mixture of hot and cold we surge through pockets of coolness and warm up again at the other end. It's like this all the way to the edge of town and just beyond until we hit the clearing before the thicket of woods. It's always this spot that cools down first on a summer's evening, and an impression that is ever marked in my memory. Yet it's just the world of impressions, and not a world of expectation I make sense of in this moment. But as we sweep into the cool blanket of summer evening air that I *expect* the evening changes, because it has always been there.

The ballpark is about a half mile out of Beaverton. Most towns around here have their diamonds right in the middle of things, usually in the municipal park, but for years Beaverton played ball in one farm field or another, and liked it that way. The bigger local family get-togethers, or local challenges formed temporary teams, and the seriously interested ball fans went to Durham to see solid baseball. Then Gary Perham's Grandpa got old and became a hazard to the road, so Mr. Perham junior suggested to Grandpa that they install a field locally and maybe start up a team sponsored by the store, after all, getting the old man off the road was going to take more than a new baseball diamond. It would mean changing his allegiance from Durham's Super Stars (out of the local tavern), to something home based, with loyalty like the *Dry Good's* staffers as team members. I guess that was about 15 years ago. Old Pops Perham has died, but the team lives!

So anyway, Gary's dad bought a plot of land north of town in a field surrounded by woods that he had resurrected as the local diamond. It's really pretty cool 'cause it's fully equipped with night lighting and bleacher seats, and a quasi-parking lot; graveled with an attendant on game nights.

At Rural Route J we turn left and off toward the field. Connor slows and turns down the narrow road. I feel his body stiffen as we near the night's game. He must be getting excited, perhaps mentally tuning up for the opposition. I hope so, I wouldn't want to be embarrassed for him or have to press a pep-talk into action afterwards. I hope to be celebrating a local victory, if you want to know the truth.

We cruise into the diamond area and skirt the edge of the playing field. Connor steers his vehicle behind the home team's bench and switches it off. I guess this means he's parking it here. I hop off and pry the buckle open, removing the headgear as fast as possible while Connor lifts the seat and removes his plastic baseball cap from the cubbyhole. He hands me his cycle helmet as he turns to the guys and the athletic activity already started on the field. It's apparent his mind is no longer on my presence but has swayed to the guys and the job at hand. I do feel a little dejected by the slight and head over to the home field bleachers. Geez, he didn't need to be that rude or self-centered, even if he does have to concentrate on the game. I turn back toward the field and holler out to his blank stare, "I hope you win. I'll talk to you later."

He grins back, apparently pleased at my support and responds with, "Okay, I'll see ya afterwards."

I look back up the steep grandstand, hoping the contrast between boards and space won't make me dizzy before I find a suitable space somewhere in the middle where I can see all plays and scrutinize the fans on either side. The stand is filling up fast with local supporters so I'm lose my lingering fear heading up the middle, row-by-row, until I am comfortably situated as close to center as pre-seated fans will allow. Unwrapping the sweater I have tied around my waist, I fold it into a square and gently placing it on the bleacher to cushion my ease. It'll cool down pretty quickly now as the sun drops below the tree line, and the night takes possession of the air.

I'm wearing blue jeans and a long sleeved blouse because the mosquitoes are vicious out here, especially around dusk as the moist, crisp air meets the dry heat of the earth—forcing its surface to cool down. I dowsed myself with repellent before I dressed because I've been stuck out here before, entirely unprotected. One time I came here with my family to watch Uncle Reese play. One season he pitched for *Dell's Dynamos* of *Dell's Quick Café*. That was a couple of years back when he was still married to Aunt Wanita, and he still had a life. I guess he doesn't feel there's anyone around to impress like that, so he quit just before she left. Anyway, I didn't listen to my father when he recommended I give myself a thorough wash of bug juice. He was right of course. I watched most of the game, that is, what I could see from the car after I smacked all those buzzers looming about the interior.

Mr. Perham has the field sprayed for mosquitoes on a regular schedule beginning immediately after the first thaw of winter snow. Apparently it's a waste of money and effort because they seem to have a massive grey cloud of mosquitoes constantly abuzz over the ball field. I would say the spray may be attracting the critters from all over the region, inviting them to settle in and multiply. Uncle Reese says that down on the field the batter is actually running hard to first base to escape the ruthless swarm that gathers while their waiting for their pitch at home plate.

Uncle Reese and Curlers haven't really got a problem with mosquitoes; neither one ever gets bitten. I attest this good fortune to their Native blood. I figure after generations of living side-by-side with the blood-sucking extortionists, a deal was struck between the god of the insect world and the Great Spirit. They came together in respect, negotiation and compromise, decreeing each family be allowed to tread unabated within their common space. Now, both Reesie and

Curlers continue to carry out the oath effortlessly, while everyone else must fight the war. Compromise must be the lesson to that story.

Hey, here comes Tammi! "Hey, Tammi," I shout out in the direction of the *Goods* bench where she's standing in front of Gary wearing some sarcastic grin. Okay, now she's looking up at the stands searching for a familiar face that would howl down for her. "Up here," I shout down. Waving my arms I stand up like a signalman directing the big engines around the yard.

She sees me, waves back and yells up, "Just a minute!"

Tammi must be doing her Marilyn Monroe impression tonight. She has on a V-neck sweater——kind of looks like her dad's, only the V expose her adolescent breasts, rather than the white T-shirt he'd be wearing beneath. She has on her favorite peach colored slacks, the ones without the pockets and zip up the back. They are close fitting and probably require some sucking-in on her part to maintain the svelte illusion. Oh well, she looks excited and natural in this flirtatious mode despite being thoroughly dowsed in bug spray too. I just hope the bug repellent isn't clashing heavily with her eau de cologne.

Watching Tammi as she promenades flirtatiously in front of Gary, overtly emphasizing her figure by running her hands up and down her hips as she talks demonstratively, probably about nothing, is just too funny. Gary seems equally enthralled with her presence, chatting and laughing boisterously all caught up with the company. Funny, but Gary doesn't appear nervous or nearly as concentrated as Connor. I'd think he ought to be out tossing the ball around with the rest of the guys.

The field lights flash on, blinding my view of Tammi and Gary for just an instant. As I focus in, the *Goods* coach is leaning over Gary and pointing to the field. Gary shrugs his shoulders and rises from the bench, apparently now ready to warm-up. Tammi blows him a kiss as he runs out to the field giving his face cause to redden. He glances around wondering I suppose, who may have seen the over endearing gesture.

From the corner of my eye I see Tammi leap over the player's bench, making me laugh at her sophisticated outfit contrasting crudely her bounding over an obstacle; the sophisticated demeanor forsaken in one momentary slip. Aah, too bad; she tries so hard!

She continues on, walking over to the side of the bleachers that ascend the grand stand by way of the stairs. She's back to grace and refinement, breezing over along the row I'm in and curtsying to a place next to me.

"Hi, Celia! Am I ever happy to see you! I thought I'd be out here all alone and smacking mosquitoes." She said sweetly.

"Speaking of mosquitoes," I say sarcastically, "I hope you've sprayed your cleavage with plenty of bug juice 'cause it could be very embarrassing if tomorrow you're seen wondering around scratching those little red splotches all over your BOOBS!"

"Don't worry, Honey," she leans over in disgust, "I know how to protect myself!"

"Geez," I continue on, "Gary doesn't seem nearly as enthusiastic about this game as Connor does. I mean, he seems playful and all, but not too concerned about concentrating or warming up."

"Well he's not very interested, ya know. His dad pressures him into playing because it's more or less the family team. His dad feels it's a good show to the community and the employees if Gary goes out for the team. Actually, Gary is a pretty good player, but I think he resents his father working out his life for him, even before he's gotten started on it himself."

"Tammi, I don't think it's all that bad, is it? I mean, Gary lives in the most spectacular house in Beaverton. He always has the nicest stuff. His family goes skiing out of state every year, and vacation in Europe or the Bahamas for a week in the summer. Geez, I have a hard time feeling sorry for him."

"Celia, it might look like a bed of roses from the outside, but how would you like to have your parents controlling everything you do, including your future? His dad even selects the clothes he wears because Gary has to look presentable or dressed in the finest from the *Dry Good Clothiers*."

"Okay, I probably wouldn't feel much like being pigeon-holed like that. I don't even know if I'd pay much attention to it after high school ended. But with all that luxury, I think I could muster playing some baseball to please them. I mean, you have to pay some dues somewhere along the way. And look at Gary, he's well dressed. It's not like they're picking out any bizarre duds for him!"

"Oh come on, Celia, it's a little more complicated than that! There's no freedom of choice here. It's probably why Gary and I get along so well, I understand how he's trapped. He's not allowed to assert his own identity or personal passion in anything. Everything he does, attempts to do, or even wears has to have the "Dry Goods" stamp on it. He's like their own walking advertisement!"

I can't believe she somehow feels her home life smacks in anyway like Gary's. Anyone with the semblance of a maladjusted home life she can identify with.

"Now wait a minute Tammi, you think your home life is anything like Gary's is a little far off base, if you ask me. What you relate to is their money and stature around here, and that Gary is paying you the time of day!" I blurt out. I suppose it's a bit harsh, but honest.

"Thanks, Celia, for showing me how shallow you really think I am!" She says in a prissy, dejected tone. "I certainly can understand how some people's identity can be lost to parents that believe they have to control everything in their grasp—or all is lost. Take a look at my old man. He identifies so heavily with being a farmer that even losing the farm and moving to town to work as a manager at the potato chip factory hasn't meant changing into a townie! No, instead he acts just like a farmer, only he's without a farm. And he's non-stop complaining about how life has screwed him over. He can't see buying me a new dress or skirt, but a set of overalls are practical in his book. Mother has to cook him three monster meals a day, including a well packed lunch, as if he's still doing heavy physical labor! We've all adjusted to town life, except for him. And until he accepts the change and he sees that our lives are forever in limbo—or until I blow this pop stand, our identities are put on hold or at least controlled by his bitterness. So for now, my identity is totally squelched in a household sitting on the edge of its seat waiting for that one person to feel comfortable in his own identity, and nobody can have their own until he does. I suspect it will never happen, which leaves three lonely people hanging on his every word.

I, on the other hand, having never identified with farming in the first place, need not hang around for such acceptance. I have my own goals and aspirations, and will be long gone before he gives the okay.

So you see, I do understand Gary's resentment. His folks are more than happy to send Gary to the best business college in the nation, just as long as it benefits the family business. Never mind he might have plans of his own, or an urge to see some of the rest of the world. The *Dry Goods* is their world, and the only one worth seeing to them."

I want to interrupt, but Tammi goes on.

"Your family may seem somewhat unacceptable to you, what with some racial tension and Reese as a kind of loose sheriff...but really, you all live a kind of tame, *normal* life. I don't even think you know how difficult it is for Gary and me!"

All right, I'm over listening to her tirade. She's sounding more like a martyr than the abused adolescent of a tyrannical, self-absorbed father figure.

The crack of a baseball off the wood of a swinging bat startles the intensity I've acquired focusing on the question at hand. I suppose it is a good cue to move our attention before I bury myself in an argument that could go on for days. And maybe Tammi is right; I really don't know what I'm talking about. I just hate letting her have the upper hand.

Durham is up, batting first. Monty Carlson is pitching for the *Goods*. He drops back to muster enough momentum to release a bullet shot off the mound so fast that I have a hard time tracking the ball, until it reaches the snug glove of our catcher, Wally Biney. Both Monty and Wally are farmers and have been *Goods* players during high school and now as family men in their twenties. Monty, his wife and kid, live at home on the family farm. That is, they live in a trailer back behind the family's old farmhouse—it was time to go modern. The Carlsons have a long history of baseball prowess. At least one person in the family has played on a *Goods* team or in a local farmer play-off for generations. They're even interested in the big national league games broadcast over the radio practically every night during the summer. According to Uncle Reese, back in the '30's a scout for the Detroit Tigers was traveling from one country team to another looking for prospects. The scout saw young Carlson (now senior), pitch a shut-out against the Pitney family and offered him a decent contract to play in the big leagues. Of course that was during the Great Depression, so any offer was probably a good one. Carlson Sr. said no, but he was that good. Good enough to have made a big league deal if he had wanted to leave the farm. Watching Monty throw three straight opponents out tonight isn't entirely unexpected. Not to go overboard though, there are lots of good players throughout the counties.

I look over at Tammi, sensing her sudden reserve after the identity talk. She's without her usual vigor and enthusiasm when Monty makes quick work of our competitors. She's probably miffed at my lack of understanding.

Connor walks up to home plate. It's our team's first attempt at getting on the scoreboard, and he leads off. Connor looks tense but directed. His form-fitting uniform with vertical stripes makes him look leaner from here. I elbow Tammi hoping she'll get charged up and nervous for Connor. His hard, blue cap shades his eyes from view, but I can feel his intense vision is so concentrated, his eyes are like two laser beams directed at the little white ball tightly tucked in the mitt of the pitcher's glove.

The pitcher winds up and ships off a fastball, but not without Connor getting a piece of it. He sends it sailing out to left field. Connor charges for first, rounds the bag before the outfielder scoops it up and hurls the ball back toward first.

Beautiful! That's a beaut! I Leap up and cheer Connor on, bouncing up and down on the bleacher boards. I end up bouncing around and check out the upper stands, hoping to see Beaverton on its feet and cheering Connor, or see the enthusiasm throughout the crowd…when instantly, I spot him! Oh god, it's him! He's looking directly at me, as if I haven't made a move without his notice. I stop dead in my tracks and for a instant, stare back, trying to place the ramifications of his presence into an understandable format for being here, now… other than for me.

I turn slowly and slink back down in my seat. "Oh, Tammi!"

"What?" she asks, still obviously annoyed.

"It's him," I say slowly, hesitantly.

"It's who?"

"Behind us, up at the very top of the bleachers—he must uv climbed up the back or something because I never saw him walking up the front. He would've had to pass us. It's that motorcycle dude. The guy that keeps following me," I say distressfully.

Tammi turns quickly around, not trying to hide her leering, to get a good look.

"Ahh, geez Celia, it is him, that motorcycle hood. You know, he's beginning to scare me. Have you talked to Reese about him yet?"

"Well no, not exactly."

"I'm beginning to worry that one day he'll come after you and I'll be hurt in the line of fire! I think it's pretty obvious that he's going to dog you for as long and as hard as necessary. I think he's trying to remain as patient as possible, since he's a stranger and you're not the usual motorcycle chic he's used to. But mark my words, one day he's just going to grab you. After all, it's only a matter of time 'til he's out of here." Tammi says, starting to make sense.

"Tammi, I'm sure you're right, but trying to explain it to someone sounds so egotistical or scare-tie-cat-ish."

"Look, Celia, if something really bad happened to you as a result of his pestering you, or, you know, like rape, then you'll wonder why you ever gave him any shadow of a doubt."

"I don't know, Tammi. I don't think he'd go that far. I think he's interested because I'm not, and he wants to be the kind of guy I could like. Well it just could never be. He doesn't live in this town and never will. He'll be out of here as soon as I relent, and I've got a future—at least I feel like I do. I'd like to think that even if I stay here and maybe marry a farm boy, at least it's something to build on. Not like what he's got in store; more highway and more chicks, and more acting tough. It's got to get a little boring after awhile. And still, getting him in trouble with Reese…well… might be more of a problem then all this is worth—at least I hope."

"Keep hoping, Celia, but I'll tell you one last time, you're only fooling yourself. That guy is trouble. I can feel it."

Just as she finishes with her warning, *Trouble* sits himself down next to me. I try moving closer to Tammi but the space between the other spectators and me are already close, and he obviously is going to force a seat next to me in order to situate himself where he has.

He leans in close, breathing heavily in my ear, "You can't really be impressed with these guys, can you? They're a bunch of twerps trying their damnedest to look like cool cats. If you really need something to look at, I can show you the real night air. Why don't you get rid of that chatty little friend of yours there, and let's get out of here? She has her own ride anyway, and she'll lose you as soon as the games over. Or, if you like, I can give her the heave-ho and lose her for the rest of the night!"

"Hey look!" I turn, looking him directly in the eyes. He looks rough but undisputedly alive, and his eyes peer longingly into mine. He takes me aback almost as soon as I've resolved to toughen my demeanor. "I can't go anywhere with you," I say softly. "You and I have nothing in common."

"I don't want to marry you," he leans in again to respond, "I only want you to spend a little time with me so I can get to know you better."

"I can't do that," I say quickly.

"I'm not going to hurt you. I'm not like that. Just because I look different and ride a bike doesn't mean I don't have some feelings."

I wonder what Tammi is thinking. She's remarkably quiet when only moments ago she was strongly advising me to get Reese.

"Why does it matter to you whether you know me or not? You're not staying around, and I'm just some small town girl who looks good to you. It doesn't matter that I might let you know me and give myself up to you, then you disappear and I'm left hoping for more. I'm the one who gets hurt…"

"You're pretty smart aren't you," he replies.

"Well, I don't try to be stupid," I say smiling.

"Maybe the problem is you think too much. It may feel real good letting me show you a nice time. Maybe that's all I want. Maybe all I want is to do something nice for someone, someone I could make feel special. Maybe all I want is to touch somebody in a gentle manner for a change, and you seem like someone who could appreciate that, if you'd just get over yourself for a minute and try trusting. But, if you want to believe I'm just out to take something from you, then be prejudice, don't give me a chance. I won't bother you again; after all, you're too good for me, aren't you?"

He stares into my head stiffly, without retraction, as I gaze down at the ball field attempting to find the steely reserve I felt was appropriate for him throughout the previous days of his existence in Beaverton. It's true. Something in me wants to know more about him too, after all, I've never met anyone like him before. He's strong and rough, even coarse, but alive and challenging—challenging to everything in my life up until now. And worst of all, good looking. Deep down, I want a few moments with him too. I understood what he means by 'doing something nice for someone,' without expectations. He could never stay anyway and I could never settle on him. I turn and look at him staring boldly, and I return the stare.

"Maybe I am too good for you," I finally say, "but I could be wrong."

"Yeah, and then again you may never know. But I think you kind of want to find out, so you see, you've got to trust me. Why would I want to hurt you? You've never crossed me. Those are the only people I want to hurt …and sometimes, I let it go. I say they're too weak. I don't need to mess with them.

Look, let's just go down to my bike and talk a little. Just talk, nothing more. I can't believe this ballgame means that much to you. When it's over you'll still be here for that scrawny guy you think is your kind. He can still take you home."

"Don't insult him, I insist. If I go with you to your bike, and talk, it doesn't mean I don't care about him."

"Yeah, yeah, I know all about that," he says.

I don't know what to think. I sort of believe he's being truthful. He merely wants someone outside his social group to talk to. He seems to know as well as I do that they live outside the world of acceptability. Maybe through me he can get a taste of what it's like to be a normal person in society. I wonder if Tammi will be totally disgusted if I leave her to go talk with this guy? On the other hand, she seems to be wallowing in resentment over my observations of her home life. In the end, we will probably wind up sitting here in silence for the rest of the game, with me trying to cheer her up and get her enthused. Now does that sound like fun?

Of course, I don't want to be heading off to this guy's bike and mayhem, but I don't believe that's what's happening.

"Come on Celia," he pleads, deep into my ear, "I just want some time to talk. Take a chance on me. You won't regret it."

I look at him again and see his calm and pleading eyes. "Okay look, I'll go and talk to you, but I'm not leaving the ballpark grounds, and I am leaving with Connor." I state emphatically so there could be no doubt about my intentions.

I lean over to Tammi who seems to have perked up, probably due to Mr. Cycle's appearance on the scene and our quiet, yet intense, conversation. "Tammi, don't go and get all excited. I'm going to go and talk to this guy for a while. I'll be back shortly. Don't let on to Connor. I'll be back before then anyway. Don't worry about me, he actually seems pretty tame," I whisper.

She begins to respond, as I knew she would. "Geez, Celia, I don't know..."

But I ignore her and turn to him saying, "Alright, you lead the way."

He gets up and jockeys down the crowded isle of fans, hands in his pockets, to the steps descending the bleachers. I'm following close behind hoping no one I know will realize I'm with this guy, or that Connor will look up and see our departure together. I hide myself behind his large frame in attempts to obscure our togetherness from everyone except Tammi, who I hope I can trust with this secret.

He continues on towards his bike without turning around, even to see if I'm still following. I stay a few steps behind, trying to appear distanced from his intent, although I am certain that I am fooling no one. We walk on beyond the parking lot gravel, worrying me a little as to where I've agreed to talk. As I survey the grounds beyond the lot, I see a shimmering metal gleam of light reflecting the baseball diamonds light, and know it is his bike. He's parked in a ravine shortly beyond the grounds, and just before the ballpark turns to woods. I feel somewhat relieved that we will be visible to the parking lot if need be, and slightly obscured from the bright lights and idlers not really paying attention to the two of us.

We jog down the short hill, him first, ahead of me, and I trailing in his broad strides. I have to admit my heart beats harder at the prospect and rebelliousness of the situation I have consented to. Certainly Pops and Curlers would see me sent to reform school before they'd have me spend two minutes with the likes of this guy. Right now I don't know why I agreed to come here, but I like the feel of his powerful presence.

"Come over here," he commands, "let's sit on the other side of my bike. Ahh, that is if you don't mind?"

"No, I don't mind. I guess I'd rather sit down." I say this thinking we'd be less visible to the people at the game.

He pulls out a pack of cigarettes and offers me one.

"No thanks, I don't smoke."

"Nah, of course you don't," he says as he lowers himself next to me. We are facing the woods and everything black. All I can see of him are highlights of an outlined form created from the ballpark lights. I can no longer be enticed by his exaggerated bad-boy appearance because all I have to go by is his deep throaty voice, softened now by a quiet and calm as I sit down by his bike; as if my capitulation snuffed out the fire.

"What is your real name anyway," I ask. "I call you the *Motorcyle Dude*, or *Maniac* which doesn't seem too nice."

"God, you want to know my name. Damn, do we have to bother with that stuff?"

"Yeah, I think so. You've asked a lot of me you know. Besides that, you know my name. You made a point of finding out what I'm called, now I think I should have the same opportunity. And, at least I'm asking the horse's mouth, not running around in some subversive manner," I say laughing.

"Well, you got me there. I guess I did snoop around for your name."

"I guess you did."

"You like to act tough don't you? It's okay with me, 'cause I like it. But don't fool yourself too much, because you don't really know the meaning of the word."

"Hey look, I'm not trying to fool anyone, it's just the way I am. No, I'm not really all that tough at all. I'm blunt or honest, and forthright I guess you could say."

"Well, I like that in a chick, especially a chick who looks like you!"

"So Motorcycle Dude, you're trying to change the subject on me, what's your real name?" I say in a determined tone.

He turns and looks at me a second then turns my face away to whisper in my ear, "It's Robert, okay? And that's our secret, understand?"

"Sure, I don't really intend to do a lot of talking about you around town or to your friends. You can count on that."

"I suppose you won't, will you," he says sighing. "I don't suppose I'm the sort of person a girl like you brags about all over town. I'd probably embarrass the shit out of you if your high school buddies were to catch wind of this, isn't that right?"

"Don't get sore. I came out here to get to know you a little better, and I do already have a boyfriend. So how did we get to bragging about you around town? It was hard enough to get you to tell me your name."

"You're right. I'm getting ahead of myself. It's just that you look so perfect, the way I always dreamed I wanted a woman to look. Not like movie star good looks, but the way you act and walk and leer at me 'cause you think I'm no good. The long black hair and eyes, I'd do almost anything to have you."

"What is that suppose to mean?" I ask irritated. "You don't even know me. You don't know if I'm a complete nerd, or if there is anything here that would be at all compatible with anything about you. You're going only on looks, and with me, I think they could be completely deceiving."

"There you go, just like a woman, trying to put a fence around the whole thing; narrow it down and put a price tag on it. All I mean is there's something about you that looks right, and I've never said this to anyone before. It kind of scares me."

"Scares you!" I say in disbelief. "If either of us is going to scare somebody, you're going to scare me. You're the tough guy!"

"Yeah, but that's kind of a simple look at things, now isn't it? You're kind of like royalty, and you know it. You carry yourself around like everyone is watching—and I like that. You're made for only the best dudes in town, and that's what you want, no questions asked. Anything else is an annoyance—like me. That's all there really is to it for someone like me. I'll never get a chance at the best girl in town because of who I am. It's scary to see that's how far down I am, and every time I look at you, it reminds that I don't have a chance."

"God, I don't know. I don't look at life that way. Everybody has a crack at a real life. You're right though, I could never really settle on a guy like you…but you could change. You could settle in and get a real job, and do a lot of stuff that would make a girl like me proud to have you as her guy."

"That's my point, Babe, this is who I am and it's too late for me. I'm not going to settle in, and that's why I know you'll never be mine. So sitting here, kinda hidden away is got to be good enough, 'cause probably it's all I'm going to get."

We sit quietly looking out into the darkness of the forest. I know he's right so putting up a protest would only mean false flattery, and he would know it. He seems comfortable and safe for me right now, and maybe kinda childlike. He looks up straight overhead, and I know he sees the multitude of flickering stars he has often seen through many nights of similar anxieties tucked deep in his heart, which he has only shared with me tonight.

I turn and ask him how he got started riding with this gang of motorcycle dudes and he replies, "Ahh it's a long story. Not very pretty either. They weren't the first set of monkeys I've traveled with, and probably not the last. We understand each other though. It ain't all that cool. Not like it looks."

"To tell you the truth, Robert, it doesn't look all that cool. It looks like trouble."

"It's funny; no one's called me Robert in a long time. I kind of like the way you say it. Yeah, well it is trouble to most people, but to us its life. We got to have some of our own laws to live by to survive, and pretty much it's all I know. Let's get off me anyway, I want to hear you talk, not me."

"Okay, what do you want to know? My life will seem like a bore compared to the stuff you're use to."

"How come you think you're such a princess?"

"I really don't think of myself as a princess, or arrogant, if that's what you mean. I have a feeling you think that's a compliment. But haughtiness, or putting myself above it all, really is not the way I want to hear myself described. I only want to be myself and find out what I can do. I guess I'm really not sure of what all that is yet, but I like the idea of exploring the possibilities. I like my friends, and the guys in town, and I guess I'll go to college, but I don't know what for, yet. If that makes me a princess, I don't know why. I do have opinions about things, and I'm not afraid to give them, if that's what you mean." I try to reason.

"Forget it," he says, "I know what it is, and I like it."

"Robert?"

"Yeah?"

"I think I should get back to the game now," I say as I hear cheers from the crowd. "My friends will be wondering where I am, and if it's nearly over, at least I should know a little bit about how the game went."

"Oh come on, Babe, I was just getting started," he says, his hot breath searing my cool summer night cheek. His face is so close to mine, I don't dare turn by head for fear of meeting his lips. Sure enough, despite my fear of such an intimacy, he places his calloused hand on my diverted cheek and strokes it gently, tenderly, then asks, "Can't I kiss you just once before you go?"

I sit there still and quiet, not knowing what to say. How can I say yes, and somewhere inside of me, I don't want to say no. I sit thinking of a million reasons why not, my heart pounding, excited by the newness, the strangeness, and how little control I actually have in his presence. But somehow I know it's not right.

He turns my face towards his as I rally for direction of my feelings. He presses his lips to mine and I find them warm, and soft, and inviting. I am lost in his overwhelming touch, kissing him back and hoping it will last forever. He removes his hand from my cheek and encompasses my whole being with his strong taut arms. I am lost as he leans over me, pressing my body to the ground. I embrace him too, never ever have I felt this kind of intensity before. We are so close, so tightly locked to each other that his massive, dense bulk on top of me is so tight I begin to fear I will not be able to breathe. As he begins to moan, I realize this has gone too far. I can't breathe and he's scaring me with his grip and kisses now pouring out and down my neck. I've got to get away!

I quickly shove his shoulders away with as much force as anything that has happened so far. I jump to my feet and give an indignant, "So long." You violated my trust, I think to myself.

I run up the ditch as if that's it, but stop and turn around when I hear no response. He's below, on his feet watching my departure quietly and says, "Don't put on airs, I know you liked it too."

I turn and run, heading for the bleachers, not looking back, and stop abruptly to walk, knowing he won't follow. I still feel odd. He's right, I did like it. It was like nothing I'd ever experienced before. Maybe because he's older, more experienced than the other guys I've necked with. Or maybe it was more exciting because he's forbidden territory in my own mind, as well as in the minds of all my authority figures, and it can never be. And then, maybe it's magic. I don't really know, but my heart is still pounding, my knees shaking and I'm burning up, no longer cooled by the summer night air.

I run my fingers through my hair to put in order the strands that may have gotten away during those few moments on the ground. The game and the spectators seem to be taking place in a world far outside my own, but as I climb the steps to the row I re-establish myself in, I awake to the explanation Tammi will surely be looking for, and Connor now playing in the outfield. As I zig and zag past feet and limbs less concerned with being stepped on or kicked than having a clear view of the playing field, I sense Tammi's glimpse of my reappearance, and her making way for my needed seat. I get there and she's ready.

"Well, where the hell did you two go? I can't believe you really spent any time with him. What's wrong with you? And you were only moments before giving me grief about my life!"

Tammi, there really isn't much to say. He's not the madman we first thought he was. He's okay. It's not like I'm going to marry him or anything. I just went to talk with him a while, nothing more, and nothing less. I can only hope you will keep this to yourself though. Like Connor, he wouldn't be the person I'd announce this to. My parents wouldn't be a good choice either, okay?"

"Okay," she says slowly, a bit mystified in tone." So, now really, what did you two talk about?"

"The usual stuff," I replied, trying to sound evasive. I asked him how he got in with this gang, and he asked me why I'm so arrogant. That's about it. There's not much else to tell."

"Ah, come on," Tammi says trying to get all the details. "You been gone for practically the entire game and that's all that happened? I saw you trying to fix your hair on your way up here, so don't try and convince me a little rolling around wasn't involved. As your best friend, I would think you would want me to know."

"Alright, I'll go through the whole thing tomorrow. I don't want to go into it right now, and I got to get a handle on how this game is going, besides."

"Well, if you want to sound at all convincing with Connor afterwards, like you may have seen the game, you're right, you better."

"So who's ahead?" I ask trying to bone up.

"We are, five to three. Connor got two hits, which by the way, he looked up in this direction after both times. I say that only to let you know he really cares about you. Anyway, Gary got a couple of hits too. It was really exciting. But anyway, this is the top of the eighth inning, thank god. It's now getting to the bored silly stage, and I make no apologies."

She's right. I'm too preoccupied with the kiss to be nearly interested in the game anymore. I hear cracks off the bat and know players are running to first base, but I don't even try to follow along. I wonder instead where he is and what he's doing. I try to listen for his bike revving up, but can't really tune out the noise from the crowd and the game. I play over and over the kiss, trying to make it feel less intense or profound. It makes me tingle all over, until I get to the part where I can't breathe.

Somewhere in my delirium I spot Connor fielding a ball. He looks sweet, and kind, and naive. And, I feel like I've outgrown him in a matter of hours. I don't want anything to have changed, and yet, it has.

Suddenly the game's over and the crowd is on its feet. Tammi is stretching her arms and paints a big wide grin across her face. Apparently she has refocused her attentions to Gary and the prospects of a little sympathetic, individual attention. That is relieving, if you ask me. I've hardly had time to process what has just happened to me, and I'm not ready to hear Tammi's version and the potential hazard I could be creating for myself.

"I'm going to head down and congratulate Gary on this victory, are you going to come to?" Tammi asks.

"Yes, but Tammi, please, don't let on to anyone about this, okay?"

"Okay, Celia, I'm not going to tell a sole, but I think you're making a big mistake. I can't believe you of all people, would be interested in a guy like that."

"Come on Tammi, don't over exaggerate this thing, okay? I only talked with him. That's all it is. Let's go see how the guys are doing," I press.

We run down the boards to the bottom rung and walk across the field to where the *Dry Goods* are gathered chatting up their victory. Connor and Gary are laughing and joking, retelling the highpoints of the game and their own version of each event. I understand the camaraderie since I run track, but the events of the night leave me distant from the celebrating. I turn my head, compelled to see whether he's gone or still watching from his dark retreat just this side of the woods. From out here in the center of the baseball diamond, all is black beyond the lights of the field. I feel his intensity still out there, watching every move and wondering what to do. I turn back to the revelers, hoping they'll be ready to take off soon and distance me from the penetrating stare of—Robert.

Connor seems to sense my edginess and comes over, puts his arm around my shoulder, "I bet you're getting bored of all this stuff, aren't you?"

"Don't get me wrong," I look up at his jubilant face and lie, "I really enjoyed watching the game, but it is getting a little old. I mean, you were really great, but it seems late, or like I've been watching for hours. I guess I am pretty close to ready to go."

I move quickly over to Tammi in order to remove Connor's arm from my shoulder, in case he's still watching from the lighted field. I don't know why, but the thought of him viewing the slight intimacy between Connor and me, is disturbing. Instead I ask Tammi, "We've had enough of this jock stuff for one night, haven't we Tammi?"

She looks at me, her eyes revealing her conspiratorial knowledge for my interest in leaving. "Yep, I think we ought to go hang out somewhere else a little less bright," she broadcasts loud enough for the giddy teammates to all hear. "You guys played great, but it wasn't like the sea parted or anything. Let's go have some real fun!"

The guys all laugh and Gary throws his mitt at her, all in fun. But it worked 'cause everyone turns and starts heading off toward their cars. Connor moves off to his bike and I follow quickly behind. I can tell he's wondering about my gesture of jostling his arm from my shoulder and whether it was intentional, or really just trying to get on our way. "Are you okay?" he stops to ask.

"Yeah, sure, I'm great," I tell him. "What makes you ask?"

"Oh, nothing. Did you really enjoy the game, or were you just being polite?" he says producing a big grin.

"No, I really enjoyed it, and you were good. I don't mean to be antsy. I've had a long day and I think it's all catching up to me. I probably could use a good night's sleep, although I don't want to rush you," I say, hoping to rush him.

I grab for my helmet that is strapped on to the backseat bars. I unbuckle it and quickly adjust it to my head to avoid further possible discussions. Connor seems to get the idea, fastens his helmet and kicks on the cycle, both at the same time. He signals for me to wait to get on 'til after he has turned the bike in the direction of the gravel parking lot, then he moves slowly and carefully over the ball field trying to protect it from tire divots and mangled grass. He's so sweetly conscientious. I follow along till we are at the edge of the ball field, then hop on behind, place my hands on his waist for balance and look beyond to the ditch in search of the other biker.

He's still there. I see him as we speed past, reconfirming my intuitive feelings of his presence. I stare into his existence and fight back a longing to be with him. Connor doesn't look over to the ditch, but instead yells out, "Wrap your arms around my waist, you're not holding on tight enough."

I do as he asks, squeezing tight and following the vision of Robert in the ravine until we are too far off to see the flicker of ballpark lights reflecting from the shiny chrome.

CHAPTER FOURTEEN

Is It Love?

Walking up the front sidewalk, I see the living room lights on and Keith's head just above the window, obviously watching T.V. He doesn't stir even if he has heard Connor's bike above the noise of the set. I don't suppose he even cares. He's probably been instructed to wait up for my return so Curlers and Pops could hit the sack early.

As I approach the steps to the screen porch, I hear someone or something go "Pssst." The sound came from the left side of the house. Then again it comes, "Pssst," as the bushes that hedge that side of the house rustle.

"Pssst, its Robert!"

Good grief, how did he make it here before Connor and me? Connor is still sitting at the front curb on his bike waiting for me to get safely into the house— before the boogeyman gets me. I turn and wave him on so he won't see me walk over to the bushes and Robert. There is no hesitation for me now; I want to see Robert again. I move up the steps waving good-bye to Connor and stop at the top until I'm sure he will leave without seeing me through to the door. He moves off slowly, not looking back, obviously buying the program. I run back down the steps and around to the side of the house. There he stands, deep into the dark shadows cast from the house and shaped by the light of the moon. Is it this night that caste's a spell so powerful my desire for his presence intoxicates my usual sensibility? Is this truly love, or am I caught up in the warmth of this summer night; the smells of the prairie thistle, the fluttering of night birds, and the angle of the moon? I know this is a daring moment—since Curlers and Pops will never see Robert as anyone but a loser. This may be too bold, but I want to see him and feel his powerful grip on me one more time. I think I have the ability to control this man in ways I'm not quite sure of, but I can feel the grip. Slinking down the steps and toward the brush, he reaches out and grabs me by my arm and pulls meet deeper into the dark. For a moment I feel as if he's going to force his will on me, but instead he draws in a deep breath and explains: "I had to see you once again. I wanted to apologize for tonight. I really did just want to talk. I know you're the kind of girl who needs to take it slow, but I can't get you off of my mind. "

"Please Robert, don't talk so loud. I think my parents are asleep, but my brother is up watching television, and if anyone hears us it'll only be trouble for me."

"I just wanted to hold you once again and I guess I wanted to see what was up with you and that guy. Can you blame me?"

"I don't know," I whisper, confused by the question but enchanted by the moment, here and now.

"Can I give you a kiss good night," he asks? "It'll be alright. It'll be the kiss that guy, what's his name on the bike, forgot to give."

"Okay, I guess that'll be alright."

"Hey, if it's not going to work out for you, it's okay," he says stepping back.

I giggle because I know he's just teasing and trying to make me show how much I want to kiss him back. "Well, I guess it couldn't hurt, can it?" I say.

He moves to me, softly and carefully puts his arms around my smaller, weaker body and bends to meet my lips as I reach up to meet his kiss. He's warm and tender and I don't ever want it to stop.

But he moves back away before I'm ready, this time. I'm disappointed, but know it really is time to go in before I'm caught out here and embarrassed. "I better go in now. Take care of yourself and I want you to know, I did like talking to you tonight when we *talked* at the ballpark."

"Sure, honey," he says walking off in the direction of the back yard. "Now, don't you go and forget me, yeah hear?"

"We'll see," I say, then stand and listen as he cuts through back bushes and into the alley. A few moments later I hear the engine from his cycle rev and know he must have parked at the end and probably in the dark away from anything that would have attracted attention to it. I turn and skip around to the front and on up the steps and through the screen door. I stop, shutting the door carefully, making certain it doesn't slap against its support and swing back into the entry-way hitting the big wooden door. Keith is still in the living room, awake and transfixed by whatever is on T.V.

I slip into the room and plop down on the couch beside him. It is almost like he's unaware of my presence. He hasn't made any kind of indication that he's even aware of my entry into the room. He looks straight ahead, silent and motionless. To see if he's actually alive, I turn and speak directly to his ear and say, "You missed a very good game tonight. The *Dry Goods* beat the pants off of Durham tonight. It was really exciting!"

"Great," he replied without enthusiasm. "I'm not very excited about base-ball, as I believe you know. What is it you want, by the way? This is a good movie, practically no women involved."

"So, it's a war movie, huh?"

"Yep."

I'm still a little too antsy from the excitement of the evening to head upstairs to bed. Keith is certainly dull as dirt at the moment; at least he's not at all interest in what I'm doing. He can't really be interested in this bad war movie, can he? He's so quiet and off to himself anymore, not like when we were little kids and played together all the time. Now Keith has little to do with Parrot or me. I guess I kind of miss him, but only when I think about it. Usually I'm occupied enough with the stuff in my life to wonder about Keith's whereabouts or his apparent lack of inter-est in my life. This gets me to thinking about what he'll be doing this year after he leaves home. Keith is moving into Minneapolis to go to school. I haven't really paid much attention to his leaving, until this moment, and now I wonder if he's worried.

"Keith, are you getting excited about leaving Beaverton for school?" I ask.

"I guess. Wouldn't you be?"

I don't know, it's still a whole year away yet so I can't really get a feel for it. In truth, I haven't started to really put together what I want to do yet. I mean, I don't suppose I even have to go to college right off the bat, do I?"

"I don't know. I wouldn't think Curlers or Pops would be too pleased if you were going to slouch around here for a year or two after graduation. I would think you could get a job up at the truck stop. Maybe replace Aunt Wanita in a waitress uniform."

"That is a possibility you know. I hope you weren't trying to be funny because there's nothing wrong with that. I could put a little money away while

I'm deciding at which angle I want to see my future. I know I'll eventually leave Beaverton, but I don't want to hit the big city just so I can leave here. I kind of feel like I'm just growing into the place, and it's mine. I know Curlers and Pops will be disappointed if I don't find something bigger for myself than a nice settled life, marrying some local boy and having a few kids right here in town. And I guess, I don't really see that for myself either, not for 10 or 15 years anyway. What do you think you'll end up doing Keith?"

"It's not so much that I want to get out of Beaverton, but I think I'd make a pretty good writer, or even a reporter, and I need a broader education for that, don't I? So I'm going to go someplace I can learn more about it, and I'm really looking forward to that. I guess I'm looking forward to getting on with it. I feel I've hung out a year waiting to get going. Really, it isn't that I don't appreciate it here, because Beaverton is just fine, only, I guess it just stopped offering me much and I knew I had to go other places to find something bigger. You know, I'll miss the family and all but I'm getting older. I'm getting antsy to start my career."

"Geez, Keith," I say, "you sound so sure of what you want. I envy you. I wish I was so clear and sure. I guess I have a lot of interests I'd like to explore and I don't really have those same urges to get my career off and going. I kind of feel like I've got a lot of time to explore the possibilities first".

"Well that's you, but I feel like I've got to get moving. I'm ready." he says. "Oh, by the way, was that you out there jabbering by the side of the house?"

"You could hear that, huh?"

"It sounded like mumbling... your mumbling. And the other voice sounded like some guy I didn't recognize. Who is he?"

"None of your business. Nothing to be concerned with anyway. He's just an admirer," I say defensively.

"You weren't doing anything strange, were you?"

"Well now, what do you mean by *strange*?"

"You know what I mean...and it didn't sound like Conner. Actually, I thought I heard Conner's motorcycle drive off before I heard the other stuff." he says, prying.

"Like I said, he's just an admirer, and he doesn't mean anything *strange* about it.

It's time to go to bed," I say, jumping up, ready to flee Keith's new found interest in my midnight rendezvous with Robert.

As I head off past the T.V. and toward the staircase, Keith can't help but add one last personal comment. "I hope you're not entering some weird rebellion age or nothing. Mom and Dad have done their best by us and they don't need any strange shenanigans."

I'm not even going to bother to respond to that comment. Who the hell does he think he's talking to. As if the only real thing I'm thinking about in this thing with Robert is how Curlers and Pops will react. If it weren't for that pressure, who knows, I might be hanging with him right now. Geez, does Keith think I'm that close to falling out of place. He must think I'm a complete idiot. Well, I don't care, it's not like I see him around any serious female situations. I don't believe he's had more than one or two dates his whole high school career. I know he harbors an extensive collection of Playboy mags in his room so I assume he likes the girls, but out of that Walter Mitty dream, he's not jumping in with both feet.

It's two days now since I saw Robert. I am going crazy thinking about him, but I know I can only see him on the sly. No one would approve, except maybe Parrot, and she's in deep with the romance novel fantasy. I don't want to talk to Connor either. He's sweet and kind and will be terribly hurt if I do him any harm. I'm trying hard to blend into the home front and not appear caste astray in a sea of confused love. I don't think anyone will appreciate what I'm going through. They'll all come up with the voice of reason and tell me no way, this ain't going to happen. And, I know they're right, but I've got to begin somewhere. I've mostly been hanging out in my room. I don't want to run into Robert and have him pressure me just yet—not until I'm sure. I'm reluctant to go out into the yard even. I don't want him to come after me here. I want to be able to figure out what I'm going to do first.

Parrot has been a good friend these last two days. She's interrupted some of her reading to hang around, play cards and listen to my problem. Somehow, I think this whole thing is kind of a cheap thrill for her. She's cruised Main Street to see where Robert is hanging, has fielded Connor's calls to keep him at bay, and we've played cards and lay out on the roof to get a tan. Tammi has been over once, but she's totally pre-occupied with Gary and really hasn't forgiven me for our family discussion the other night at the ball park.

It must be ten o'clock high and I haven't gotten up yet. I'm so far off my schedule, the whole town may be wondering where I am. It's kind of hard to believe Robert could be so crazy about me. He must be lonely, or those fast girls he has regularly on his arm are no longer interesting. I suppose he might like the challenge of someone like me…

"Say, are you going to get out of bed soon?"

It's Curlers storming into my room, not even knocking first. "I don't suppose there is anything you'd like to talk with me about. I've noticed you're loafing around the house the last couple of days which seems definitely out of character for you Celia!"

She sits down on the bed and begins to stroke my head. I run the whole situation through and take a good guess at what her reaction will be. Quickly I decide I prefer to deal with the affair my way, avoiding any unwanted freak outs.

"Nah, there's nothing particular going on. I'm just taking time out to think about my future after high school." I figure this is a good time to lay it on her since it gives her something to concentrate on other than the real problem at hand. Can she deal with child number two leaving home, likely before she's ready? Maybe a year from now she'll have it worked out, emotionally.

"Well you're right Celia, it's getting to be time you really decide what you want to do with your future. If there's anything your father and I can do to assist you in the decisions you have to make, please speak up."

"You don't have to worry, I'm sure there will be a lot to settle. I'm not even sure I'll want to go off to school right after I graduate. Maybe I should get a job around here for a year, while I make sure."

"I think your father will be highly disappointed if you remain in Beaverton. We've long hoped you'd want to see a lot more of the world than this."

My father will be very disappointed? I think to myself. Geez, I wish she'd speak for herself. What does she want from me? Never mind, maybe I don't really want to know.

"In the meantime, Celia, it's time to get up. I want your help with the dirty laundry this morning. You can think about your future plans while you're folding the clothes.

Ugh, this hanging about may have been all wrong. Maybe I should have hung out somewhere else. Nay, she would have nailed me, one way or the other.

I make creases with my finger along the cotton shirt creating a diagram that shows me where I will make my folds, then toss the finished product into a basket sitting next to me in the basement by the dryer. I am bored, but without a place to go and not wanting to be seen, I'm willing to fulfill my obligations.

Parrot is sitting in a corner by a giant spider web taking one of a number of breaks from our duties. I don't care, I 'm enjoying the crease process. She's whining about something obscure and I've decided to ignore it. I've tuned her out as I exact my folds and achieving complete glory in laundry room procedure. Of course, there is the highly conceivable possibility that I will be engaged for the same duty next time as a result of my current outstanding work. I won't worry too much about that now however, I can always go back to my old methods.

"Are you about through there, Sis?" says Parrot.

"Oh, I've got five or six more of Pop's shirts and then you can do some."

"Come on Celia, I'm getting so bored! Let's do something else for awhile."

"Geez Parrot, I'm in no rush and it isn't like you've pitched in to make it go faster. Besides, what have you got in mind?"

Let's make up a picnic and take it out back. You know, over by the rhubarb patch, kinda like behind the garage where we can't be easily spotted. We can put on our swimsuits and sunbathe, read some magazines and just luxuriate."

"Okay, sounds like about all I'm good for anyway. I wonder what we've got in the refrigerator that's good, and the boys have tossed aside for the rest of the pack?" I ponder.

"I know there are still potato chips and grapes, and maybe some egg salad left-over from yesterday. We've got lemonade or orange juice, so it's not all that bad. Thank god Curlers likes her lemonade and egg salad or we could've ended up with PB&Js with water."

I quit the crease process and finish out the chore with the usual quick 1-2-3 fold and drop that last one in the basket. I ask Parrot to grab one end and we head up together, ready to disappear into the reverie of food, the warm sun, and a pile of fresh teen mags Parrot subscribes to. We drop the basket down by Curler's bedroom door and head further up the hall to our rooms to change. I yell back from my door, "I'll grab the quilt from the linen closet and meet you down in the kitchen. Don't forget the mags."

"No way, they're the most important part. There is a really cool article in one on how to put on perfect toe nail polish in three easy steps. You'll love it."

Curlers is in Durham grocery shopping. It's quiet in the house for a lunch hour. Keith is somewhere. He could be in his room. He's quiet anyway, making it hard to tell if he's around. Peanut is with Curlers, probably putting his two cents in on each of her selections and is taking over around about the cereal section. We'll be basking on the large star quilt long before they get home.

It's calm and quiet out here. I know even Parrot is appreciating the serene, restive quality out in the summer air without anyone conscious of our whereabouts. Sure we've got an army of ants, a few annoying flies, but I feel as if I'm the odd one, temporarily basking in their world of flitting and feeding. They land on the bright white magazine pages to explore. Do the pages have pollen? Can I eat it?' Okay, the mosquitoes can be hell, but mid-afternoon they're asleep in their bogs and don't come out for blood until dusk.

"Hey Celia," Parrot says in between bites of sandwich, "how about tomorrow we head out to the Old Mill and do some swimming? Maybe we can get the car if we ask early enough."

"Sounds like fun to me," I say as I watch a big black ant crawl across Parrot's belly without much response.

Parrot has on her pink bikini and a pair of cat-eyed sunglasses. Trés glamorous. She's looking ten years older, and by her aloof demeanor, I know she's enjoying the fantasy. Parrot looks good in a bikini, whereas, my torso is short and my legs long so that a full suit breaks up the look better. I'm a bit envious because everyone thinks bikinis are much more alluring.

I flip through the latest installment of teen hunks looking for someone handsome yet brainy, dressed like a regular guy and without attachments to some movie star girl.

"You know that guy from "*Medical Doctors in Action*"?" asks Parrot. "Man, I think he's so cute. It says here, he sees Melissa Shue of "*Sands of the Mandela*." Can you believe that? I mean she's so doggy compared to him. I would love just 5 minutes in a room with him!"

"Oh yeah? What would you do with five minutes? Give him a hickey?" I ask.

"Maybe, that could be a possibility if he's up for it and found me attractive."

"Okay," I respond, "it's not like we're talking about reality here. I'll take ten minutes holding hands with George Thompson of "*Bill Finley Lives Forever*." I can just imagine us walking slowly through a tall pine forest looking deep into each other's eyes. I wouldn't even have to talk or try to be charming. We would just know we were right together." I say, picturing that guy as Robert and wondering idyllically through a cool path under huge pines with aromatic needles below my feet. I can't seem to shake his image from my mind. I don't know why, but I have a feeling it won't be long before he actually comes to the door looking for me. Hopefully it won't be today.

I flip quickly through the remaining pages of the mag and flip over to roast a little on my back. I pick up another mag and try to keep my mind on the subject at hand. Connor has called once this morning already, and I'd like to ask him to back off for a couple of days until I sort this thing out, but I'm sure he'd just opt for going his own way. I guess I can understand that. He'll see Robert as something really bogus, and if I could entertain the idea of having relations with him, well, I am probably not right in the head. And, maybe I'm not. But who can rationalize this stuff. One day you're walking down the street just taking in the sights, and the next, the strangest kind of stuff happens; you're in love with what some may call a total looser. The thing is, I know Robert isn't a total looser. I can see he has more to him; a tender remorseful side that makes me feel like he needs someone like me. He genuinely is living by his feelings and his wits. It seems not too many people understand that. It seems maybe more people should live that way, instead of like cookie cutters; already molded and shaped by an imaginary wall that comes down around them.

"You know," interrupts Parrot, "maybe I'll spend a day with Uncle Reese in the squad car. I'll bet he gets mighty bored by himself, almost as bored as I am around here this summer. Next year I'm going to apply to some kind of summer camp program. Maybe I'll find something intellectually stimulating like, *The Great Heroines of Romance Novels—A Four Week Intensive Study*. I could start hounding Pops right now about it so that next year, when it comes time to pay for it, he will be emotionally ready."

"Personally, I can find enough around here to keep myself occupied, but I can see you need some outside stimulus. I do think it's a good idea to get a jump on Pops to cover next year's costs. It'll take that long to get a grip and actually fork over the dough, but you could make it happen."

We fall silent and I begin to examine the idea of going to the Old Mill for swimming tomorrow. With one car in the family I must plan ahead for an afternoon's use. I'll call up Tammi tonight to see if she wants in and descend on Pops just as he's feeling relaxed and ready to kick his shoes off after dinner. It may not be as bad as all that. Sometimes he's perfectly congenial about letting loose with the keys. It's got to be better than driving us around and chaperoning on a regular basis. I think one more day of laying low to figure out this romance stuff should be enough, then I've got to get back out into the world. After all, there are only two more months of summer, and it seems only one summer and two more months of real life before I totally own up to responsibility. I can't kick around the house in a fog of confusion much longer. I'll have to make a firm stand one way or the other. I guess I pretty much already know what that is, but...

We got the car without too much fussing or cajoling, 'cause Pops is within easy walking distance from his job and didn't need to go anywhere on business. Parrot is cruising the vicinity with Uncle Reese, but she should be back before too long. Tammi is in and has decided she can tear herself loose from Gary for a cool afternoon swim. We were nearly sequestered with Peanut, until he thankfully put up a fight to stay home and manage his night crawler business. Hanging out waiting for buyers is the ultimate boredom, and granted, he will have some business, but it couldn't be nearly as bad, he thinks, as listening to the monotonous girlie gab of his sisters and their friend. Not to worry, the feeling is mutual; we don't want to listen to the torturous whines of an eight year old not getting his way, nor worry about drowning potential since his swimming skills are so far just fair. Curlers is probably hoping for some time to herself for a few hours without the demands of her loving children. Peanut will probably disappear shortly after we take off, heading down to Tammi's brother, Trevor, and Curlers will be left to fish out the 'crawlers hibernating deep within the rich, dark soil in the box in the garage. Or realistically, she will ignore the doorbell altogether and the summer's fishing enthusiasts who come for bait—it depends on her mood, although she claims to be allergic to dirt.

Parrot bursts through the door, her cheeks flush, panting something about what an enlightening experience. She must mean her ride in the cruiser. I try to think why she would identify with it so much—maybe because some aspect of it was sneaky.

"You know, detective work could really be my bag. Uncle Reese is a lot more on top of things then you might expect. He's deceptive, covering up with his clowning around or being an uncle, but really, he knows what he's doing. I wonder if he'd mind my hanging out with him more often—kind of learn the ins-and-outs of the business through him. By the time I graduate high school, I could go right into service, working the area for crimes."

"Parrot, I think your imagination is working overtime," I say. There isn't any real crime going on in the tri-county area to warrant even keeping Uncle Reese on full-time, practically. Anyway, let's blow. We're going to pick up Tammi, then stop at the *DQ* for burgers on our way to the Mill; unless you and Reesie already ate lunch."

"Nope, quite frankly, we didn't have time. We were doing some pretty heavy research, so I've worked up an appetite. I'm going to go put my suit on and get my babysitting money, then I'll be right down."

"Don't forget to grab a towel, alright? I don't feel like sharing mine."

Parrot yells back, "Don't worry! I'm on top of it!"

I guess the morning with Reese hasn't worn off. I imagine she will be playing the junior sleuth for the next couple of days, or for the rest of the summer if he lets her tag along on a regular basis. Actually, it's a good thing for her to do. It gets her out of the house and into some real living.

I carefully back out the driveway aware of Curlers' eyes peering from behind the living room curtains. I guess if I have an accident in front of the house, she wants to be there to see it. We pull up at Tammi's and I honk the horn. I hope she's ready because I hate to have to go up to the door and get her. If by chance her Mom or Dad answers the bell, a sinking feeling will permeating from the frown or scowl that masks the anguish they regularly walk around with. I hope they overcome, one of these days, soon.

We sit there staring straight ahead, idling the motor and hoping to hear the door slam and Tammi running down the front walk. I sit a minute or two longer than turn to Parrot, "You want to go up to the house and get her?"

"No thanks," she replies, "there are psychos living in that house. You go get her."

"Psycho might be a little bit strong a term for Tammi's family. Depressing, maybe, with the hard times they've been through and all, but they mean well."

"That's a dandy explanation, Sis, but I ain't going in alone," Parrot says.

"Oh, alright, I'm going in," I say turning off the car and swinging the door open. I trot up the steps hoping my effort at short-and-fast will continue and carryover to the delay within the house. I lean on the buzzer with extra force and swiftly the front door is jerked open by Mr. Townsend.

"Good afternoon Mr. Townsend, is Tammi ready to go?" I ask as sprightly as possible to someone as expressionless as he is.

"No," he says turning and walking off without explanation.

I open the screen door and walk into the din without an invitation. I blink to adjust to the lack of light and spot Tammi's younger sister stretched out on the living room couch. "Have you seen Tammi?" I ask.

"Yeah, she's in the kitchen," she says without taking her eyes off the TV set to see who might be inquiring.

Geez, I'd sure hate to live with these deadheads. They might not be psycho but they sure might be zombies. Maybe Tammi is right; running as far away from them as she can, might well be the only thing that saves her from becoming just like them.

128

I cross the threshold through the narrow door into the kitchen. Tammi is going through dishes ninety miles an hour and hasn't heard me enter. "Hey Tammi, do you need some help?"

She jumps back, startled at my voice. "Geez, Celia, you scared me! I guess I'm concentrating hard at getting these done. She whispers, "It's not like anyone else around here can't help out. They managed to find this task just as I was ready to leave. Sorry to make you wait. They're mad because I seemed too excited about getting out of here for the day, so they thought they'd throw a pile of dishes in for good measure. But look Celia, if we both grab a towel we can have these dried and out of here in just a few seconds. You dry only, and I'll dry and put away the bunch since I know where to stick 'em."

She's talking and moving about as fast as Tammi does when her energy is up and into a challenge. It's almost like she's not really relating to me, more like she's speaking to herself, motivating the inner Tammi to forget the outside world; pushing the inner gears to machine-like speeds—not to question but to do.

We are done in what seems like no time at all. Tammi grabs my arm and her towel from off the kitchen table and we nearly trip trying to escape the kitchen threshold at the same time. She holds onto my arm and charges for the front door, not waving a dreary good-bye or even mentioning the fact that the dishes are done and in their place. I hesitate in expectation of some hassle going out the door, but Tammi slams it shut and yanks me down the steps. She finally releases my arm from her surge and I stop dead in my tracks trying to reclaim my own momentum.

Parrot hollers out the front seat window, "What took you guys so long? I'm sick of sitting here waiting. I almost went home to find something else to do."

"I had to do the damn dishes!" Tammi yells back. "I wonder who will replace me as all around maid when I'm gone? Or will the place just fall apart?"

"I don't know," I tell her, "but now a swim will really do us good. Not that we weren't just playing in water and drying off in there."

Finally we're catching Route 2, heading south. We're on the road, happy as clams with Tammi's momentary interruption in schedule already forgotten. Parrot is digging into a bag of potato chips we've brought to snack on; waiting must have built up an appetite. About five miles out of town, we intersect Route 43 east. I slow down as we approach and make the left turn that will take us 10-miles up to the swimming hole.

We know we're going to get there now. We ease back into our seats and feel the pull of our nylon suits below the outer cover of our summer clothes. Tammi is tugging at hers in the usual spot where it hikes up between the butt crack. Her suits are usually her mother's hand-me-downs and sink and stretch in the opposite places. Awkwardly, Tammi is a whole head taller than her mother, so it's no wonder it pulls up the middle. But despite all of Tammi's complaining about her lack of respect around the house, she has never mentioned why she has to wear her mother's ill-fitting swimsuit. I think this is one thing her mother has done for her that she actually likes; sagging brassiere and exposed butt are hardly noticeable.

Tammi says, "I hope there's some good male entertainment here today. Taking a dip is fine but I don't expose this much of myself every day. Not that I'm looking for compliments or anything like that, just a little appreciation."

Through the rear view mirror I happen a glance back at Parrot's face. She's giggling and pinching her nose, obviously not terribly appreciative of Tammi's figure.

Drifting off the subject to the reeds and cattails that grow tall and resilient along the road, I realize they sway like long strands of hair in the breeze, so dense that a body could surely hide a foot within and not be seen from any point, including above. It must be damp and probably wet on the marshy floor, as it is in so many areas around here. I guess that's why stuff like wild rice grows so well in the area—wild rice and mosquitoes. Pot holes of wetness pop up everywhere, especially the closer you are to one of the lakes. Real lakes too, thousands of lakes of all sizes, not one of those big sink holes or reservoirs someone took a fancy to carving out from the middle of dry earth. We have the real thing around here, surrounded my marshes with eddies, and unexpected drop-offs with nests of herons, pelicans and loons that line the edges in the safety of the grasses.

As we approach the Old Mill, a line of cars and motorcycles are parked on the gravel lot that precedes the steep hill down to the beach and mill pond everyone swims in. Obviously, we aren't the only ones with this idea of taking a dip.

"I guess we won't be lonely," Tammi laughs.

Parrot edges forward from her back seat and checks out the view. "Know what I think? Celia will have her hands full. It looks like that motorcycle club is out for a bath. Geez, I hope the water is safe for swimming!"

"Ah, come on Parrot, give me a break," I say.

"Seriously," she answers, "this isn't that big a swimming hole and the bunch of them are usually severely dirty. I thought they were doing their bathing in the river?"

"So, does this mean we're opting out of the swimming idea?" I ask, even though my heart is starting to catch on to the idea that Robert is probably here, and I'm not quite prepared. That's okay though, I can adjust.

"No," they both shout.

"I like a crowd," says Tammi.

So I turn the car into the lot and find a spot off to the far left of the motorcycles. I figure it's not as obvious as if my intentions were to run into him here in the first place. Maybe it'll be a nice surprise. I don't know, I still don't think I'm prepared to make any kind of decision for or against him. If I'm ever going to have a relationship with Robert it could be a battle of wills with the whole town. They will all feel sorry for my folks, since they've been such good examples of parenthood, and they'll think I've gone to the dogs. Now, if I decided to go with Connor, everyone will have us wrapped up with a baby carriage anchored to a nice little spread of our own. I don't like the results, either way.

"I packed some potato chips, but I left my lunch on the kitchen counter and I'm hungry," says Parrot.

"Were you going to eat before or after swimming, Parrot?" asks Tammi.

"You know Tammi, I thought I'd stuff a couple of sandwiches down, some chips, maybe some lemonade, a candy bar and then dive in. If I didn't immediately cramp up, it would be a great testimony to swimming on a full stomach."

"Oh, so you're trying to prove something to the world, or are you just feeling suicidal?" says Tammi, equally as sarcastic.

"Where should we set up camp?" I ask, breaking in.

"I like a blanket down on the grass just before the beach," says Tammi.

"I don't know…, I like being on the beach," says Parrot. "It's easier for people you know to spot you from a distance."

"Well in that case, I'd rather be on the grass," I submit.

"Oh whatever," says Parrot, "then why ask me anything?"

"Parrot it's not like I'm trying to be contrary, but I don't know if I want to immediately be spotted by everyone I know. If anything, I want to spot them first, THEN decide whether or not I even want to talk to them. At the least, I won't be caught by surprise with a blank look on my face."

"Geez, aren't we special!" says Parrot.

131

"It's not that, Parrot. Suppose Russ Tomlichek, you know, the guy I dated before Connor, comes up from behind and gives me one of those bear rubs he thinks are so cute. I'd probably clobber him as a natural reflex action," I explain.

We stand at the top of the hill that looks down over the waters of the Old Mill. Only the beach is visible from up here as this side of the pond is shaded by tall trees canopying the area for picnickers, and those of us who wish to be partially secluded. If we hope to get hot sun, we can always get in the water where its reflective rays will tan our skin another degree. I can understand Tammi not wanting to lay out on the beach; her skin is not just fair it is totally white, even translucent during the dead of winter. It would mean listening to whining and moaning all the way back to Beaverton if she's not careful about exposing herself to summer rays. Parrot and I are a golden brown all year round, so capping it off a little deeper is sort of a natural summer phenomenon and hardly noticeable. Tammi goes bright red and must sting by all the fuss she displays, but I know it can't be pleasant, and that's not even touching on the freckles that pop up as a result.

We descend the hill down to a flat green plot with lush soft grass. We veer a little right so Parrot can absorb the ray of light that is now poking through the branches of the trees and Tammi, on the other side of the blanket, can lay in the shade as well. I fit somewhere in between, which is good because I can avoid being spotted so readily by onlookers. Speaking of onlookers, Parrot and Tammi are scooping out the territory for familiar bodies and not doing much to hide their interest. I guess I don't blame them, if it weren't for my "above it all" image, I'd be cranking my neck to see who might be worth checking out. Since I can't bring myself to do that, Tammi and Parrot are welcome to, and will happily report back. Obviously neither one is going to go in swimming until they know exactly who is present and accounted for.

"Do you guys have to be so obvious," I ask.

"How do you expect us to know who's here if we don't take a good look around?" Tammi replied firmly. No one is going to stop her from looking.

"Man, look at those motorcycle guys, and their girls! I guess you could call them girls," says Parrot. "Geez, they're grabbing each other and holding them down, like they want to drowned 'em!"

"Good, that's one less problem around here," says Tammi.

'*Motorcycle guys! Red alert*' I think to myself. I look off in the direction of all the noise, splashing and commotion, straining to see if Robert is in the crowd. I don't expect he'll be moping around wondering where I've been and if he has a chance with me at all. It's hard to distinguish one body from another, what with the distance and the splashing water…

But there he is, and my heart sinks. 'It doesn't look like he's missing me' is the right description for someone carrying an Amazon on his shoulders, complete with miniature cut-offs and a brief bikini bra. My heart seems to weigh a ton, so heavy that I couldn't get up if I wanted to. He looks like he's having the time of his life, and so does she. I guess my questions don't really need answering, and I'm certainly not going to chase him down. I shouldn't feel bad, we never really even got to first base.

"Will you look over there!" says Parrot. "It's that crazy biker guy, Celia, the one who had his eye on you. He looks pretty well entertained today, doesn't he? He seems to be having a good ole time with that slutty biker chick. You suppose it's his regular girl? I hear that the guys in motorcycle gangs don't just have one girl, they share or pick up chicks whenever they can. Imagine being passed around in that crowd!"

"I guess you're not the only chick in town, now are you Celia?" says Tammi. "What do you suppose is his deal: chasing you around like that and generally spoiling our fun? Do you think he's just out for some laughs at the expense of a small town girl, or hoping for another notch on his belt? I guess he's not as desperate as he seemed to act, now is he?"

I don't know what his deal is? And it wasn't as easy as all that they made it out to be—at least not for me. I guess I don't know Robert terribly well, but I believed him when he said he felt like I was something special to him. Could he really have been dishing me out a line? I guess I owe Connor a big apology, an apology he probably doesn't even know he has coming. All he probably senses is my withdrawal from the fun we started out having at the beginning of the summer.

"I guess I don't really have much to say about it," I respond quietly, giving Parrot and Tammi a reason to peer a little closer at me. I suppose if I had made a definite, emphatic statement regarding his degenerate place in society, they would not be giving me the hairy eyeball right now. They don't realize he was more to me than that. "You guys don't need to stare at me like that, and I don't want to talk about it either."

"Okay by me," says Parrot, "I'm ready to get wet. What do ya think? Anyone else ready to go?"

"Sure, let's do it," says Tammi.

"Okay, you're not leaving me here to mope in silence, I'm going too."

"I can't believe you really saw anything in that guy, Celia," says Tammi.

"Are you trying to say you were really going for that guy?" asks Parrot. "Geez, that's pretty okay, if you ask me. I am your dear beloved sister, and I can't believe you won't let me in on this Celia. I guess that has something to do with you dragging around the house for the last couple of days. Yeah, sure, now I get it... Girl likes bad dude, bad dude wants good girl, good girl and bad dude can't make a connection 'cause good girl is, well, good girl is, good! Guess you can tell I know my romance themes, can't you?"

"I didn't tell you, Parrot, 'cause I didn't want good girl's parents catching wind of bad guy until I knew what I was doing, got me?" I say.

We reach the water's edge, just past the gravelly beach the town has laid down for easy access. We're all too chicken to run or dive in. The water is cool at first, so we stand mixing little eddies with our legs and waiting 'til we can handle the next level. We are not alone, for the beach is not secluded or a hidden oasis, but is teaming with local kids and some of their mothers. I would say girls out number boys because the boys are back at the farm workin' on tending the crops and the cattle; then, around 5 o'clock or so, a few'll trail down here to rinse the soil, sweat and soot from the days labor. It's those younger kids you have to watch out for. The ten and eleven year old boys who can't resist splashing water all over you while they're chasing a buddy right up your swimsuit practically. Those kids I want to get up and dunk myself. If you want some peace you've got to swim out beyond the shallow waters of the kids. Robert is off to the left where the only way in to this part of the beach is off some big rocks. You can stand up as long as you're standing on some of the big rocks that line the bottom. Otherwise, it's over everyone's head.

As we attempt a graceful waltz in deeper, I feel the moment the bikers have looked over and captured us in their vision. I would think we were of interest only because of how our figures fill out our suits, and lack of male companion-ship. But I can feel Robert watching intently. His very stare pierces me like an arrow, and I know in an instant he's still mine.

I dive in, disappearing from view, too excited by my realization and it shoves me fearlessly into the cold water where I make like a dolphin and soar. Resurfacing, I can hear the squeals of Tammi and Parrot in disbelief of my coura-geous jump. "Oh, come on you chickens, I'll be ready to get out by the time you finally take the full plunge."

I turn around and dive in again. It's the perfect temperature, once you start to move around. I stroke up and down and tread water now out to the deeper depths. It's so perfect out, I feel almost suspended and weightless as the water holds me buoyant, and I imagine little fish swimming about my giant mass in their domain. Once I'm out far enough, I grab the chance I've been waiting for, to see what Robert is doing over by the rocks.

He's watching me. The girl is off his shoulders and the gang is splashing away without him. He stands waist deep on one of the gigantic submerged rocks, scanning the surface of the water to see where my head pops up. But I've spotted him first and can see his interest is with me. He now sees my head and realizes I am watching him. He waves hesitantly and I re-submerge, swimming back in toward the beach. I'm too embarrassed to publicly display my interest in him, nor do I want to be called over to join in with the rest of his party, which from any vantage point looks like beer drinking and bottle throwing into the refreshing waters of the Old Mill. It's that kind of offensive disregard for the life of the pond that gives me the chills.

As I gain a shallower perspective, I see Tammi and Parrot floating lifelessly through the murkier shades of worked up water. They are serenely lost to the moment, to the comfort of buoyancy, and have obviously tuned-out the shrieking children bouncing up and down just a few feet closer into shore. I purposely splash water on both of them, which prompts them to an upright position and hollering things like: "Hey, that's no fair!"

"I'm heading up to my towel," I yell back, trudging up the sharp little rocks that poke at the soles of my feet as I hasten out; the quicker the less torture, I believe. I grab my towel and dry quickly off to embrace the warmth of the sun that cuts between the large branches of the majestic elm we are settled next to. I look over in the direction of Robert and the bikers. I zero in on him in his cut-off blue jeans, climbing out of the water and onto the large rock jutting out into the water. He stops and looks over at me, then turns and moves over to the path that circles the pond. He's coming here for me, I guess I know that. I look over to the beach where Tammi and Parrot are working their way up the sharp gravel toward the seclusion of our spot under the big tree and their towels. What will they think when Robert approaches and I don't blow him off? I guess I'll have to defend myself. Or once they get to talking with him, they'll realize he's more than they want to believe he is.

"Brrrr!" says Parrot. "It's that run between the water and the towel that makes it hard to get out, or get back in." She grabs her towel and throws it around her shoulders, shivering while the goose-bumps decide it's okay to recede.

Tammi is running up behind her and seconds the statement. As she flings her towel around her body, quickly drying as she works it around, she's the first to notice Robert's approach. "Well, I suppose it was only a matter of time before we should have expected a visit from him, right Celia? I hope this doesn't mean we can expect the rest of those dudes to follow up behind him."

"I hope he has all his teeth and he speaks a reasonable amount of English," pipes in Parrot.

"Oh please! He does have all his teeth and he's a lot sweeter than either of you have yet to know. So could you give him just a little bit of a chance? I know he didn't come on very well with a first impression, but he's okay." I say in his defense.

"I can say the bod is in pretty good shape, and that helps," says Parrot.

"It might help," says Tammi, "but it doesn't change the fact that in the end he's a loser."

"Shut up, Tammi," I squeeze out between my teeth as he walks up.

"Where have you been?" he asks me, as if he's entirely oblivious to the presence of my companions. "I've missed you. Are you trying to avoid me?"

"No, I've been laying low, that's all. This is my sister Parrot," I say turning from his captive eyes, "and this is my friend Tammi. As I recall, we've had a few moments together before." He looks down at me unresponsive to my introductions or last comment. "Do you want to sit down and join us for I while?" I ask, looking up at his dripping shorts and wet hair.

"Not particularly," he responds. "I was kind of hoping I could talk to you a little in private. It's been awhile since we last talked and I'd like to catch up on what's going on. You two ladies won't mind if I just chatted a few minutes in private with her, would ya?"

His tone seems a little odd, yet I can't put up any resistance since I feel like I owe him some explanation, and I truly want to see him. Maybe I don't care for the way it feels; like he's taking control. He sounds almost authoritative and demanding, and I have a very little voice in the outcome. But still I want to see him.

"I don't know," says Tammi. "We all came out here together and are enjoying each other's company. Couldn't you get together another time?"

"What do you say, Celia?" he says turning back to me. "Can we talk a little bit, in private?"

"Yeah, I guess that'd be all right. Hold down the fort, girls, I'll be back in a bit." I get up and wrap my towel around my waist while waiting for him to lead.

"Let's go this way, he points further down the path it seems he's already on. He grabs my hand, and I feel small and awkward in his. Who besides Tammi and Parrot see me linked with this guy? My reputation is shot if this gets out.

He makes me feel like a real woman, and I like that, but I can't really carry on a relationship with him in front of the whole town. I guess I know that now—I haven't got the guts.

"Let's go look at the Mill, okay? It's kind of a cool old building. See," he says as he stops and looks at me, "it's not so hard to be with me, is it?" I smile back at his handsome face and deep blue eyes, but can't respond. "I really missed you these last couple of days. I didn't like getting the brush off."

"I wasn't brushing you off," I say, "I need some time to think this thing through."

We walk intently on in silence as the distance between me and my friends at the beach separates us from easy earshot. I like our solitude and privacy, without anyone able to see us together. I relax more now and enjoy the excitement of being with him. We reach the rickety old mill. The little brick building leans to one side, as pieces of its structure have fallen to the ground, the wooden roof swaying into the middle of the single room inside. The grasses around it are thick and tall, no longer trodden on by regular guests. Everyone comes out here now and again; teenagers anyway, looking for a secluded spot to drink, or smoke, or make-out. The lock that once kept the backdoor secure has long been busted apart, and not even Uncle Reese has bothered to replace it. Nothing bad has ever happened here. I suppose a girl or two has gotten pregnant, but I think that's as deep as it goes.

"Let's go inside to talk," he says. He seems so familiar with this place that I wonder what has brought him out here before. It's obvious that he knows where he's going and how he needed to get here. "Let's sit down on the bench inside."

I follow him without hesitation. I've come this far, and although I like the attention, I'm going to have to tell him we can't see each other.

"Can I touch you?" he asks. "I've thought about you all the time, hoping you'd give me a chance. I just want to take you in my arms and press you close to my heart."

He doesn't wait for my response, but leans down and kisses me hard against the lips. My knees melt and I drop slowly onto the bench some visitor has created. He follows me down, holding the kiss steady. I don't know how I will be able to tell him about my decision since it sort of feels like I could be changing my mind. He draws back his head but not his grip and says, "That wasn't so bad was it? I've felt like holding you like this for a long time, and now it's finally come. Your skin is so soft against mine, I wish we could be here without anything on between us; not swimsuits, nothin'. Just you and me, the way it should be with two people like us." And then his lips meet mine again and I am lost inside his strong embrace. I feel my towel part and his large hand wonder along the back of my leg. Slowly, I begin to come to, in an effort to prevent him from going any further. *I'm not ready!*

"Look Robert," I say sweetly as I pull away, "I've got to get use to you before I can do anything else. This feels nice, but what happens after this? I'm not very fast, I'll admit that. Really, I'm down right slow compared to what you're used to."

"What I'm used to!" he says sharply. "What do you know about what I'm used to? All I want is a little of your time, a chance to be close and feel good with someone. Stop acting like your too precious for me!"

"I'm sorry, I don't want you to feel like you're really odd, but for me you are very different from any of the guys I've known before. Different than the people I know around here altogether. You're more aggressive than any of them. Any of the situations you might get into with me will be easy for you to get out of. All you have to do is leave. But I stay here to live it out, at least 'til next year. I don't want to go too far and then regret it when it's too late."

"Man, what are you talking about? Yeah I'm different alright, but maybe people ought to have some respect for that, instead of acting like I've got cooties or something. Why can't they see me as a positive influence, as someone just checkin' out the world in his own way? All those good, fine citizens out there thinkin' that I'll rape their daughters or stab their sons to death in a gang fight. Now is that how I seem to you?"

"You don't seem like that *now*, but when we first saw you over by the river that day, you didn't come off altogether friendly. I think I've only started to discover you have a tender side, and a person who thinks about the whole world, not only about himself."

"Yeah, well that's all fine," he says, interrupting the positive input I want to make, "but I'm right here, and this is who I am, and you're right here with me now. I haven't forced you to come here. I figure you've come because you wanted to. Have we got that straight?"

"I guess," I say hesitantly. His sudden change from affectionate to demanding is a little disconcerting. I feel my body tense up and focus on the question of whether this is where I want to be.

"Hey relax. I just want you to know that I'm here for you, and I want you to see that you're here 'cause you want to be with me."

He leans in and kisses me again, and I crumble in his larger being. The feeling is so good and satisfying I don't want to let go, or risk his irritation. I think I'm over my head. Maybe this isn't quite right, but I can't let go of the completeness of this feeling. My arms wrap around his shirtless torso and hold in the volcanic heat I sense within his uncovered frame.

His strength lowers me down against the bench as he presses into me with weight and desire. I don't know about this position, in this moment. Somehow I know I've gotten myself into this, and even if he feels so overwhelming, I want to back out. What are Tammi and Parrot doing? I would think they'd begin to wonder where I am. I wouldn't want them to find me in this position 'cause they'd have their doubts about me for sure.

He starts caressing my arm and pulls at my swimsuit strap. *Wait a minute!* He jerks up away from me, and in an instant, pulls the top of my swimsuit down to my waist, lowering himself quickly down on top of me. He sighs in some kind of physical relief and I freeze as his body presses harder onto mine. I let go of the pressure I used to hold onto him and press my hands against his body trying to move him away, at least long enough to pull my suit back up where it belongs.

"Don't fight it," he says softly, "I'm not going to hurt you."

"I'm not interested in this!" I say, "It's time for me to get back to my friends."

"Forget your friends, you're with me now."

I try rolling over and indicate to Robert it's just that I want to be on top. He concedes, still pressing hard against my lips, his hands finding their way to my breasts. It's my moment to run...

Quickly I jerk away from his chest, pressing hard against his thighs with my knees. I reach and fling open the door, breaking away down the path toward the less wooded swimming area and the tall elm tree that I hope Parrot and Tammi are still under. I don't even look back but stick my arms through my suit straps and pull it back up over my breasts, just before the clearing. As I reach the edge, I listen for his footsteps behind me while catching my breath trying to look unscathed. I don't hear anyone gaining behind me. He must still be at the Mill waiting for his passion to recede.

I suck in a deep breath and toss around what I should tell the girls. I don't suppose Robert did anything against the law. I mean, it wasn't rape. I did consent to take a walk with him, but clearly he is more than I can handle.

Tammi and Parrot will be easy. I'll tell them Robert and I went for a walk... period. What else do they have to know? I want to confide in them, but Tammi especially, will blow it up so huge the whole town will be in on it—except Connor.

Okay, I trot down the incline from where the woods opens over the valley that rolls gently into the Old Mill pond, park, and beach. The tall elm under which Robert implored I come speak with him, still somewhat shades my two best friends. I don't want to show it, but they lend needed comfort. I wish I could share my gratitude for their being here with me. I know if I were to tell them the truth, they'd back me up in any way and support whatever it takes to put Robert out of the picture.

As I walk up quietly from behind, both Parrot and Tammi are snoozing—at least it looks that way. Parrot's face is using the Victoria Holt romance as a shield to the afternoon sun. I imagine her forehead, cheeks and chin are stuck to some dull chapter, in between some ubiquitous tip-toeing through the tulips with a prince, a not so fair maiden, and a unicorn grazing not so far afield. The pages, now pasted to her sweaty face, will stick until Tammi or I point out she's wearing the print.

Tammi is laying facedown, her legs splayed loosely apart while her arms are gripped tight to her sides. She could be dreaming..., probably not of anything particular, just reviewing how she plans to make a splash somewhere other than Beaverton, or, at the very least, living larger than her world has so far allowed. Geez, I wish it were that easy for me. How did I get to this spot? Yesterday was so simple. The summer had all I wanted to include in it; Connor, bikes, hikes, girlfriends, summer dances...and now this. Oh well, if, if, if... First explanation is now coming up for Parrot and Tammi! All their insults and questions will prepare me for anyone else who might get wind.

Where is Keith when I need a big physical brother to defend me? What's the point in a brother if not to tell some guy they're over-stepping their bounds— that they're OUTA bounds? That would sure eliminate my folks, or Reese making a big thing and calling me on the carpet.

As I stand staring at my friends, I hear Robert's footsteps along the path. I'm not even going to turn around and acknowledge his presence. He ought to know I'm not interested in his rough behavior. Shoot, we've hardly had a conversation, let alone third base!!

"It's not over," he shouts out to me as he stalks past. Since he's only got his cut-off shorts on, it looks like he's taken a wrong turn from the outhouse to the lake.

I'm not even going to respond. *It's not over?* Please, it hadn't even *started* to get *over!*

Out of the corner of my eyes I noticed Parrot and Tammi look up as Robert threw out what sounded more like a threat, than a lover's lament. I know they'll be right on top of it as soon as I hit the blanket. I stand for a moment watching him descend back into the lake and his friends. What are my days ahead going to be like? Is he going to show up the moment I step out the door? Will he threaten Connor? Does he think he has some special rights? I hope this doesn't include some outrageous jealousy issues? I should've read all of Parrot's romance novels; maybe they could provide the answers I may shortly need.

I don't care how you look at it, he was crossing boundaries without any consideration for my feelings. No respect. I guess this is a taste of what everyone talks about concerning respect. I didn't even have time to explain. He just went for broke and no regard for what I'd have to say, think, feel…all of it. Geez! Bring on the dancing girls already! Try not to give a thought to what I'm all about! I feel like screaming this at him as I watch him dive back into the water, popping up to splash at his friends. He doesn't even turn to acknowledge me as I stare at his antics. He knows I'm watching, I can feel purposeful neglect.

"Well that's interesting," pipes up Parrot from over in left field. "What's this, 'it's not over!' Was there anything started to *be* over?"

"Oh, I don't know. He's just acting tough as if he's got something going on!" Geez, I can't believe I'm saying this, to my best friends. Have I lost it? Why don't I want to tell them the truth? I have nothing to be ashamed of. I suppose because for a few seconds I gave him an opening, and I was wrong…

"Um, I think a little something most have gone on," kicks in Tammi. "I mean, who just yells out, '*it's not over*'? Come on, break the news, we can handle it."

"Well, it's not all that dramatic, but okay." I guess it's better to give them something to rummage through, than to keep it all in. One day I'd have to spill the beans because it'll keep coming up.

Just as I'm pulling my story together, and about to give the girls an overview of what took place between Robert and I at the Mill, out pops Uncle Reese from the same area of the path Robert and I took to the Mill.

"Good afternoon ladies. Don't look so shocked, it's just me. Uncle, doing his rounds, protecting the neighborhood from scoundrels and thieves. Say Celia, when you get a chance…, maybe later today, could you stop by the station? I would like you to go over a few things with me."

"Oh, okay Uncle Reese! Do you want me to clean the place or file some papers for you?" I ask quickly, trying not to give Reese an opportunity to talk about what he may have seen at the Mill. I'm not so foolish as to believe he didn't get a good look at Robert and me, now that I've seen him lumbering out of the woods around about the same place and time we'd been there. He might have made it seem like he'd been just going through the woods, not even taking the path to the Mill, but I know Reese is keeping an eye on those guys, and remember, I asked him about Tiny.

"Well, maybe", he replies. "I need a youthful perspective on a few issues I've been rolling around." Reese is looking ravaged, probably as a result of ducking through bushes, tall grasses, and peering around trees. His face is sweaty and a bit warn, I imagine from keeping his little pug nose to the grindstone, I hoping not exactly on my trail. "I think I can make better sense of it all if I had some teen, female, half sensible, half foolish motivation regarding a few issues I'm reviewing around here," he continued. "I hope to get an early jump with a few clues to the logic of youth."

I wonder what Reese has on his mind...

"Hey, I can help you out," says a suddenly perky Parrot, now sitting straight up and ready to move on to something with a little intrigue.

Reese moves fast with a quick response, "I'd love to know what you think Parrot, but I need someone with a year or two more of experience. I've already spoken with your mother, and she says she's taking you shoe shopping tomorrow."

I know Reese is telling a big whopper, but Parrot looks happy just to imagine the possibilities. She's not quite onto Reese's habit of making up a good story rather than being on the level in order to get his needs met, and not get into a timely confrontation just to pacify the inquisitive. I hope one day soon though, he'll ask Parrot to clean out the holding tank, or scrub the jail's floors. She so wants to be somehow involved in some police action.

"Well, good to see you ladies, but I've got some distance to go before I can pull the cruiser into the garage. Please carry on with what you were doing, and I'll see you later, Celia, right?"

"Oh yeah, I'll be in, Reese. I guess I can meet you late this afternoon—say around 4:30?" I want to seem interested because Reese will really go ballistic if he finds I'm hiding anything that can disrupt his work, or could harm me in a way he can help to avoid.

"Okay", he shouts back, "I'll make sure I'm back at the office then."

Damn, I think to myself, I'd sure like to turn back the clock, say, two weeks. Connor and I would be on! Hands down. No complications with interlopers. I might even have been here at the mill pond with Connor, instead of the girls. With my crazy, stupid feeling that Robert may just want a friend, I put my dear Connor on the back burner. I don't know what he thinks now. He hasn't called, and I haven't pursued him either. He seemed really interested, but maybe because my energy has wandered off, so has his.

"Celia! Celia, I'm going back in the water, one last time," yells Tammi, stretching out like a cat waking from her nap. "Anyone care to join me? I want to cool down, but then I'll be ready to hit the road... Oh, and I haven't forgotten your boyfriend troubles, girl!" she yells back at me as she leaps to her feet. Tammi's got on a one-piece chartreuse colored swimsuit that is so obviously secondhand and worn out—stretchy fibers now limp. Remarkably, she doesn't seem to care. "You promised to tell us about it, and I'm holding you to it. You owe us an explanation. Still, I've got a date later on, so I'm going to need to pamper myself before Gary picks me up. Come on girls, join me!"

CHAPTER FIFTEEN

Growing Up

I drop the girl's off and head straight for the Beaverton "correctional facility", aka, Uncle Reese's office. I floated some idea to the girl's that Robert and I had talked at the Mill where I'd told him a relationship was pretty impossible for us. That's the reason he said, *it's not over*, because he can't accept that we have nothing in common. I left out the part in which he pulls down my swimsuit hoping for home plate.

Now Uncle Reese on the other hand, is probably going to ask for a full explanation. Shoot, I'm surprised I didn't get a sense of someone prowling around and spying on us. Still, I should have known, afterall, these guys are on his list of public enemy—"numero uno." Naturally, he's on their tail. Most folks in this community know Reese isn't any sit-around cop. If anything he's too nosey! I'msurprised he didn't call me into his office the morning after the ballgame. I suppose he saw me sneak over to the bushes to talk with Robert that night after Connor dropped me off. I guess that was kind of innocent. It really wasn't until Tiny's disappearance that any of this started to be a real problem...well, for me anyway. I don't know, maybe I'm just jumping to conclusions. Uncle Reese might just want me to file some papers for him.

I pull into the jail's rear parking lot, 'cause now I want full privacy from any lurking boyfriends, family members and chatty town folks. Nosey. I never have liked all that talk, especially if I'm not able to clue my friends or family in first on what I might be up to. Shoot, it's usually pure innocence. Robert has already given me the impression he's got a right to be jealous! Really not cool! That's a big clue, right from the start, why he's not for me.

I push open the back door and walk into the dark cool of the back end of the jail facility. I saw the cruiser parked in the front so I know Reese has already made it back from the Mill. "Hello! Uncle Reese! It's me, Celia!" I shout even before I reach the big room he usually sits and where his desk is located.

"Good afternoon, young lady," he responds, "About time. Have a seat. We've got some stuff to discuss."

Geez, he's sounding kinda cryptic. "Okay, whatcha got on your mind, Uncle?" I say slowly as I drop into the usual seat across from his desk.

"I know all about you and that cycle gang leader, so don't interrupt 'til I'm done," he responds officiously.

I nod my head and I'm trying to look like my ears are straining to hear his every word and detect every innuendo. Uncle Reese has on a fresh change of uniform and he's looking a whole lot better than he was an hour or two ago when he slipped out of the woods all dusty and sweaty. There's no doubt in my mind that he'd been lurking behind some trees, maybe even crouched down on the ground. Now that he's made it clear he knows about Robert and me, it's probable he's seen us together, if not in the Mill, at least going to and from.

"I'm totally unimpressed with your selection, missy!" he continues, "and especially knowing a little bit of what's been going on with the whole gang of motorcycle dudes since they've blown into town. I suppose all you high school gals think these guys are a lot more exciting and oh so dashing in dirty t-shirts and leather, dust blowing up and lending a little more ambiance to slow ole Beaverton. I'm sure that rooting Connor on at one more ballgame is just not that exciting anymore."

"Now Uncle Reese," I protest. "It isn't like that…"

"Hey, I said hold on until I'm finished, and I've got a lot more to say," interrupts Reese. "Okay, let me cut to the chase. I've had my eye on the whole lot of them since day one. They've been acting like their blowing into the neighborhood is just a sightseeing tour, but I know it's been a bit more than that, whether it was suppose to be or not. Maybe they were just passing through, then one day went by, and then another. Anyone would've gotten suspicious. The whole town is talking and asking me what it's all about. I've had little recourse. I couldn't just throw them out for looking menacing. That's not right either. Joe Bronowski living on the corner lot up the street looks menacing, but that doesn't mean I can kick him down the road, or lock him up for any ole thing. But, it wasn't long before these biker guys started trying to charm the pants off of me. Now why would a couple of bike-riding, interlopers, hopefully riding in and out of town in a matter of a day or two, want me to think they're sweet?"

"Well, supposing one falls for a town girl?" I suggest, only alluding to the truth.

"Don't interrupt," he challenges. "That made me all the more suspicious. I know we're a fascinating bunch around Beaverton, and I can get this jail loaded up pretty quick on a Saturday night, what with a "Shnabie" celebration and busting up brawls out at *Emerson's Surf and Turf*, but it's a rare opportunity when folks feel a need to brown-nose me. No, no, no, no...I instantly felt the crew meant to take advantage. Yeah, the Mill is a nice little swimming hole, but they can do a lot better than this further south. The burgers at Dell's or Emerson's are not necessarily state-of-the-art, and I checked with Emerson and he says they aren't going for the Turf in *Emerson's Surf n Turf*. Now if they were hanging to repair their bikes or double-dutching at the laundry mat up by Deer Stream, I'd be less suspicious. I've been on their trail since around the day you said Tiny was missing. I haven't necessarily forgotten about Tiny, but I have been carried away with who's who in the cycle world. Interestingly, a few have left or disappeared, while one or two others come and go, and the rest maintain an existence down by the river. Like the day you said Tiny disappeared in that area, the crew seems to have put up stakes down amongst the river reeds.

Now, it seems too late for me to say keep far, far away from that bunch; they've got nothing good in mind, because in my close observation of the more active ones, I've just happened to see you hanging with one particular biker boy—and I don't me Connor!"

Uncle Reese eyes me with a look of disgust that quickly turns to a knowing smirk. "Yeah know, I probably seem as old as the hills, Celia, but I was a youngster once too. I liked all the hot sassy babes, believe it or not, so yeah, I can see the attraction. I'm more than a little cautious about who I'd choose to be seen around town with these days...not only because I am the law around here, but I don't need more crazy drama than any sane person ought to sign up for in a lifetime. Listen missy, I've made enough wildly ridiculous selections in the relationship department this family should be required to handle. When I see you sneaking around to meet this poor confused soul, I truly understand." Reesie says all this with an intensity that assures me he's now cutting through all the build up, and is working his way to making it clear he means business. Not only are his jet black eyes piercing, but he must feel it's important to lean inward toward me in a chair, opposite him across his desk. I get the point, and hope that at any minute someone will walk into the office and distract him from any and all points he wants to emphasis. All I care to do now is head for home and straight up to my bedroom. Today has been too much. I've already gone swimming, grappled with Robert, made excuses to my best friends, and, prepped for a scolding by Beaverton's law enforcement official, my Uncle Reese. All I can do is wait it out.

"Sure, I get the wild, windblown, blonde tresses and the brooding constant pout, and quite a six pack. Give me a break! Just where do you think this is going? Is he going to clean up nice so he'll be good dinner company for your folks? Okay, don't answer either one of those questions, 'cause if you come up with some crazy answer…well, no telling what measures I might have to resort to. Did I see you at the ballpark? Yes. Didn't I see you sneaking out of the house to meet him? Yes. Did I see you two running into the Mill earlier today? Yes. And that's the final "affirmative" I'm ever going to confirm about you and this dude from here on.

Okay, let's get real. We have some serious issues with this young man; "man" being the key word there. I say "we" because I feel not only do you have some responsibility here, you may find yourself in some danger YOU may not be able to handle without MY back up.

Reese looks at me with that pointed, '*You can't challenge this 'cause I know way too much about what you'd rather I didn't know anything about*' look. He's right. I can't challenge any of what he's said so far. Pops, but especially Curlers, will go ballistic if they knew I'd been spending this kind of time in any connection at all to bikers. Even hanging out chit-chatting for no particular reason would bring on a never ending lecture, probably brought up and reported on year after year 'til I'd finally have to lash back at them. Keith, Parrot and Peanut will forever bring this up. I know it!

Behind all my thoughts of future embarrassment, I hear Reese still working the biggest annoyance in his recent career… "Forget being named nicest girl in Beaverton. You're going to challenge the opinions of all the upstanding citizens. You will be a full on new member of the other side of the tracks. I love the "other" side of the tracks, as you know, it's certainly more entertaining, but no one had a choice over there. You have a choice. Never forget that. What your parents created for you was a choice. Are you aware of that? If anything is important it's that you weigh where you come from, where you want to be now, and how does this affect where you are going? Like it or not, other tracks don't have the benefit of knowing they have a choice; forces of nature, insecurity from themselves and their families make it hard to chose anything else, nobody committed to their lives, and boosting self-esteem. You know you had more than that, and I think you need to start honoring some of the choices your folks made for you!

Again, he's back to eyeing me with that intensely-knowing glare. Am I getting it? That's what this look is all about. Am I getting it? And my answer: well, gee, I guess! I know in my *mind* that Robert is all wrong. I'm sure of it, now that he physically tried passing my boundaries without any concern for dislike, or fear of where he wanted to go. I'm not even sure I wouldn't have gone all the way if he had changed his approach, and that scares me to know. In my *heart* he's exciting, I suppose because he's bigger, older, more sure of himself, and something of a man. So yeah, the idea that it's me he wants is hard to turn my back on. I know everything that Uncle Reese is telling me makes sense, but I don't feel it like the way I feel Robert's excitement. What am I suppose to do—ignore my feelings? Suppress? This is so hard. I guess the only thing that can make me cut the cord, for reals, is knowing that my parents will be so ashamed, so bummed out by anything I might have to do with him—no matter how I feel. Oh Uncle Reese, stop talking. I need some time to think, by myself.

"Now, to get to another dangerous issue in all this," he continues, "this group has made an even bigger mistake; they unfortunately opted to take care of their pack issues here in my jurisdiction".

"What do you mean, *pack issues?*" I throw into his dialogue, because all I've been thinking about is the *me and Robert* issue.

"I'm getting to that," Reese says quickly, not wanting to be interrupted, but also clearly getting excited. What's this all about that he's burning through a lecture and now on to police business?

"Like I said, I've been on their trail since day three. When you came in with an all-points-bulletin about Tiny, I'd already been onto it. I couldn't stop for a dog loss, or get anybody all upset and spoil my investigation. I'll talk about Tiny in a minute, so try and follow along with where I'm going on this. Like I said, I'd noticed they'd spend a lot of time down by the river, not just camping out, but they'd sit and wait up along the railroad tracks. Once the 11 o'clock train whistles through the area, they'd immediately break off; go to lunch, play around at the Mill, race up and down some country road around here, or chat up some of the local girls.

Of course I was wondering what these knit-wits could want with the 11 o'clock train... It doesn't even stop here at Beaverton, but it does slow down. I wasn't seeing additional bikers get off, or one of them catch a ride on down the line.

Then came the day a white bundle got thrown from one of the empty cars."

"Oh yeah, I kinda forgot about that!" I say, immediately thrown back to the morning Tiny went missing. My stomach is not feeling so good and my butt must be full of concrete because it's as if I'm stuck here forever to wallow in biker dung...

"Oh yeah, how time flies when you're distracted," Reese pipes back sarcastically. "Well, hold on to your hat little lady, because there's more.

I missed seeing the large white bundle getting tossed from the train, but I did catch up with it the next day, the day Tiny went missing. It must have arrived the day before. This I have seen every day since then. When the train slows down, a small brown package is tossed to one of the dudes. They have a little place they bury things close to the track. I'm not quite sure what it is because I haven't been able to get a close-up look. Since that first toss, they've always had someone guarding the stash.

I do know, however, what was in the big white bundle. I missed the river toss, but the body turned up downstream a couple days later. Some young boys snagged it while they were fishing and reeled it in. Low and behold, we've now got a dead body, and you, the only eye-witness to the toss."

"Ahh shit," yeah, I know this is Beaverton law enforcement and my uncle, but I can't help but curse 'cause it seems to me like things just keep going from bad to worse.

"Yep, it's a lot of shit all right. I'll double that. Still, don't let your mother know I've approved your foul language and all."

"Ahh, come one Uncle, this is seriously stinky, and I'm as wrapped up in the middle as an innocent bystander can be," I pout.

"Yep, I agree, and that's why I've come up with a plan. So listen up. I don't want to have to repeat myself. I'm not sure I even like this plan, but I have a feeling it will work," he grumbles.

"What do you mean, there's more?" Good grief, all I expected was an 'I'd better stop seeing Robert, or else.' I had no expectation there'd need to be a *Plan*! This all seems self-explanatory. Is there a plan to lay all this out gently on my folks? I was kinda hoping all that could be avoided if I promised to stay away from motorcycle types and head off to college when everyone says jump. That really doesn't take much planning, that's more like barking orders. Apparently the scowl on my face and the tone in my last question gives Uncle a chance to pause and think where he's going next with this private little chat. I'm kinda surprised because it sure seems as if he had the whole issue all wrapped up. All I thought he'd need from me is a statement to the effect that I'd straighten up and walk within the lines according to him and my parents. Plan? Well, let's hear it.

Reese squirms around in his chair, looking at the ceiling, and then again back at me—kinda like "the hairy eye-ball" sort of look. And finally he gets to where he left off.

"Yes, there's a plan. There has to be a plan. There's a dead body involved that might have been lost and forgotten if it had turned up in Louisiana at some point down the road, but it didn't, it showed up a couple towns down the river. As of last week, the FBI was able to link the dead man with these beautiful boys right here in town. According to inside dope, these guys had been traveling together, and in order for the FBI to get backup info on this gang's interesting activities, they followed the guy in the white sheet. Enough said, except, in order to nail these misunderstood waifs, someone is going to have to rat. Yep, someone is going to have to explain, or picking them up will be wasting time. Yeah, the FBI say they had a mole on the inside, and he was connecting the bikers with drug running, there just hasn't been enough material to make an arrest. Before they can make a strong case, their mole goes and turns up wrapped in plastic and a white sheet down the river from here.

What? Are you getting squeamish?"

"Hmmm…geez," I'm concentrating on his story, "this is really, not even remotely close to what I thought they were up to. I mean, biking around *acting* bad, maybe even getting into serious trouble, but I guess I excused it all because he seemed so sincere," I sound so whiny!

"Look it, kid, too late for confusion. These cuties are dangerous. They've been playing at this racket for too long. I think this guy Robert likes you enough that you're a distraction to the dangerous games they're playing. I think the game might be a little routine, and you're a reminder of his manhood. In my book, manhood out trumps playing games for a bit of cash.

Here's the plan: I need you to get close to this guy. Yes, I know he went way overboard today, even for you. Yeah, yeah, yeah, I saw it all, but I've got to keep a close eye on the whole scene. The state and the FBI are sending out agents to circle the town and keep them from injuring innocent bystanders. Great… How to get the whole town upset, and give away the case. These folks will get a good feel for all the agitation, and beat it quick. But I've got them…This is my place… I'm no fool, or background material for anybody. I think I can nail these waifs and get them a definite booking in a state or federal facility, and I think *you* can help me to do that."

"Really?" I can't imagine how I'd fit in at this point.

"Really!" Reese responds without hesitation. "See, you're actually my ace in the hole. I've got the trump card, and that's you. In other words, I've got his manhood. He's not really through with you until he gets what he wants. He'll keep after you as long as we allow him to live in peace around the neighborhood, and I plan on doing exactly that until I get a confession. That's where you come in."

"What? That's where I come in! I thought you were telling me strictly to bow out!

"Now, come on, Celia, it's not that complicated," says Reese, knowing he's sheepishly needing me to play dumb on one hand, yet, we both know he can't accomplish the hero's journey without me. Team work is what he's got to count on me for. I get it. It's not that complicated.

"Geez Reese, what do I get out of all this? You really won't be that close to capturing even one of these guys if I hadn't spent some time with Robert. You know, this makes me feel like a Judas! Really does, you know. I can feel some sides of Robert are lost and lonely, and you act as if I should treat him like he's probably always been treated, and show no interested in a guy who just wants some understanding of a tossed around and out boy who rides a bike. Yes, as I'm sure you know, he went too far at the Mill. I just wanted to get to know him better, and maybe do a little necking. I felt like there was more to him, something deeper that wanted to get out, and he could tell it to me. Now you want me to betray the one connection he has in Beaverton that might give him some belief in a kinder, sweeter Robert."

I'm feeling somehow betrayed by Uncle Reese, "What about me?"

"Well, Celia, I'm glad you said, "might" give him some belief, because I'll bank on the FACT that he's delivering you a line, a line that probably works with any chick he chats up, in any town he rides into. If you want to use psychology on his "syndrome," yeah, he probably learned to get by with the, "I'm misunderstood" charm, from an early age. It may have saved him from his parents, but you're not going to change all that. He's done it too long, and as cute and charming as he is to a newbie like you, this guy runs this gang. Yep, he's the leader of the pack—the alpha male."

But Reese, how is this different than the dudes who come running wild off the rez every weekend. They hit *Emerson's* like a whirlwind, then sooner or later, there's a fight, usually in the parking lot 'cause someone gets jumped. Next thing ya know, someone is being taken to the hospital. You let everyone else sleep it off in the jail, and later they slide back home. Once every couple of years someone actually gets beat to death, but nobody is asking some teenager to squeal." I say in an agitated protest.

"Huh, you'd be surprised! A drunken fight between a couple of booze-swillers making fast with the lip and flailing arms is one thing, but outright sober plans of murder is different. To top the whole mess, dropped off in my lap, these boys are drug runners, not revelers forgetting their depression at the other end of a bottle at *Emerson's*," Uncle Reese quickly clarifies. "I want you to know, Tiny turned up too!"

Oh no, my heart skips just hearing he knows where Tiny is…and it doesn't sound uplifting. "Where?" I demand.

"Very close to the wrapped bundle downstream. Seriously close to the dead body," he answers, not sugar-coating a thing.

Tears rupture like a broken water line that froze at 10 degrees below zero. I don't know why I thought Tiny would surely be found alive. She was the best dog ever. I can see her sweet little face looking playfully up at me, hoping for a game of chase, or better yet, a doggie treat. Who in their right mind would hurt such an innocent, perfect, little being? WHO?

"There's no doubt in my mind one of those biker maniacs played kickball with her!" Reese continued. "Sorry, Celia, but if it takes this kind of graphic brutality to get you to see what is actually on the ground running, then I'm telling you what we're really up against here. This group, including, and maybe especially Robert, is willing to hurt or destroy whatever gets in their way. So, do I have time to lay down some respect or even pity for these monkeys? NO! Will reeling them in to get em off the back roads and highways be easier with your help and cooperation? YES! Should I wait for bigger, maybe better law enforcement backup? Maybe. But if I know the State boys, and even the Feds, they'll be in here with some big ole abstract plan that will end up backfiring with that Robert dude sticking his hooks even deeper into you, and a chase looking like the Keystone Cops. I'll end up taking the fall for their failure. Believe me, I'm not going to let that happen. I know my territory. I've got the bait, and we'll quietly reel them in."

"Okay, Uncle Reese, enough said. Count me in. What do I need to do?" I'm ready. After hearing about Tiny, open the chute! Talk about bucking bulls! I'll give 'em a ride alright!

"Whoa, slow down! This has got to be done right and with precision. I've got the whole thing orchestrated; all I need you to do is follow directions to the T. No hotheaded stuff, or it won't work, right? Okay then, here's my plan."

CHAPTER SIXTEEN

Hanging Ten

I thought about Uncle Reese's plan all night long. I barely slept as I reviewed his instructions and thought about Tiny's horrifying end. How could those bastards for one second think of kicking even the scariest most horrifying animal, unless it was rabid? Tiny was so sweet and fun. She was all about love and having fun; full of kisses and nestling in around someone's feet. Okay, she may have had a yap that rang through my ears like being locked into a tin can with the shrill sound bouncing off the cylinder walls. When I lost her that day along the river near those bikers, she was using all the punch she had barking at their presence. Still, they've got to be missing a couple smart genes. She was just a small sweetheart of a dog who'd eventually lick them clean. They don't know who they've messed with. People underestimate Uncle Reese, but he always, always gets his man... or woman. Tiny will get justice. I don't even care if I have to take a couple hits, Tiny will not have died in vain.

I awake wrapped and tangled in my sheet and blanket. When I did drift off, I must uv done some battling if my messed up bed says anything about the quality of sleep I had.

It's six a.m. and I've got to get dressed in order to get this plan rolling like Reese worked out. Am I scared? Yeah, I'm scared, but even more I'm angry.

Charming! He played me like a real small town fool. All he had to do is flatter me. He "likes 'em like me'!" Please! How could I have been so blind? Man, he almost got the whole kahuna! To think! Then what? He'd a hit the road. Man, I could've ended up with a child by him. I don't want to jump too off the beaten path here, but isn't that how it usually happens? Yeah, I'm nervous, but it's time to straighten things out.

I know what I've gotta do. I've run it through my mind all night. Like Uncle Reese says, I've got to slip out of the house without disturbing anyone. That won't be that hard now that Tiny is dead. Back when I'd walk her in the morning, she'd get excited knowing we were off for an early morning run. She'd run around my room whining as I'd get dressed, then whip down to the back door and bark frantically until I opened it and slide out into the fresh morning dew. Of course, any of the light sleepers would hear the whole routine; never my mother though; she sleeps like a brick until it's absolutely time to descend to the first cup of the day with no moments in between to evaluate dreams, cozy up in the blankets, or reflect on the new day. She thinks all one does if they lay in bed too long is trip down memory lane, re-evaluating a lot of the past that's best long gone. Still, she's never up until 8 o'clock or there abouts.

As for Pops, well he's a light sleeper so I've really got to tip-toe around and get out of here now…early. Parrot, Peanut and Keith aren't even in the equation.

I got everything together last night. I've got my clothes, make-up and tooth-brush all on my chair in front of vanity, and a glass of water ready to rinse the toothpaste out after I brush. I'm not even going to use the bathroom 'cause it might be too noisy. I'll have to wait until I hit the woods for some morning relief.

Uncle Reese asked that I do a particularly "fine" job of putting an outfit together; something tight and colorful and short. I've got to get Robert's attention and then some. I've got my shortest cut-offs and a hot pink tank top with a bikini on underneath that was really too small a couple years ago. I hope I won't have to show it, but if I have to pull off the tank to lure him in, baby, I will.

Okay, now just my purse. I found this little cloth one that looks like a pocket with a long stringy strap that I'll lace over my head and sit cross-wise on my opposite shoulder. It's got the tape recorder in it, a little small black thing no bigger than a coin purse. It's truly perfect for what Reese needs. I just hope no one asks for anything like change.

Okay I'm dressed and ready to go out my rear bedroom window. It's not that hard to slip out of, and no one can hear me either. I push open the lower window and it shoots up fast without any real effort. Both upper and lower window panes sit horizontal as I crawl out on the roof—no problem. I'm sure no one has even heard a thing. My room is at the far back of the house, almost on its own, placed above the back porch. Someone would have to either be sleeping or awake on the porch for anything to be heard from my room.

Out on the rear roof that slopes out from the lower den and kitchen, I make a wild jump to the big cottonwood a couple feet away from the back of the house and catch the nearest sturdy limb. Yikes, I feel the bra portion of my bikini hike-up nearly to my neck. Good thing it's too early for anyone to be up and notice. I'm about to pee in the bikini bottom and shorts, so I need an easy landing. Geez, it's hard being a girl! I tear up my palms a bit making the swing from the limb to the ground. Now, get me to the woods where I can make a quick pit stop off in behind some trees.

I take off for the pasture that leads on to the path Tammi, Parrot and I took just a week or two earlier and first really met up with the motorcycle gang. It seems like forever ago now. As I get close to the woods that hide a view of the path and the railroad tracks, as well as the river, I scan the horizon for a quiet and protective spot to relieve myself. Nothing jumps out from here; I best just head for the path that's canopied by the tallest of cottonwoods and willows. I know I can find a more secluded spot on the other side of the trail. I spot a desolate expanse and dash in its direction, finally reaching the canopy of trees racing down the far side incline and push down my bikini bottoms and shorts all in one quick motion. Just as I squat down, I hear rustling within a few quick feet. Too late to jump up. I try to take care of business as quickly and quietly as possible all the while wondering if someone can see me. Maybe it's Reese already on the scene; or one of the gang standing watch for interlopers; or Robert, up early, too restless to sleep. Whoever it is, it'd be nice if they'd give me a little privacy!

As I yank up my bikini bottom and shorts, I spot the guy. It's not Uncle Reese or Robert, but one of the gang rolling out of his sleeping bag. I don't know why he's located this far from the crew, but I don't like the leer he's got for me. I suppose I gave him a full shot of my rear end and he thinks it's funny. I think I was right the first time; he's some kinda lookout for the rest of the crew.

"What are you doing lurking around here this early in the morning?" rumbles out of a hole in his now stone-cold grimace.

I'm not sure what to say, but he's not distracted, he's standing in wait of an answer. I've got to get my act together. I've got to get into "the Plan." One of the dudes has landed in front of me a little sooner than anyone anticipated, but I've got to go along with any variations to make the plan work. Still, who does this guy think he's asking? ME! What am I doing walking on MY path? He's the intruder!

"I'm walking here!" I shout back. If he really knew what I was adding in my head to that short reply, I'm sure I'd have a fight on my hands; so, I'm moving down the path quickly yet as casually as I can to not have any confrontation with this pocked-face gang guard. This guy is dark and swarthy, and perhaps with cleaning up, a comb through the hair, he'd be just another townie, but he's all smoky from campfires. It looks from his hair poking straight up on one side that he doesn't care much for appearances. Actually, I'd say all this grubby, bad teeth, and probably bad breath, "tough" is ideal—not "attractive." Man, if Reece hadn't talked me into this plan I wouldn't even know this sissy was now keeping the likes of me out of my own back yard. And if Tiny were still around, I'd have made this discovery a lot sooner. I don't know what I'd have done, but it wouldn't have been so easy to set up shop here—I'll tell you that.

I stretch out my stride and pick up speed...yet I hear his boots mooshing along in the early morning dew, not too far behind me. I want to look back just to see exactly where he is, but I don't want him to think I'm concerned one way or the other of his whereabouts. No matter what I'm doing here, I don't need some stranger thinking they can escort me anywhere. Not after the loss of my Tiny. I'm heading directly for their "take advantage of a local high school girl" leader, and I can get there without his bodyguard holding my hand.

I feel a paw land on my shoulder and jump forward a foot or two. "Hey! Wait up honey!" I hear him blurt from behind. "No one's open for business yet! You're going to have to take your walk in a couple hours when the crew ain't bunked down."

"What? Where am I? This just happens to be where I live. I've walked around here for as long as I can remember. Besides all that, I'm kinda looking for Robert."

"Robert? Who's Robert?" he asks looking surprised I'm not crumbling at his tough guy demeanor.

"Robert is your big leader, isn't he? You know, he's got the black bike with the orange flames on his saddle bags. You know..., blonde, cute...m i s u n d e r s t o o d," I say with obvious sarcasm.

"Oh, you mean Boogger."

"Boogger? No, I mean Robert, with the spider tattoo on his right arm."

"Sorry honey, I don't know what he told ya, but that's Boogger. Only one around here with orange flames on his side bags. Yeah, he's pretty enough isn't he, but don't let his blue eyes fool ya, he doesn't like getting his wake up call for another hour. You can buzz off 'til later, or sit it out here by my camp for when Boogger feels like talking."

Until he feels like talking! Who does he think he is? "Well, he invited me over here when we were out swimming yesterday. I'm just checking out his invite," I sound assured but trying not to sound demanding. I want to get the plan rolling. I want to get back to my normal life, the life that was at my pace, enjoying my friends, and maybe Connor—if he's still interested. I can see now that Uncle Reese has been right, these guys aren't really what I want in my life. No prejudice intended, especially on his part, but if I chose riding down this road just because the "cute one" is paying some attention to me, I will lose my youth to some gang playground, even lose the respect of my family; which may not mean much to me now, but Reese insists one day it will all make sense.

"Well, if you're some type of security guard, I'm surprised Robert-ugh-B-o-o-g-g-e-r didn't tell you I might be coming around," I say to throw off any doubts that I've been beckoned to the pack leader. I turn immediately toward where I think Robert is bunked down by jumping off the path and cutting through the reeds while making a beeline to the center of the biker encampment.

I don't hear the guards footsteps or reeds brushing against another as would be if he were trailing somewhere behind me. I think he bought my supposed invitation from Robert. Good. I've got a little space and relief that walking straight for the encampment—uninvited, may actually go down like I envisioned.

My only problem might be Uncle Reese. He wasn't going to be down by the river until 7 a.m. I'm still feeling I've got to get to Robert ahead of time to bring to terms the feelings he made me believe he had, or was it all Old Mill—all sex. I thought there was more. I thought he really wanted someone like me—more home town and well, they say, grounded. I don't want to back him into a corner, like the plan requires, but show him I really care, that love can, or coulda been in his life, if he allowed it. So I guess what I'm asking is, was this just sex and I was some sort of toy, or did he think we had a real connection—maybe friends even? If I was being played, than jokes on me. I'm a joke and Tiny's dead—and that's sick! I want him to own up. One way or another, he's still going to jail.

Okay, that's not a part of this plan, but I've got feelings too, and that seems to be left out of all Reese wanted of this quick move to bring the bikers in. Problem is, I care about Robert. Okay maybe not *in* love or even want some romantic kind of relationship, after all, he didn't even ask what I wanted at the Mill, he just thought he could take. I think his life has been rounded with more negative than positive. Geez, in what other direction could he have chosen?

Uncle Reese has a tape recorder tucked in this little purse, not even the security lookout seemed to care about. According to this plan, I should have it turned on and recording during the full discussion I'll have with Robert. Pretty much the whole dialogue will be to get Robert to lay out what's been happening with this gang since he landed in Beaverton, and at the utmost, what kind of business the gang's been into all along.

Reese thinks he can crack this case with me as the "sitting duck." Well, I'm not that concerned with everybody's investigation. Yes, I know there is a strong case against these guys if one of them will just admit to murder, drug-running, and threatening the lives of anyone who tries to stop them. I can see just by the security guy's question about why I'm walking in my own neighborhood that they think they can come on in and intimidate folks while they carry on some sort of fool's game. I'm not intimidated. I want my freedom back. I guess it's just me and Reese who have the sense to set it right. Still, I want to hear Robert, or Boogger's words for all this.

Geez, I haven't been down to the river where the water, reeds, railroad, and path to town all meet at the same point for awhile. Looking around it feels different with pup tents up and a big fire pits, bikes all lined up in formation just outside the circle of sleeping bodies. In a few places guys, and at some spots their girls too, are sleeping out in the open in bed rolls or sleeping bags. I scan the inner sanctum for Robert. I'll have to wake him up, and I know it'll be a shock 'cause what would he think I wanted—plus getting past his guards. He's going to think I changed my mind about sex.

And for me, I've got to be on top of turning on the recorder to tape this conversation for Reese's purposes, which will take some finesse. Yeah, I'm committed to the plan, but I'm not the end all. I guess you could say it feels like throwing a bone to the dogs.

Anyways, I want to talk to Robert before Reese zones in because for him it's all business. I need to know from Robert that I wasn't just a piece. I gave him some of my heart—I mean, I gave the best I could give, and that does stand for something. That's got to be more than selling drugs, or another girl, another town. That's gold as far as I'm concern. He's got to recognize if he could give that to me too, we've exchange something special, and I won't be just another person who sold him out.

Okay, there's his bike and it looks to be one of the few parked next to a tent. The tent is kinda beat, and despite having a shabby looking towel and wash cloth draped over the back peak, it's got some colorful patches looking like souvenirs from exotic locations: Vegas and Reno, Nevada, Laconia, New Hampshire, Sturgis, South Dakota, Las Cruces, New Mexico, and a few more points I've never heard of. It doesn't matter; it kinda gives his sleeper some distinction— other than the beer bottles haphazardly kicked around the campsite.

I don't know how I'm going to get the tape recorder on without Boogger hearing it. Hahaha! Boogger! I can only guess how he got that name. Uncle Reese is absolutely going to be here by 7 a.m. I know he'll have guns drawn, hauling a_ _ to bring these guys in—with me as back up providing some kind of confession from their leader—Robert.

It's going to take some finesse, I know that, but whatever it takes, I want his true confession of what I meant to him, and then, what this crew has been up to. I want to be true to Uncle Reese too. He's the best law enforcement officer this side of everywhere. He means good for everyone, and he really means that. If he feels it's in the best interest for the public and the perpetrator to be taken off the street, that's his goal. If he thinks all someone needs is a good tongue lashing, then no matter what the public says he'll do his damndest to give a good lecture and keep that person out of the system. It's hard for me to think anyone might see him more as, *the Spoiler*, a name that gets tossed around town once in a while. If people only knew how concerned and conscientiously he executes and believes in doing the right thing. So, I've got to back him above what I might personally feel about Robert. I do know Robert hasn't got my back, although I might have his, and truly Uncle has mine.

I bend down and tap on Robert's tent pole to try and wake him up before I unzip the flap and barge right in. His tent is placed in the thick of the camp. I suppose situated for protection, and I feel, because it also lets everyone know who's in charge. No answer. I half whisper, "Robert. Psst, Robert! Wake-up… it's me, Celia…" Nothing. Okay, is he even in here? Again only louder I try, "Robert. Psst, Robert! Wake-up…it's me, Celia."

Now I hear some whispering. Actually, it sounds like a female voice. Maybe some girl actually occupies this spot and not Robert at all. What would his bike be doing parked right here if that were the case. Then I hear a male answer back, and I'm sure it's Robert. My heart sinks for just a moment. Yes he's got a girl in there with him. Really, is that supposed to mean anything at this point. I want some meaningful answers I may not get.

"What are you doing here?" comes from the other side of the fabric.

"I really want to talk to you about something. It's important!" I say almost overly emphatic.

"It's a little early isn't it?" he replies, as giggles emphasize he's got girlie company. Reese and I hadn't actually considered an issue of someone camping with him. I don't know why it hadn't been considered. Maybe we were both lost in the notion that he really, really just wanted me. I'm such a fool.

"I guess for you it is, but I'm always up early. I like walking along here, remember? Still, I want to talk to you."

"Geez, what time is it?" he says while I believe he's stalling for time just to clear his mind.

"Around 6:30," I respond.

"Really, do we have to do this now? I mean, I'm sleeping here. How did you get past security anyway?" he asks, sounding like he's coming back to earth. All those distant stars he was traveling to in his dreams are now just that—distant stars. Well, I think that's where he's been, but that's denial. He's probably been smooching with the little lady on the other side of this canvas.

"I'm sorry my timing seems to be off, but this might be the only time I have left to see you. I'll be heading down to the Cities and I didn't have much of a chance to talk to you after the Mill. You seemed angry or frustrated and I don't want to part mad. Maybe we can make up." Wow, that's working my way a little too close to some untruths. I guess the idea that he's got a girl with him, and probably always had, makes me want to corner him in all his deceptions, one way or another. I hoped to go into this whole business as clear and honestly…and compassionately as I truly feel he deserves, but I'm having a hard time separating myself from him as a vulture, and me as the prey.

"Alright, alright, but just a minute," he slowly shouts out, "Trixie here has to find her stuff and scoot." Trixie, or whoever she is, grumbles while at the same time I can hear her fingering around for her stuff, pulls on her pants 'cause I can hear a zipper go up… and then an effort at putting a top on, I think.

"I don't really appreciate bein' awakened at this hour just 'cause ole Celia goes out for a walk this early, and then has to speak to you. She had her chance," says the girls voice from inside the tent.

"Yeah, I know, Sugar," replies Robert. "Still, gather your stuff and scoot. I'll see what gives later."

Hmmm… The girl's voice sounds familiar. Man, I hope this isn't a townie. Yeah, I could've made the same mistake, but with all the spare gals riding with these dudes, why pick on us. Not only that, but who's out sleeping around with Robert, kinda, my Robert?

The zipper suddenly comes ripping down the front of the little tent. Out steps Candice Johnson. Yeah, I know her. Her mother is sort of loose, but attractive and simply nice. Well, Uncle Reese had a short thing for her not long after his divorce. When he was seeing her mom he took me aside and asked that I make an effort to be friends with Candice. I kinda did, but she was more trouble than fun. I think she just needed more attention from her mom, but her mom always wanted to be out getting attention for herself, from the guys. Funny, I would've expected to see Candice's mom crawl out from this dude's tent over Candice. I guess nobody really is thrown to far from the nest.

"What's up Celia?" she says as she rises from the ground. She looks me over as if she can't imagine what the likes of me would be wondering around a biker's camp this early on any given morning. "You've got something going here? Your Uncle Reese knows about this?" Wow, Candice getting nosy.

I don't answer because it's really too frivolous for my work at hand. I've got to effortlessly turn on the recorder in my mini shoulder bag before I replace Candice in the tent. This thing has got to work. I look into the little bag for the RECORD bottom I purposefully placed pointing up so that I could push it quietly, yet resolutely on. I'm now prepared to work Plan A as I watch Candice glide off towards the bushes by the river, probably to pee. This is the point I take the opportunity to press quietly down on RECORD. Whatever is about to happen, my systems are go.

"Ahh, didn't you come to see me Celia," hollers a masculine and sleepy voice from the sagging little interior of this green, regulation military-style tent.

If anyone is watching me from around the biker village, I can't stop. I push on the recorder button and pull the purse flap shut, snapping it closed. "Yes", I reply while bending down and onto my knees. I peer through the opening created by the canvas door that Candice flipped over the tent wall. Robert is lying on a flannel lined sleeping bag dressed in well worn t-shirt with the sleeve holes cut large for comfort and a pale yellow pare of wrinkly boxer shorts.

"Hey Chick, fancy meeting you here! You're the last person I'd expect to see looking for me at 6:30 in the morning at my end of the world," he says while studying the tents ceiling.

I think to myself, wow, this is what Robert looks like first thing in the morning. His eyes are squinty, yet I know now what it means to have bedroom eyes. His drowsy, droopy lids are really quite attractive, or sexy enough to get my heart revving up—throbbing even. His blond hair is seriously matted and sticking straight up on the side that was probably facing Candice. Geez, I wouldn't be surprised if Candice shows up nine months from now "with child" as Curlers would call it.

Asshole! What does he care? If Uncle Reese has his way, Boogger isn't going to see much of that child, should Candice be unfortunate enough to receive his genes, so to speak.

"Yeah, well you know, this has always been MY stomping ground," I reply with a new mustered confidence. "Until you guys moved in, I walked through here with my dog Tiny every morning. Hey, by the way, Tiny disappeared around here a week or two ago. Have you or any of your guys seen him?"

"Man, girl, is this why you're waking me up this early in the morning? Did I see your dog?"

"No, it's not why, but since it's come up, I ought to ask. Tiny is my little pupster and everybody loves her, not just me. If you guys have her, or know where she is, it would mean the world to me," I say almost pleading for any information Robert might hold.

I'm a little worried about the tape recorder. Right now I can feel the tape rolling in my little purse as it plops solidly on the plaid, flannel sleeping bag like a thump upside a head. I guess that also says there's not much cush between the flannel and solid ground.

"Geez, whatcha packing in there, rocks?" asks Robert. "You're not going to thump that over my skull when I lean in for a kiss, are ya?"

"No, silly. Just a change purse in case I want to stop off at *Dell's* after my walk." Man, a quick lie here, a quick lie there; so wrong, and maybe it's right in order to bring some justice to my dog, and whoever's been thrown in the river. But I'm playing at their game: lies and manipulation, and so maybe I'm wrong here too. Am I therefore qualified in the category of: not any better than they are? In many ways, but I'm not out getting what I need in deceptive ways... except for today.

"Robert, I come in peace. I know yesterday you took off mad from the Mill because I wouldn't go as far as you wanted, right? Yeah, I'm right," I say, answering my own question.

"Whatever. It don't matter to me," is his comeback.

"Wow, it doesn't matter to you? Well gee, Boogger, why did you make such a huge play for me? I mean, I had a boyfriend and was going along with this summer just the way I wanted to. No pressure, then you came along. I didn't even like what I saw at first. Remember the day you chased us down these very railroad tracks? That was definitely NOT love at first sight."

"Hahaha, oh yeah, that was funny!" he laughs. "You were three little bunny rabbits hopping off into the woods. You shoulda seen when you guys took off how your fluffy bunny tails stuck straight up in the air. Ha-ha-ha-ha!" He laughs and eyeing me for a reaction.

I just stare straight into his eyes, trying to figure out if he's got any true feelings for me at all.

"Hey look, I thought it was cute! You were hot in those shorts, girl! You've got to admit, you got it going on. You know what you're doing, trying to turn us dopes on to you. What else would you be doing here this morning? You want some action from me too. I hope you weren't jealous when ole Candy girl left. I've got more for you, don't worry."

Oh my GOD! What the hell is he talking about? What nerve! If he's just out for sex…well, what kinda fool am I? Me, or Candice? Either or? What was I thinking…he might like me?

"Let me taste those juicy lips, girl. They're looking mighty sweet this morning," he adds.

Robert's been leaning up on his elbow while I've been sitting cross-legged and facing him straight on. He reaches up and grabs my neck, forcing my head tight into his, until my reflexes kick in and I lurch away, catching his warm breath and musky scent, and engulfing my own ethers. Oh no, I can't let his overwhelming sexuality get to me. Where's Tiny? I repeat to myself over and over. I need to in order to stay on track. Also, I'm plenty aware of the tape recorder. It's grinding away a documentation of this full conversation, and do I really want to pass on this increasingly sleazy dialogue. All Uncle Reese really needs is a confession. All I really want to is a confession of the game he's played with me. I want to hear him say that I was just another piece in game of "Lonely Hearts." Increasingly however, my big concern here is the tape will run out before either confession gets made. Well, that and he'll hear the tape click off when it hits the end.

"Geez, girl!" he shouts back to me, reacting to my rebuff.

"Hey, Robert, what do you think was going to happen with me in the long run? Were you going to ask me to head down the road with you? Were you going to come back for me when I could get myself free? Or, were you just going to take my body and run off? Did you think of me like that? Like I said, I had a boyfriend. I had things going on, and you got in the middle of that, as if you saw something important in me. Well, you seemed like this big interruption was important to you."

Robert didn't even take enough time to think about my point of view or the emotional questions that come along with relationships. Why didn't he think about me, or these honest questions?

"Hey Celia, what's up with all this? I didn't make any promises. Why are you acting like I owe you anything? This was all supposed to be fun. Shoot girl, I could claim that you're the one who seduced me. I never said I'd be staying in this pip squeak of a town. Shoot this isn't just too small for me, it isn't me at all. No girl is going to get me settle for this! I was just sampling girl. Damn, couldn't you tell?"

"Sampling?" I respond, and not really needing an answer. "Well, I guess you guys just push yourselves around don't you. You look all messed up and hope that all the regular folks will be threatened by the tattoos and greasy hair. As you can see, that doesn't mean much to me. I'm looking for the goods. That's how I was raised. You can look any way you want, but I need to see what's on your inside before you'll scare me. And for real love, okay, I get it. I'm nothing but what you can use up while you're heading down the road. I can handle that 'cause I've got places I want to go too that may not include felons. No, I don't want to kiss you. There's nothing behind that but an empty pit. You know, I started out asking you about Tiny and you didn't bother to answer. I know why you didn't answer. You didn't answer because you know what happened to her, and where she's gone will need to be a confession."

"Hold on now sister," he says sounding more like the day has seriously begun, "I didn't answer 'cause if you mean that little yappy dog who pulled in here one day, don't go accusing anyone one of foul play. Ole Panda Bear, laying lookout, had to bury it a week or two back after he ran her over with his bike. He didn't mean to, it just got to chasing him up the tracks, and splat! If that's the dog you mean? No harm, no foul on anyone's part here. It's what happened.

Come on now cutie, let me see some sugar. I don't want us to part without me showing you how much I appreciate what you have to offer," he says, once again trying to sway me with some false interest in connecting to me.

"So why are you pulling out of Beaverton, Boogger?" I ask.

"Hahaha, who told you to call me Boogger? I like how you call me Robert. I don't want my special girls calling me Boogger."

"That dumb security guy camping out near town didn't even know who "Robert" was, until I described you. He said, oh, you mean B-o-o-g-ger!!" I am trying to get on with this conversation, but all the while I'm thinking of Tiny and how she wound up chasing one of these fool's bikes. That was my fault. She

165

would never have even been out here if I hadn't taken her. And if I'd bothered to look for her and not gone home without her that day, she'd be with me right now.

Robert reaches for the back of my neck again, only this time he puts his strength into it and pulls me forcefully to his lips. His lips are ready to get what he wants, and no effort on my part can stop him. He knows he's got the power to take what he's after and I squirm while thinking more about the tape recorder and a confession than how far he's thinking of taking this. His lips press into mine and force me to lay back on the tent floor, as he moves on top of me. I'm searching for a way upright when a rough-graveled voice, obviously altered by too many cigarettes, hollers into Robert, "Hey Boogger, what's the game plan? Word up from Cedric in the Cities is we got to meet Cali by noon tomorrow outside of Billings. They want all the cash and we can make the exchange then. And they want a serious explanation on why we got rid of Sonny."

"Hey, Hey!" Shouts Robert. "Don't you know I've got a guest in here with me?!"

"Oops, sorry boss," whimpers this guy, lowering his tone. The heavy, acrid smell of a thousand smoked cigarettes wreak from his hair to his boots, along with clothing that without serious bleach couldn't possibly rid him of used, smoked cigarettes. Even buried under Robert, the odor is now wafting throughout the tent.

"Get lost Dewey," hollers out Robert, as he rolls over and exposes me to Dewey's mistake. "Get everyone rolling. We'll want to fully break camp in an hour, so if you dudes need breakfast and coffee, get it done now." Then, without catching his breath, he turns back to me, "Now, let's get back to us," and he uses his arms to press my shoulders back down to the tent floor.

I'm not even concerned because I'm sure Sonny must have been the guy I saw wrapped in the sheet and tossed into the river. "Robert, why was Sonny killed?" I ask out loud, surprised at my own bold determination to get to the bottom of Boogger's real personality.

"He didn't do what I asked," he answers quickly. "Why are you so nosy? I deal in serious business and anyone challenging my orders, or making too many mistakes, means they're hurting me and may even get me killed. But as you heard, we're out of here in an hour. Isn't it time you showed me how much you're going to miss me?" he presses down hard on me to make his point. "Now come on, girl, I'm over this game. Don't make me take what I'd rather you'd give up gently, because I know you want me too."

I reach up and pull Robert's head down to kiss. I've got to do something to play for time while I think of how I'm going to back out of here. I'm not giving anything up, and I'm pretty sure I've got all the material Reese is looking for. Seriously, at this point if he doesn't, it's too bad. Robert seems to know what he wants and he intends to get it now...before he breaks camp.

I gather all my strength and push Robert over on his back as I roll over on top of him—still locked in a kiss. Damn! The tape record and my little shoulder purse are stuck under him. The strap pulls at my neck making it awkward and painful to straighten out and still hold onto this kiss. Robert feels under his back. He must know he's lying on top of a hard little box packed into my purse—a purse that's just large enough to hold the recorder and snap it shut. It must be biting into his ribs–what with his and my weight pressing down on the purse. I'm just hoping our weight isn't going to damage anything I've recorded so far. My question is answered; he reaches a free hand under his back and twists to extract the purse, accidently knocking me off—while we still hold the kiss. He grabs the purse and CLICK, the recorder sounds OFF!

Instantly our lips go limp and our eyes open, staring momentarily in recognition of what just happened. Whoa! That's it, *I'm outa here!*

I'm to my knees and back out of the tent like a horse realizing it's been cornered in a small stall. I'm halfway through the door flap as Robert registers—*she's recorded this conversation!* He looks surprised and betrayed. I don't care. I just need to move out of camp in a real hurry! Uncle Reese is supposed to be waiting for me on the dirt road to Route 2, immediately over the other side of the mound created for the railroad tracks.

I spring to my feet, striding out for what I hope is Reece's position. Charging through the thorns of the tall weeds and grasses, my knees and calves are cut as I try to jump through to the edge of the pasture and bottom of the railroad mound. I can't look back, nor want to hear Robert's footsteps behind me. If Reese hasn't arrived on the scene yet, I'm in real trouble.

I'm zigging and zagging past bikes, makeshift cooking setups, towels, cloth lines and camp trash. Right when I jump over a turned over plastic bucket, I hear Robert shouting out from behind me, "Stop that girl! She's stealing my stuff! Bring her over here! Stop that girl, NOW!"

I put it in overdrive. I know those guys will do whatever Boogger asks, and I'm sure if I look back I'll see a couple of them popping their heads out of their tents to see who he needs brought in. If I look behind me, Robert may be eating up space between us. I'm nearly at the point where the road and the train tracks meet. I just have to run up the dike. I can hear footsteps bounding on the ground behind me but no wasting time to see who may be gaining.

I pray Uncle Reese is on the other side with the squad car. Just as I make the short hill, I feel an arm grab my shoulder. Agh! No, I can't stop. "Uncle Reese," I shout, "Uncle Reese, help me!"

"No one is going to help you! Give me that purse! NOW!" I hear Robert demand. "I'm coming after you one way or another! You're not getting outta here with or without that purse, so ya best stop here, girl!" Robert spews.

I squirm around and wriggle loose from his pinching hold on my shoulder and trip up to the top of the track. "Uncle Reese, help me!" I shout. He's not there. Why isn't he parked at the edge of the road! Damn, I'm a goner!

And just as I feel his hand catch me again, I see the large, beautiful, white cop car speeding down the road toward the two of us. It's Reese at last! Hall Ass! PLEASE!

But Boogger's arm grabs my shoulder again, forcing me backwards down the incline. I'm not goin' na go down though and hang tight to the purse's shoulder strings.

"You're in trouble," I yell back at Robert as I make a rabbit-like hop back up toward the track. "Reese, hurry," I say out loud, but with no real energy left to scream out to the stocky little brown man now running toward me. "Where've you been, man?" I holler.

"I had to make some calls for back up," he hollers. "Get in the car, we've got some arrests to make. Did you get the tape? Tell me you've got some kind of recording!"

I pull on the cruiser's passenger-side door and look back to see what's up with Robert. All that's left is his blonde head disappearing below the other side of the tracks. And as he disappears I hear him shout, "Scatter, NOW! Police are here! Move! Move!"

Yeah, he's right about that because back in the direction of town come the sounds of sirens—multiple police sirens. Here comes backup. This is why Uncle Reese was late. He must have convinced all neighboring law enforcement because they're moving in like buzzards aware of a fallen carcass, and ready to feed.

Sitting quietly alone in the cop car, and watching Uncle Reese sneaking up the incline, I feel relieved and sheltered from the turmoil outside. There's turmoil inside here too, inside me. I know Robert's not all bad. Somewhere in the mess of things, and down some far distant road, he was a little kid wanting to make good. Now he has another idea of what making good is. He may never have had a chance to exercise control and power before, and now the kind he's got is crazy…and harsh; not willing to see what positive creativity might be. True, it's false power and control he thinks he has, at least from my perspective, but this morning I could see by the way he's got his crew set up, he in some personal ego-boosting mindset, believing that he's got value. In some man's world, he's got control. I'm think it's the prison world where this stuff works. I can't actually say he knows anything about girls, women, or he has the ability to nurture something or someone. I don't suppose he's actually trying to find meaning in female relationships. He's either let that go, or hasn't really spent time getting close to any of us. It shows. But if Uncle Reese has a grip on what looks to me like a situation that will end right here in Beaverton, Robert's not going to be getting any other practice soon. And somehow, I feel bad for him—for never having the opportunity to feel comfortable trying something else.

Looking back up to see what's going on outside the car, I see Uncle Reese signaling to me. His hand is waving me down. I can read his lips mouthing, GET DOWN!

I hit the cruiser's front seat, my head lands in the middle of its lengthy expanse to the passenger door as I spot a couple of empty gum wrappers I'm sure Reese tossed quickly aside as he headed out here this morning. Then loudly I hear him shout, "WE'VE GOT YOU SURROUNDED! STEP AWAY FROM YOUR BIKES! YOU ARE ALL COVERED BY 100 OFFICERS AND THEIR DEPUTIES WITH AUTOMATIC WEAPONS! PUT YOUR HANDS OVER YOUR HEADS-**NOW**! WE KNOW THERE ARE ELEVEN OF YOU SO LET'S SEE ELEVEN OF YOU STEP FORWARD! I SAID ELEVEN! I'M ONLY SEEING NINE! WE ARE PREPARED TO USE TEAR GAS FOR ANYONE NOT OUT OF A TENT, NOW!"

At that, the whole show goes quiet, and I lay on this beige Naugahyde seat that spreads across from passenger's door to the driver's. All this excitement and hardly sleeping last night…, I shut down…, and sleep.

Right in the middle of this sweet dream about Tiny, Uncle Reese pops open my door. "Okay Celia, you are this one man's hero. You were over and above what we needed. I'm so proud of you because you've been able to see this in the big picture, and see your future, even though I know this guy got under your skin. Down the road, if you'da stuck by this guy, you'd be living in chaos and maybe heading for the place he's probably going to. Oh, and sorry about that slow rescue. I meant to be here 10 minutes earlier. Really I did, but the county didn't want to pick these guys up and transport them to their facilities until tomorrow. No room at the inn, I guess. But please know, I would never have let him over this train track with you harmed in anyway. Got me? Now with that said, could you hand over that tape recorder? Also, I've got to ask you to walk home because these cruisers are going to have to take each of these winners back to their town jails until sometime tomorrow when we can check em in to bigger facilities."

"Oh great," I think out loud. "So I've got to consider he's in this town 'til tomorrow. I'm not scared, but man, Uncle Reese, he's going to be in the back of my mind, and I'll kinda feeling guilty. I'm just wishing this was over and done..."

"I know, Girl, it'll probably be uncomfortable until time proves to you what's happened has been for a reason, a good reason. You're already strong and it'll make you stronger. For these guys, going to the slammer, they'll remember that some young lady thought they were worth something, and that will stick with them the rest of their lives. If it changes their future, well, it already has. If they make different choices from now down the road, that's something YOU can't predict. So remember that, and if you need to talk more about it, I'll be free the day after tomorrow, alright?" he says patting me on the cheek.

"You always say it just right, Uncle Reese. Thank you, I say purposefully while reaching up to pinch his cheek back. You're always here for me. I LOVE YOU!" I yell back to him, and run off for home.

www.ingramcontent.com/pod-product-compliance
Lightning Source LLC
Chambersburg PA
CBHW021102130626
46554CB00002B/496